WALTER

CASSANDRA ANTHOLOGY

Volume One

Books One to Seven

Brooklyn Maxwell

Welcome to the world of Cassandra. Cassie was my very first Femdom heroine and her first book my very first venture into the world of erotica.

Cassie's adventure begins with her exasperation with her boyfriend which manifests itself in a spanking over her knee. This is the start of her erotic journey into BDSM and Polyamorous relationships.

Cassie meets Peyton and so begins her second love affair with plenty of spanking thrown in.

You will find Cassie not only exploring the use of many implements but also her own sexuality. This ultimately results in her desire to experience a spanking for herself with surprising results, from an older woman.

Cassie's journey is by no means over and perhaps I will come back to it one day, with some new episodes.

In the meantime, there is plenty here to love and enjoy, in this special print edition just for you.

I hope you enjoy reading it as much as I loved writing it for you.

Brooklyn

Cassie learns to spank (Book One)

Cassandra watched Nathan walk down the path just as she always did and get in the car, the little red sports car that she had bought him. She was thirty-something with long dark hair that fell in a wave down her back, and she smiled all the way from her full bow-shaped lips to her brown eyes as he turned and waved goodbye. Her slim but curvaceous body was barely covered by the satin robe that hugged her figure like a second skin leaving nothing to the imagination. Her rounded breasts lightly lifted the fabric showing their shape and the nipples standing proud through the cloth. She raised her well-manicured hand with its pink nails and waved back.

"Bye Nathan," she called out and smiled again but more seductively this time. "Don't be late home."

"I won't." He blew her a kiss, started up the motor in his red Mazda MX5 and pulled away, the sports car making a satisfied purr as he accelerated.

She smiled to herself thinking of his kisses. Maybe, she indulged him too much, she mused. A woman of independent means since her husband died over two years ago. She had loved her husband deeply and felt so bereft and alone. Then Nathan had come into her life, young, virile, blonde with just about the right amount of muscle in all the right places. But he was no airhead, he was studying for his master's at university and he had an enquiring and agile mind which was so alive. He entranced her own mind first and they talked for hours, read poetry and laughed together before she surrendered to his body and also his magical fingers, she quivered spontaneously at the thought of their morning lovemaking. Her mind drifted to his kiss and his cock moving inside her.

She had been barely awake and him in all his 'morning glory' thrusting harder and harder as she gasped and enjoyed the sensation of his stiff thick engorged shaft filling her up with joy.

"Oh, Nathan, oh fuck, oh God, oh fuckk!" she cried out as he lay between her legs, fucking her faster.

"Cassie, oh, shit, fuck, Cassie, oh my God," he breathed in guttural tones, while his toned body thrust deeper and deeper.

"Oh, God, oh, oh, oh, oh, oh, ohhhh!" she climaxed wrapping her legs up and around his back.

"Ahhhhhhhh!!" his answering loud gasp presaged the pulsing of his cock as he orgasmed, and she felt his warm spunk within.

Recalling it in technicolour, Cassandra could hardly wait for later and just thinking of it made her wet. They made love often and although her friends teased her about her 'toy boy' he had made her whole again. She loved him, she cared and doted on him and he took all her indulgences with ease.

The little Mazda was a birthday present and even though she chided herself she could not help it. Marriage to Leonard had been a staid affair. He was wooden in bed and not in the right way. He did not believe in his wife's pleasure and she thought this was how it was meant to be, and she loved him passionately in spite of it. Later she found out from friends what 'Wham bam thank you Ma'am' really meant and was ashamed she had tolerated it all these years.

The first time Nathan had placed his velvet lips between her legs and found her clitoris with his soft warm tongue she was lost, she had cried for all the times she had missed out on the tender pleasures which sex afforded. However, the lost sex was soon made up in abundance with Nathan.

Leonard had died of a heart attack late one night in the office. His colleagues were sympathetic and said he had worked too hard. He left her more than comfortably off, a rich woman in fact with substantial life insurance payout, plus the house, and other investments he had made from which she could live off more than comfortably and in style. With no mortgage, and plenty of disposable income, she was sitting pretty. She didn't have to work again if she did not want to. She discovered what Leonard had lacked in the bedroom department he more than made up for in his bank account and investments. So, for *that,* she could be grateful and for Nathan. A woman of leisure she spent her time painting, or writing poetry, reading all the books she'd never read. Others might see it as an empty life, but Cassandra was happy enough on her own, with Nathan, most of the time.

Shutting the front door, she went to the kitchen walking barefoot on the tiled floor, enjoying the sensuality of the smooth cold porcelain on the soles of her feet. Pouring herself a glass of orange she leafed idly through the day's mail. She imagined they were most likely bills and other uninteresting things. But, unwilling to put off the inevitable and chewing a piece of toast laid thickly with peanut butter she picked up a knife and opened one at random.

It was just as she thought, as was the next and so coming to the third she glanced at it and then stopped swearing under her breath.

"Oh my God! The little ..." she gasped as she took in the total line of the bill for the mobile phone, she most generously provided Nathan. It was a four-figure sum and though she could afford it, a wave of annoyance came over her. In one whole month? She could hardly believe it. Though Cassandra had money she was quite thrifty with it too and unnecessary expense annoyed her.

For one thing, it was not the first time this had happened. Only last month she had spoken to him about it. Nathan was into extreme sports, which she helped to fund, and he had pals all over the world, pals whom he generously called using his mobile she had bought him and that she paid for! He had been less than contrite last time they discussed it and in fact when she persisted in asking him not to spend so much time on the phone or try to organise a better way of doing it then he had become a little childish, to say the least.

"Why can't you just Skype or use Viber, or WhatsApp or something, anything but the phone?" She had asked, not unreasonably.

"Oh, come on Cassie, some of these guys are halfway up a mountain when I call, do you think they have internet coverage? It's just easier this way. It's just a small thing really, I mean this is my hobby, don't you want me to be happy? Maybe you don't, it's not all about you, you know, and it's not like I spend ALL your money, give me a break…"

"But you do..." She had tailed off about to say 'spend all my money' but what was the use, she was the one who had allowed it. She had pursed her lips on the retort. It was the downside of being with a younger guy. He was so good for her and to her in so many ways and so immature in so many others. Like a child, she thought and a very naughty child at that.

"If you are going to be like this, I am going to play Xbox until you calm down, and fine, I'll pay it if you want, it might take me a while but…" he started to walk away to his den. She had given him a room for himself, a man cave, a den where he could retreat and do his man stuff. She wasn't into computer games or whatever else he did in there. He played online with mates from all over. This she didn't mind. It was the phone bill which irked her.

"No, I don't want you to pay and Nathan don't you walk away when I am talking to you! Nathan, we need to discuss this properly." She had been cross and couldn't help herself, self-control was something she sometimes found herself losing around him and he had carried on walking. Her final admonishment, "I am warning you Nathan!" had come out so wrong, and so lame.

He had stopped for a moment. "And what? Cassie?" He had fixed her with his melting blue eyes and smiled. "What are you going to do? Spank me? I am not a child you know."

"Well, you know what," she had snapped back. "Maybe I just ought to do that!"

He had laughed then and said before turning away. "Now that's funny, you may say you'll do a lot of things, but the trouble with you, Cassie, is you never follow through, so I think my arse is safe for now. Even if you were thinking of doing it. But I doubt it. Could be fun though. So, I've heard."

She had watched his retreating back and felt the truth of his words. It was true she never did follow through. She threatened things sometimes when she was mad at him, but he always brought her around. She tried to make him sleep on the sofa when he came home late after drinking with his buddies, but one kiss and she gave in. He ran up a big clothing bill on the credit card she paid for and she said she was going to cut it up, but she never did. Just like always, he would win.

The truth was, she was afraid. She wasn't sure he really truly loved her and though she was truly smitten she was afraid to lose him, most probably to a younger woman, if she stopped paying. If she pushed him too far then maybe he would walk away. Generosity sometimes brings its own problems and those on the receiving end begin to take the giver for granted. She had spent an awful lot on him and in return, he gave her affection, sex, faithfulness, made her dinner often and comforted her. In fact, she did not ask for much, but she liked having Nathan around, he completed her.

She liked to spoil him, and it gave her pleasure, but he could be so careless, and he sulked if he did not get his own way. He had his own money and his course was paid for on a scholarship, but she had given him a lifestyle he couldn't have imagined before he met her. Once he'd finished his master's, perhaps he'd get a well-paid job. Cassandra hoped so. She didn't want him around the house all day and with his spending habits she might end up with nothing if she didn't reign him in.

His words came back to haunt her, "you never follow through". Never follow through, that's what he thought of her. The last thing he had said was like a challenge. My arse is safe for now. What else did he say? It could be fun? Was he tempting her somehow, to do it? Was it a fantasy of his, after all? She pondered this for a bit until she brought her mind back to the present and the phone bill dangling in her fingers. She dropped it onto the countertop. He always knew he could get round her.

Cassandra went upstairs to shower with thoughts running wildly through her head. Naked under the hot water she let it soothe her mind and allowed herself to drift. She soaped herself running her hands over the smooth skin and started to wash her hair.

"What are you going to do? Spank me?" She was remembering suddenly what he had said. Why did she think of it in particular? And somehow the thought of him naked across her knee came into her mind. Her fingers moved down between her legs and found her clit as she pictured herself repeatedly slapping his reddening backside. She was getting hot and bothered at the thought and her fingers moved more urgently as she lost herself in the fantasy. She loved his tight bottom at the best of times, but this was something new, something almost deliciously naughty. As her fingers worked almost frantically now, she started to moan, and she could feel her orgasm was close.

"Oh, fuck, oh God, oh, fuck, oh, oh, oh…" That beautiful moment of release was just about to break when the jangling of the phone intruded into her consciousness.

"Oh fuck!" she cursed brought back from the brink and feeling frustrated. Stepping wet and naked from the shower she ran to the bedside and picked up her phone from where she had left it.

"Hi, babe." It was Nathan, ringing her from the very same offending mobile.

"Hi." She was a little breathless.

"Whatcha up to babe? Have you been playing with yourself again?" His laughter tinkled teasingly down the receiver.

"Maybe, I just had a shower, and I *am* naked," she teased back.

"Mmm, I hope you were thinking of me."

"Maybe." The image of him lying over her knees flashed back into her head, her face reddened at the thought of it and what he would think if he knew.

"Sure, you were," he laughed. "Hey, I just wondered if you would mind, some of the guys are going out for a drink tonight and asked me to come, I know I was going to cook dinner and all that, but would you mind. Babe? I will make it up to you I promise."

She was silent for a moment, ordinarily, she would have given in but somehow today she felt things were different. They had to be different.

"Babe?" he said tentatively when she hesitated longer.

She took a deep silent breath. It was time for things to change. "Actually, darling, I do mind and I would rather you didn't."

"Oh." He sounded disappointed. "Well, I guess if you had plans…" He tailed off still obviously hoping she would relent.

"Yes, yes I do have plans for tonight, so please don't go out, Nathan."

There was a pause and then a cheeky laugh. "Oh, oh I get it, well hmm, okay, I will be home as usual then, look forward to it." She could almost feel him winking at her over the phone.

"Yes," she said her mind was racing. "Yes, please do."

"You OK, babe? You sound, different, is everything OK?" There was a note of concern now in his voice, she realised she had sounded a little, formal.

"Yes, yes sure darling, everything is fine, I'll see you later, bye." She blew a kiss down the phone and disconnected before he could respond.

Something inside her had snapped or perhaps become very clear. Her heart was beating fast the more she thought of it. She definitely had plans now, maybe it was the episode in the shower or perhaps it was his attitude on the phone, but she had decided to take matters into her own hands and yes, she was definitely going to follow through. The thought of spanking Nathan had taken hold of her imagination in a way she could not have bargained for.

Her trip to the local mall was pointed and somewhat brief. She had come with an express purpose and she arrived at her favourite shoe shop. Shoes were a passion of hers and she had many already. However, she wanted a pair for a specific reason, a brand new pair for a brand new Cassandra. It was fortunate sandals were still in season. She headed for the row of flip flop style sandals and ran her fingers over a few. She did not know what made her think of using a sandal in particular, for spanking, but it just seemed like the perfect instrument, and as a bonus, she could also wear them, at least inside.

"Are you looking for something special?" asked a pretty blonde shop assistant a little younger than Cassandra.

The woman was younger than Cassandra with blue eyes, sensual bow-shaped lips and a heart-shaped face. Her blonde hair was tied up and Cassandra found herself wondering what it would be like hanging loose. Cassandra glanced at the other's figure which was slim, with smallish breasts and she was wearing high heels. Her feet were rather sexy. The assistant was waiting for an answer with a smile playing on her lips. Cassandra jerked her attention back to the sandals.

"Do you have any of these in erm, leather, you know with leather soles?" she asked.

"This is our leather range," purred the woman indicating some sandals with thin thongs. "They don't really do them with leather soles these days."

The assistant watched her with interest. It felt almost as if she was checking Cassandra out. In the heightened state, she was, it began to make Cassandra feel a little hot. Cassandra picked one of the sandals up and ran her finger over the sole. It felt almost sensuous coupled with the images of Nathan's bottom in her mind. It wasn't leather as she'd been told, but it was thin and flexible, the synthetic sole felt rather nice to her touch. She tapped it lightly once or twice on the palm of her hand. She imagined it might well sting if she did it harder. The thought of this gave her a thrill.

The assistant was still regarding her under a lidded gaze smiling all the while. For some reason, Cassandra didn't mind. In fact, she liked it. She smiled back. Cassandra selected a pair in her size with shocking pink thongs and tried them on. They felt good on her feet and the sandal fitted well in her hand when intended for the very different purpose she had in mind.

Cassandra had attractive and well-proportioned feet. She kept them in good condition with regular pedicures. She had shapely ankles, and perfect toes too. Nathan liked her feet and told her they were sexy. The shop assistant seemed to like them too and couldn't take her eyes off them. Cassandra walked around in the sandals, starting to feel a little flushed.

"They suit you, you have nice feet," said the assistant.

"Thanks."

Cassandra slipped them off and handed them to her.

"I will take these thank you."

"A very good choice," said the woman. "I think you'll find they will do very well for what you want them for." Her gaze held Cassandra's for just a second too long.

"Does she know?" thought Cassandra. "Does she know what I am going to do? Oh my God!" The idea of it was quite a turn-on. It brought up confusing feelings which Cassandra pushed away, she had enough to deal with carrying out her plan.

She accompanied the woman to the counter, and paid with her credit card. The woman tore off the receipt and put the sandals in a bag. She wrote something on the back of the receipt and put that into the bag also. Then she handed it over to Cassandra.

"Thank you" Cassandra flushed slightly.

"Have fun," said the assistant. Cassandra could have sworn she had winked but it was too quick for her to be sure.

A little later, she had also added the purchase of a sheer pink satin negligee to her shopping. Cassandra then headed for one more particular shop for another vital item and then home her attention on what was to come. She was almost shaking with excitement, alternating with waves of trepidation. She kept running spanking scenarios through her mind, wondering how it would all play out.

When she arrived home, and after a lunchtime snack, she went upstairs to prepare. Taking the receipt from the bag, she saw on the back of it the name 'Peyton' and a phone number written in pen.

"Oh God!" Her hand went up to her mouth with a little gasp.

That was what the shop assistant had been doing. Cassandra had forgotten but now staring at it in shock, other more intense thoughts entered her head. Her lips on those shapely lips, kissing. Her hands-on those pert and full breasts. Details she hadn't even clocked about the woman, she now recalled exactly. Cassandra's breath caught in her throat. A finger slid down to her pussy told her she was very wet. She felt bad, very bad. She belonged to Nathan, didn't she? How could she be thinking of kissing a woman, and… other things?

After staring at the receipt for a long time, she folded it and put it away in her bedside drawer under some other papers so it couldn't be seen. Cassandra could not bring herself to throw it away. Somewhere in the back of her mind was the conviction she would one day end up dialling that number. She put it firmly out of her mind. It was time to prepare herself thoroughly for Nathan. She wanted to be ready to give her unsuspecting boyfriend what he really deserved and what he deserved was a sound spanking. Even the words were quite erotic to her when she repeated them in her mind.

***

A few hours later Cassandra was sitting in the living room waiting. She sipped a glass of Chardonnay delicately which she had just to steady her nerves. Nathan's car drew up outside and her mouth went dry. Her heart was racing in anticipation of what she had planned. Would he even let her? She adjusted the pink negligee and smoothed it down, crossed one leg over the other, while the pink sandal dangled from her toes. Her nails were carefully painted a delicate pink shade and she had straightened her hair, and smelt of her favourite perfume. She had spent a long time at her toilette, making sure her legs were super smooth, and she felt beautifully feminine, just how he liked it.

She wanted this to be special, perfect. She wanted to be extra sexy and delicious. She wanted him to want her badly, but even more, she also wanted very much to spank his backside and just once make him see she was not a pushover. The words 'you never follow through' rankled with her and she wanted him to see he was wrong about her.

She wasn't really sure about the spanking part. She had tried out the sandal several times on her own bottom just to feel what it was like with short sharp spanks and it certainly did sting. It also made her very aroused, not only by the sound but by the sensation it gave her. This was going to be a new experience for them both.

She heard the front door close and jerked back from her reverie. Then Nathan was in the room. He stopped for a moment, taking her in, breathing her and consuming her with his eyes. She almost lost her nerve there and then and just wanted to take him to bed. He had those bedroom eyes you hear about, and many ladies had succumbed in the past she was sure, and as she did every single day.

Nathan gave a low whistle and said, "I am glad I didn't go drinking with the guys after all."

Cassandra wondered if he would still think so in a little while but instead, she poured a glass of wine for him and said, "Why don't you come and sit down?"

"Why don't we skip the aperitif and go on to the main course?" he countered.

"Not yet," she said. "First let's talk, OK?"

"Talk?" He looked at her quizzically but sat down and took the glass she offered sipping the wine. "I'm all for action baby, not talking."

"Me too, and there's going to be some action for sure," she replied. "But first I want to discuss something important with you, please, Nathan?"

Cassandra could have kicked herself. She still sounded like a pushover, begging him to sit and talk. This was supposed to be her moment to take charge. So far, she wasn't doing it very well.

"OK," he said with resignation and waited.

Cassandra was pensive for a moment summoning up the courage to say what she had rehearsed all of this time in her head. As she sat there opposite him, he noticed the sandals and that she was idly and rhythmically flexing her toes making one of them slap against the sole of her foot. For some reason, this action and the sound was turning him on, and he watched her foot for a moment, watched the slap, slap, slap of the sandal.

"Are those new?" he said finally as she didn't speak.

Her foot didn't stop, and she noticed he was getting a decided bulge in his trousers. She smiled at the thought of his hard cock and what she wanted him to do with it but then she had to bring herself back to the matter in hand.

"Yes," she said, "I bought them today and this," indicating the negligee.

"All for me?" he asked smiling.

"Oh, definitely for you."

"Mmm," he said rolling his eyes lasciviously. He looked as if he was humouring her waiting for what happened next. They sometimes played games and they both liked it, so perhaps he was thinking this was a game.

She made him wait a little longer. "Don't you think they are sexy?" she asked him finally.

"Yes," he said. "Very sexy and I love your outfit, I can't wait to slide it off you and get to that luscious naked body underneath. Then I'm going to fuck your brains out, you horny little bitch."

This kind of talk usually drove her wild and it certainly was having an effect even now. Cassandra sternly took herself in hand in her head. It was now or never, she had to instigate what she planned or consider herself a failure evermore. So instead of answering his sexy banter, she reached down beside her and picked up the mobile bill. She gently tapped it in the palm of her hand.

"Do you know what this is?"

She looked him in the eye and once more dangled the bill from two fingers, trying to muster up a little sternness for his benefit.

"I could hazard a guess," he said, obviously not sure how he was supposed to respond.

Summoning a bit more assertiveness and knowing her sexual pull had his attention at the moment, she continued, pitching her voice quite low.

"Could you now? Could you really?" She paused for effect. "Would you like to know what it is?"

"I am sure you are going to tell me." He teased her with a slightly uneasy smile. This wasn't the Cassandra he was used to, but he was willing to play along with her game.

She smoothed open the sheets of paper without speaking and passed them over to him.

He took them and perused the contents. It was the phone bill. He shrugged and passed it back.

"It's my mobile bill," he replied being non-committal.

"We talked about this before didn't we Nathan? Or rather we didn't talk about it because you wouldn't listen."

"Are we going to have an argument about this, Cassie?" He rolled his eyes. "Because if we are then it's just going to spoil the mood you have so carefully been preparing."

This was the spur she needed. His arrogance which came out every so often. Taking her feelings for granted.

"No, no. Nathan, we are not going to have an argument." She kept her voice steady, all the while her heart beating wild flutters in her chest as she built up to what she was going to say.

"OK that's sweet, so then why don't we just go upstairs now, fuck and talk about this later?" he said bluntly. His manner had changed, it sounded very much like he was going to go into a sulk.

"Oh, I am going to let you fuck me, Nathan. Very soon."

"Let me fuck you? Let me… what the…" He stood up looking exasperated. "Cassie, I don't know what this game is you're playing but…"

Cassandra suddenly snapped.

"Sit down!" she ordered him sharply. Cassandra had no idea where this came from. Neither did he as his eyes widened at her tone, but he resumed his place, nevertheless.

"Nathan, I love you, I love you so much, but this is the last straw, I just can't do this, I can't let you take me for granted so much anymore do you understand?"

He looked at once contrite and guilty as if he knew exactly what she meant and how much she did for him. His voice took on a hectoring tone, pleading almost.

"Babe, aw come on, babe, hey, look I don't mean to make you feel that way, I am sorry, come on, honey, let's kiss and make up."

"Nathan, last time we spoke about this I asked you not to use the mobile for all these calls and you didn't listen, you wouldn't even talk about it and you also acted like a little child and threw a tantrum."

"Well I guess I was a little out of line," he ventured. "But baby, baby how can I be serious about this when you're sitting there all dressed up like that?"

"You were *very* out of line and you told me I never follow through on anything, didn't you?"

"I am not sure I am following you, Cassie."

His brow furrowed in a way she usually found incredibly endearing, but she ignored it.

"It's just there really needs to be some payback, darling, that's what I have decided." She smiled at him disarmingly.

"Payback? Payback? Well, what did you have in mind exactly? You know I can't pay this bill all by myself? You know I don't earn enough for that? I mean what is it you want me to do?"

"Well," she hesitated. "I have been thinking about this and you even mentioned it yourself, I don't want your money but what I think you do deserve is… a good spanking, honey." She had finally said it, it was a huge relief to her all at once, she suddenly felt much more relaxed.

"What?" he said, "Come on Cassie, this is a joke right?"

She shook her head, and her heart was still in her mouth.

"Oh, darling, I just want you to appreciate me a little more and it's just… well, think of it as being a way of getting things off my chest," she said persuasively

"I… I err…" He stopped. "Is this a game?"

"If you like, honey." She smiled at him. Getting up, she pulled him towards her and kissed him softly feeling him melt a little at her touch.

"Oh God," he moaned. Her lips nuzzling his did the trick. "OK, OK fine then let's do it if it will make you happy and then… let's fuck."

She pulled back, a little triumphantly. She was surprised after all at how easy it had been to get him to agree.

"So, if it's a game you will have to play by the rules. I will be the Mistress and you will do everything I say, OK?" Cassandra fluttered her eyes seductively. She could play the wiles when she wanted.

He looked at her suspiciously.

"Just a game, right?"

She nodded eagerly feeling a little guilty at her subterfuge. It was a game, in a way, but perhaps it might turn out to be just a little more than that, it depended upon how carried away she might get.

"Sure, fine, whatever." His breathing was a little forced and she could see he was somewhat turned on. Perhaps his hint at spanking earlier wasn't really a joke, perhaps he did have a secret desire after all.

"OK," she said. "Then, let's begin."

She stood up drawing him up with her hands. She closed with him and pushed her hands underneath the back of his shirt feeling his bare skin. Her mouth came up to his and she spoke in a whisper. Somehow, she was starting to enjoy the feeling of the role she was about to play. First, though, she wanted to prime him properly, arouse him before spanking him.

"What did I just say was going to happen because of your mobile bill?" she breathed seductively.

"I… I don't know," he whispered back, and she could feel his hard cock inside his pants pushing against her. Her chest registered the beating of his heart and it sounded quite rapid, like hers. Her pussy was incredibly wet already and when she squeezed her thighs a little tighter, a little wave of delight ran up her body.

"Is that right? I think you do know Nathan, or would you like me to remind you?" she said quietly.

"I guess," he replied softly, it was obvious he wanted her badly then, he was stiff as a board and his shaft was now pulsing against her soft body.

"Don't be smart with me, Nathan," she told him and at the same time, her nails dug quite sharply into his back. His eyes flew wide open. He hissed as he felt them, though she knew he always loved it when she did that.

"Ohh," he said involuntarily.

"I told you exactly what was going to happen didn't I?" she said prolonging his suspense, biting his lip gently.

"Oh God," he said. She knew he was totally in the moment. His hands went up and down caressing her naked back and she tingled at his touch.

She lowered her voice a little more, pitched it really sexily. "I said I was going to give you a good spanking, that's what just I told you didn't I?"

"Yes, oh yes, now I remember, you did, it's difficult to remember anything when you're doing this to me you sexy bitch. I just want to fuck you… so much."

His breath was very ragged now because she was arousing him in exactly the way she knew. His mouth found hers and he kissed her deeply and longingly, she knew he wanted her but this time he was going to have to wait. She wasn't going to let him fuck her, not just yet.

She was utterly aroused, horny and wet as fuck. She wanted to fuck him too with almost irresistible longing, but she wanted to play the game out. Somehow, she felt the sex would be even better for doing so.

She pulled away from him a little and out of the kiss.

"You are coming to the bedroom right now," she said without preamble.

"OK," he replied, in no state to refuse her.

"I will be fucking you, Nathan, but *that* comes later, much later." She smiled at him playfully. "First though, I am going to give you something you've definitely had coming to you for a very long time."

"I know, I know, you told me, why do I get the feeling I wish I hadn't agreed to this? You're enjoying this aren't you?" he said with resignation.

"Let's go then."

She turned ignoring his remark and held onto his hand. He ventured nothing more and followed her as she almost dragged him along urgently upstairs. She took him into the bedroom, shutting the door behind them.

She let go of him and said, "Stand there and wait."

He did and watched her with unbridled lust in his eyes as she walked over to the dressing table and picked up her chair. It was a wooden quite plain chair without arms. It was convenient she had the chair she felt. It was just fit for purpose. Perhaps somewhere in the back of her mind, she had always thought of this use for it. No, that was just silly, she told herself.

She carried the chair to the centre of the room her eyes on his and deliberately placed it on the floor facing him. The room was quite large, and they had the biggest bed possible. Cassandra liked white, so the furniture was white with gilded panels. There were splashes of colour in the furnishings and the quilt cover.

The carpet was a creamy beige. She fluffed her hair a little and then wondered if this was still making him as horny as it was her. She didn't have to worry. She could see it in his pants.

Cassandra walked slowly and sensuously from the back of the chair to the front and sat down. She made herself comfortable, then once again smoothed her slinky nightwear nice and flat. He had been watching her walk and had been listening to the slap of the sandals against her soles. She noticed the sound too which was suddenly very arousing.

"Now then, Nathan," she said looking at him sternly, but also trying to keep the smile off her face, it was so hard not to smile at him. "You have been a very naughty boy, haven't you?"

"If you say so," he said a little defiantly, perhaps feeling this was his part, and he leaned back against the door folding his arms.

"I told you, don't get smart with me, Nathan. Now I want you to do exactly as I tell you, when I tell you. In this room you will refer to me as Mistress or Mistress Cassandra do you understand?"

He nodded slowly his eyes still a little rebellious, but she could see something else in them, something full of anticipation, almost as if he was starting to enjoy it.

"I want you to take off your shirt for me, nice and slowly, sexily." She smiled sweetly.

He didn't move right away. There was a part of him which didn't want to submit to her quite so easily. Cassandra realised she would need to up the ante.

"Didn't you hear me?" she ordered raising her voice. "I said take it off now!"

He regarded her with some surprise at her assertive tone. She was beginning to surprise herself. Holding her gaze the whole time, he peeled off the shirt very slowly, sensuously like a slow striptease. She watched, running her tongue over her lips involuntarily as he revealed his naked torso. His abs were hard and well defined as were the muscles on his arms and chest, not overdone but defined, nevertheless. He had some tattoos which she loved. She never tired of looking at his body, it was a huge turn-on for her. He cast the shirt aside.

"Good boy," she said approvingly. "Now undo your belt and take down your jeans and take them off, nice and slow, just the way I like it."

This time he obeyed immediately and pulled the belt out with deliberate precision flicking it out and onto the floor. He undid the trousers and turned away shimmying them down rotating his hips like a stripper and then turning to face her teasing her with his eyes as he removed them.

She noted the by now huge lump in his boxers, something she was well acquainted with.

She pointed at his feet. "

Socks!"

He took them off and finally was standing there in his boxers looking at her a little more shyly. He seemed somehow vulnerable like that.

She looked him over and was satisfied.

"Leave the boxers, I will take them down myself."

Her moment had arrived. She reached down and very slowly slipped her right sandal off her pretty foot watching him all the time with deliberation. Sitting up again and holding it by the heel in her right hand, she tapped the sole of it lightly against her left palm.

"You know I bought these specially today, nice and flat, thin, flexible and hard, just right for your tight white arse, Nathan. I can't wait to try them out." She teased a finger up the sole of the sandal as she spoke.

He smiled giving her a look of apprehension and also dripping with lust.

"Come over here and stand beside me," she ordered, indicating her right-hand side.

He walked over to her slowly and stood waiting on her right, looking down at her. She hesitated, this was it, she could stop it now and change her mind. Part of her wanted to and the other part desperately wanted to give him a spanking.

She had thought of nothing else for most of the afternoon and it consumed her, the idea of it and how it was going to feel for her and for him. She had to do it. She had to go through with it. She was feeling very worked up now. The whole build-up to this had left her soaking and it really was all she could do to carry it through to a conclusion and not fuck him right away. However, if she did not give him a spanking, she wouldn't get another chance.

His thick cock was hard and standing out straight inside his boxer shorts, but she pointedly ignored it although she desperately wanted it inside her. She loved his cock the feel of it, the size and thickness of it. She tore her mind away from it and to the business in hand.

"Bend over my knee, we're going to do this properly," she told him firmly.

He hesitated which goaded her just a little and she knew this was the final moment of commitment. Even though he thought it was a game, once he was in that position he was submitting to her will and to her sandal. A slight shiver of anticipation ran through her.

"I said get over my knee, NOW!" She spoke sternly wondering once more where the inner voice had come from.

"OK, fine, I am doing it, I am doing it, for fuck's sake, Cassandra," he said a little petulantly. He wasn't used to her ordering him around like this, game or no game.

Nathan gave a shrug, knelt down and settled himself across her lap. Cassandra was feeling a little breathless and so aroused, she couldn't think straight. It was amazing she had him like this, at her mercy. It was a powerful feeling indeed.

Cassandra ran her hand over his arse lightly and then pulled down his boxers to his thighs to reveal his smooth white naked bottom. The tight well-defined bottom she loved so much. Placing the sandal against his right buttock, she moved it around a little, but lightly so he could feel the sole running over his skin. It was quite sexy, at least to her, and she shuddered in contemplation of what was coming next. She felt him tense a little anticipating it too.

"Oh God, Nathan. Now you are going to get it. I am going to give you such a spanking, the spanking you so richly deserve. I've been thinking about it all day. I'm going to spank your bottom until it's so fucking red." Her voice was low and somehow vibrant. The thought of it, listening to herself, almost made her want to cum without having laid a stroke on his backside.

This wouldn't do, she tried to get a grip.

Nathan said nothing but she could feel his heart was beating fast on her lap and surely, he must be wondering what she was going to do, and what it was going to feel like.

"You've been a naughty boy, haven't you?" she said to him.

He still said nothing.

She raised the sandal to what she thought was about the right height took a deep breath and brought it down swiftly against his arse, lifting it off again as soon as it struck. She wasn't sure if it was right but the experiment on her own behind had told her this would sting far more.

It made a resounding "SMACK". A red mark sprang up immediately and she looked at it for a moment and then spoke.

"I said, haven't you?"

"OW… yes!" he said.

"Yes what?" she said

He did not reply.

She brought the sandal down again with a resounding "SMACK."

"Didn't I say you are to call me Mistress?" she asked him.

"OW… OW Cassie, fuck, I mean, Yes, Mistress" he replied this time "Look do we really have to do this?"

"That's better and yes we do, Nathan," she said to him. She was beginning to get into the swing of it. "So, can you tell me why you are getting a spanking?"

"I don't know," he said to her.

She raised the sandal again.

"You SMACK don't SMACK what?"

Even with only four spanks his backside was already going a little pink.

"Owwww… I said I don't know!"

He was either being deliberately obtuse or deliberately difficult. She wasn't sure which, but she wasn't about to stop. In fact, a small part of her had started to enjoy it. The sound of the sandal on his naked flesh was extremely hot and turned her on.

"Really? You really don't know after our little talk just before? Well, maybe this will remind you!"

She raised the sandal with determination then and let fly with a SMACK, SMACK, SMACK, SMACK, in quick succession alternating from right to left buttock cheeks. More red marks appeared to her satisfaction.

"Owwww," he said.

"I didn't hear your answer." Then getting into her stride repeated her tactic with the sandal… SMACK SMACK SMACK SMACK!

"Okay Okay," he gasped. "I do remember really, it's because I've done something you didn't like."

"Oh my God, Nathan you really are making this hard for yourself," she told him. "Yes, but what SMACK have SMACK you SMACK done SMACK?"

"Owowowowow Jesus Cassie… I mean, Mistress, I ran up a big mobile bill OK, I admit it I was wrong to do that."

"Good boy!" she acknowledged and raised up the sandal yet again.

SMACK, "OW", SMACK "ooh", SMACK "OUCH", SMACK "Ohhh"

Another four in quick succession, each time she smacked a little harder. With each smack, he began to vocalise the effect on his reddening arse. She was pleased that at least the sandal appeared to be getting through to him where her simply talking had not.

"But I've admitted it, can't you stop now?" he complained.

"Yes, you've admitted it and that is why you are getting spanked!"

She paused for a moment.

"Hmm, your bottom is getting so nice and red."

She admired her handiwork so far. Cassandra couldn't credit how she took on this role so easily and how she had aimed the spanks to ensure maximum coverage of his tight little buns ensuring the redness spread evenly over them.

"So happy to oblige," he said sarcastically.

Surely his behind was smarting by now she thought and contemplated stopping but another part of her was into this and she wanted a little more, to make him pay just a little bit more. Oh God was that bad? A pang of guilt hit her but not so much as to make her want to finish it quite yet. Besides, she felt he wouldn't have quite learned a lesson if she didn't repeat it a few more times.

"It's my pleasure, and don't you think you deserve it?" she said.

"I…erm." He obviously didn't want to buy into the spanking *that* much.

"I SMACK can't SMACK hear SMACK you SMACK." Her response was swift.

"O wow Owwww… yes, yes I guess so if you say so," he finally said begrudgingly.

"Didn't SMACK I SMACK tell you SMACK to call me Mistress SMACK?"

"Yes, ow, sorry… yes, Mistress. If you say so."

"I do say so Nathan and I said there had to be some payback. And there is going to be. A lot more than you think."

SMACK, "Ouchhh", SMACK "OWWW", SMACK "OHH", SMACK "owww"

She rained further spanks down on his bottom which was starting to take on a nice crimson colour.

"Oh god, isn't this payback?" he gasped.

His arse must surely be starting to sting now she thought and wondered if it was an arousing sting. After all his hard-on had not lost any of its stiffness, she could certainly feel it between her thighs. She was tempted to squeeze but decided against it. His cock could wait until she was finished with his bottom. Part of her suspected perhaps, he was somehow enjoying this.

"This is payback Nathan but not all of it, yet."

SMACK, "fuck", SMACK "shit", SMACK "oh God", SMACK "OWWW"

She couldn't stop herself from continuing, a strange but nice feeling of power somehow gripped her as she gave in to it and perhaps latent desires dormant all these years were coming to the fore.

"It's not?" he said when he could speak.

"No, it's not… until I decide it's enough. You obviously need this and it's obviously doing some good, at least you are paying attention, which you never do."

SMACK, "OWWW", SMACK "Nooo", SMACK "ooohh", SMACK "FUCKK"

"Oh my god," was all he could say. "I thought this was a game. I didn't think games were supposed to hurt."

The whole thing was so erotic now she could hardly stand it, she wanted to fuck him so badly. It felt like a primaeval force was unleashed inside her, she was so wet, she could feel the dampness on the seat, her breathing was more than a little ragged.

"Oh well payback needs to hurt a little, darling, and perhaps it needs to hurt quite a bit more," she mused and then, "Hmm… well it might be just about enough for now."

She felt him instantly relax. The devil was in her and as an afterthought, she added, "But then again, just maybe one or two more for good measure won't go amiss. I'm enjoying this by the way."

SMACK, "OOHH", SMACK "shit Cassie", SMACK "fuckkkk", SMACK "OWWW"

"You bitch!" he said, rather unwisely.

"What did you say? Did you call me a bitch?" She raised the sandal again and peppered his backside with spank after spank.

SMACK, "ouchh", SMACK "OWWW", SMACK "ohh oww", SMACK "oohh"

SMACK, "OW", SMACK "ohhh", SMACK "ahhh", SMACK "fuck"

The afterthought had turned into several more spanks as she unleashed herself on him. The upset and annoyance he had caused her in the past weeks came to mind.

"Christ! FUCK! I thought you said one or two, that was a lot," he complained when she stopped.

However, he must have bitten his tongue on any more retorts, after the last volley of smacks.

"I lied!" she laughed teasingly. "So, are you sorry for what you did?" she continued, feeling she should gain some complicity from him in the exercise.

"Yes," he said almost without hesitating and undoubtedly wanting to end his ordeal.

"Really SMACK you SMACK are SMACK? You don't sound sorry Nathan, let's see if this will help you to decide. Also, my name is... Mistress! SMACK SMACK."

"No, wait... Cassie... I meant Mistress, no, please, Mistress," he said but it was too late.

"I'll show you just how much of a Mistress I am, Nathan. You deserve every one of these spanks and more. That phone bill was a grand, Nathan. A grand and I'm very angry about it, as you're finding out. I'm going to spank your bottom until you are truly sorry."

SMACK, "AHH", SMACK "OWWW", SMACK "Nooo", SMACK "please"

SMACK, "oohh", SMACK "Ahhh", SMACK "OW", SMACK "ouch"

He cried out after each spank hit his bottom, and he was obviously feeling the spanks which gave her an immense feeling of satisfaction.

"Oh no please!!" his arse was scarlet, and she could feel the heat coming off it and by the sound of his voice, it was stinging like mad. "I really am, I'm sorry, babe... I am, no more please babe that's enough."

"Hmmm, well now, you sound a little bit sorry, but I get to decide when you've had enough not you, and I don't' think you've had enough just yet," she said assertively warring with her lust for him and her enjoyment of the feeling of newfound freedom she had unleashed within her. It was in some ways hugely enjoyable and the frustration which had built up inside her was melting away with every spank she gave him.

SMACK, "OHHH", SMACK "OWWWW", SMACK "NOO", SMACK "AHHH"

SMACK, "OOWWOW", SMACK "Ohhh", SMACK "fuckk", SMACK "Ahh"

"Oh god, Cass… Mistress, please, I am sorry, really," he said and sounded like he really meant it.

"I don't think he's going to help you now," she laughed.

SMACK, "OWWW", SMACK "oh shittt", SMACK "fuckk", SMACK "ohhh"

He gasped and shouted at each spank. She felt perhaps she should really finish it before she really got carried away. It could easily happen if she continued much longer.

"Another six, Nathan, just to make sure you remember this lesson in future."

He said nothing, but she could tell he had had enough.

She measured each smack, waiting between each one making them count, and smacking as hard as she dared.

"One" SMACK, "OW"

"Two" SMACK "OWWW"

"Three" SMACK "FUCKKK"

"Four" SMACK "AHHH"

"Five" SMACK "Jesusssss"

"Six" SMACK "OWWWWWWW"

She was panting herself, a little from the exertion. Her arm hurt she realised. It was time to call it quits. She rested the sandal on his back and ran her hand over his arse, it was so unbelievably red and hot.

She felt somehow satisfied and inexplicably whole again as if by this very act she was no longer a pushover. Now a more urgent need was pressing, she needed to fuck him so very badly and she couldn't wait any longer to do it. She threw aside the sandal onto the floor without looking at where it landed.

"OK, that's it for now. I think you've had your payback. I'm certainly satisfied you're sorry," she told him. "Stand up."

He did so, he looked somehow relieved and red-faced, a little bit like a naughty little boy. He rubbed his backside which she figured must be stinging quite badly.

But his cock was so very, very hard and she could see it was wet with pre-cum. He had liked it. She was sure now he had enjoyed this submission to her will. She had certainly done so. He probably wasn't going to admit it, however.

She stood up too and took his hand saying nothing but leading him to the bed, and then she pushed him roughly onto his back. He didn't resist and from the expression in his eyes, she could tell how much he wanted to feel her hot and dripping wet pussy surrounding his hard cock.

In one swift movement, she divested herself of the negligee and kicked off the other sandal. She climbed onto him and straddled him, very slowly but quite urgently lowering herself and guiding his shaft into her. It slipped in with ease and she let out a loud moan and is she sank down onto it.

This was one of her favourite positions and she knew it wouldn't be long until she came. His eyes were closed, and his breath came in spurts, she began to move up and down his shaft quite slowly but wriggling until the head of his cock was just moving up and pulling on her clit and she fucked him. He reached up to her soft pliable breasts and fingered her nipples knowing that would drive her wild. It did and it was also at *that* moment she started to ride him almost uncontrollably and she was screaming out it felt so good, so hard and she felt so full. Each time as she came down, he raised his hips up to meet her and arched his back.

"Oh God, Oh Nathan, Oh God, Nathan, oh fuck, oh shit, oh fuck, oh God, oh, oh, oh, oh, oh, oh," she shouted as she felt the rising tide coming up to wash over her. The wave broke and she started to climax harder than she had ever done before. "Oohh Nathan! Nathan! Nathan! Ohhhhhh!"

She screamed, cumming so loudly that had it not been a detached house with a nice long drive the whole street must have heard it. She pitched forward onto his chest and his arms came up to hold her tight and kiss her lips hard.

"Cassandra you are such a fucking bitch," he whispered, but it wasn't meant in hurt, it was filled with love and affection. It was as if the spanking had somehow brought them closer in some weird and kinky fashion.

"I know," she replied, and she thought to herself 'but until today I did not know just how much.'

He lifted her up gently and she did not resist, he turned her over onto her stomach and she automatically got up on all fours. This was another position she loved, she loved to feel him fucking her doggy style and ramming himself deep into her. She could tell he was really in a mood to do so.

"You've had your fun," he growled. "Now it's my turn"

Almost roughly he slid his shaft home and she gasped as it went in so far and deep.

"Oh GOD!" he cried out as he felt the slick wetness of her pussy on his hard cock. "OH GOD I NEED THIS, I am going to fuck you Cassie, so fucking hard, you bitch! You fucking bitch. Fuck, fuck, fuck, fuck!"

"Yes! Yes, Nathan fuck me, I want you to fuck me!"

He held on to her hips with both hands and he began slowly, savouring the moment. She could feel him pulling right out to the tip of his cock almost teasing her and then going back in deep. It was unbearable but so deliciously beautiful. Slowly he began to go faster and harder, she loved it, his hard cock rammed her again and again and his balls slapped against her backside each time.

"Oh Nathan, Oh god Nathan…"

"Cassie, Jesus, Cassie, God I love to fuck you, oh God," he cried out and now he was going fast and hard. Cassandra was shouting with pleasure, but he was lost in that moment before he would shoot his load. His cock was pulsing and she knew he was close. Suddenly he rammed home with such force that she was pushed forward onto her stomach as his orgasm broke, she could feel his cum spurting hot and juicy inside of her, she loved it, loved that feeling.

"Aaaaaaaaaaaaaaahhhhhhhhhhhhhhhhhhhhhhhhh hhhhhh" she could hear him crying out so loud and so vocal, a guttural roar, until finally, he subsided.

They lay like that for quite a while, him on top of her, their skin glistening with sweat and her hair all wet. The sex had been incredible, electric. She hadn't felt so turned on for a very long time and her orgasm had been unbelievably good it seemed to go on and on forever.

Their breathing slowed and she slipped around to face him, he enfolded her, and her arms slipped around him drifting into sleep.

A little while later it was dark outside and, in the shadows, she looked at his face. His eyes opened and they kissed, long and slowly and tenderly.

"You know I love you, Nathan, you know that don't you?" she said.

"Yes, yes I do, Cassandra, and I love you too."

She smiled, her pearly whites glistening at him, he didn't say it often and she pulled him to her and hugged him tight.

"I am sorry I took you a little for granted," he said.

"Really?" she asked him, almost surprised at his honesty.

"Yes, yes I am," he said.

"Maybe I should spank you more often," she giggled.

"And maybe you shouldn't," he retorted but he was smiling. It didn't seem as if he was really objecting too much to it after all.

She leaned back and turned on the bedside light.

"Turn over and let me see your arse," she told him.

"For fuck's sake," he said with a laugh, but did as she had bid him.

"Hmm, it's still so, so red," she remarked running her hand over it lightly.

"Well that's hardly surprising," his muffled voice replied.

"Did it sting then darling?" she said playfully.

"Maybe," was all he would say, he was very macho deep down and wasn't about to admit too much.

He rolled over and looked at her.

"Anyway, you've had your payback, now haven't you?"

"Mmm maybe," she teased her eyes dancing.

"So, it's probably enough of that game?" he ventured.

She was silent for a moment and then looked at him with the tease still in her eyes. Absently her hand began to play with his flaccid organ.

"Well now, it depends," she said.

"On what?" he eyed her uncertainly but with a tinge of anticipation.

"On how you behave in future, darling, of course, don't you think? I mean if you take me for granted, don't listen to me, things like that, then maybe I will just have to spank you again."

She was smiling but also thinking of the events of the day and of the riding crop she had also bought which was for now safely hidden in her chest of drawers. It would be a shame never to try it out she was thinking, but not today.

"Oh, I will be exemplary from now on, babe, you'll see," he laughed.

She laughed too and leaned in to kiss him.

"Maybe," she said as her mouth moved to meet his. "Just remember… if you ever see me wearing those sandals again."

"Remember what?" he whispered.

"The spanking you just got and the spanking you'll be getting."

She kissed him softly and felt him go hard, something else entered into her mind. The lips of the buxom blonde at the shoe store. Peyton. What would her lips feel like?

Cassandra didn't know what had happened. All kinds of feelings had risen inside her. The spanking was a catharsis somehow. She had a feeling this was just the beginning of something, she just didn't know what.

Cassie spanks again (Book Two)

Cassandra flicked the rabbit onto pulse as she lay back naked on the bed. The rabbit was a recent acquisition with her newfound fascination for expanding her sexual horizons. She felt the pink latex shaft throb deliciously inside her while the little rabbit fronds teased her clit sending the exciting sensations through her whole body. She moaned softly pushing against it harder arching up her back a little.

She liked to start on the pulse mode which alternated vibrations and then stopped, almost like Nathan's teasing tongue when he was going down on her. She carried on in that mode until she could stand it no longer and pushed the button to make the vibrations continuous but not too strong. She had used it enough times to flick the modes with ease.

"Oh, oh my God, fuck!" she gasped. She was alone in her house and could shout as loud as she wanted.

Images were playing through her mind, as they seemed to do a lot these days. The spanking she had given Nathan was uppermost in her thoughts recently. As she recalled the SMACK SMACK SMACK of her sandal on his bottom, she got closer to the edge of her orgasm.

"Oh, Nathan," she whispered to herself, "I want to spank you again, and again, and again!"

She pushed the button to maximum strength which would take her right to the brink and beyond in seconds. Her pelvis began to buck involuntarily against the fronds sliding up against them fucking her own vibrator.

"Oh, oh, oh, oh, fuck, shit, oh God, oh, I want, oh, ohhhhh!" she let out a scream as the wave of her climax rushed through her filling her head with a cloud of pleasurable sensations. Just for a moment, she hit another plane, and the present melted away as the waves washed through her again and again. She held the rabbit in place until she could no longer stand it. Then switched it off and lay still while she recovered from yet another masturbation session which seemed to be becoming more frequent.

When Nathan came home, she would fuck him at least once that evening, and he did not object at all, in fact, he was as horny and virile as any male around. He seemed more than happy she had up the ante on the sex and since the spanking, he had been very attentive to her. There had been no further reason or opportunity to use the sandals which were presently on her feet.

She was keeping those particular sandals purely for spanking but could not resist wearing them. The tan and pink strap flip flops with synthetic thin soles made her feel sexy, and she remembered what she had done with them to Nathan's bottom every time she put them on. Cassandra liked to wear them around the house but put them away before Nathan got home. She had promised him they would only appear if he deserved another spanking. She had taken to wearing the sandals whilst masturbating, as it turned her on.

Feeling relaxed after zoning out, she removed the rabbit from her still slick pussy and wiped it clean before putting it away in the drawer. The trip to obtain it had been interesting, to say the least. It was the very first time she had ventured into Ann Summers. Her sexual awakening had begun with Nathan after the staid sex life she had with her husband. Nathan had taken her to new heights of pleasure and initiated her into oral sex, and many new exciting positions. She bought sexy underwear to wear for him, and high heeled shoes. She still never ventured into the more uncharted waters. She had never watched any porn, nor looked at a sex shop online before the spanking incident. Until then she had not realised the desires buried deep in her psyche and like a very latent sensuous flower she began to blossom.

She had examined sex toys online with interest, and avidly read some accounts of using vibrators. She was determined to buy one and try one which is why she ended up in Ann Summers where she felt she might be able to get some good advice. After a lengthy time inspecting all it had to offer, and particularly the fetish wear and spanking implements, she had shyly asked the shop assistant for some help. The assistant proved to be very informative and knowledgeable and not the least fazed to be consulted. Cassandra had left clutching her purchase with excitement and feeling incredibly naïve.

The vibrator, after its initial charge, got regular daily use, but Cassandra was too shy to bring it out and show Nathan. She fantasised about using it on him or he on her, but she wasn't ready for it yet. Unlike most women in their thirties, who had probably done everything already, sex was a novelty to her. She knew there was so much more for her to explore.

Cassandra stopped daydreaming and stood up. In the mirror she caught a glimpse of her slim frame, she had a good figure with nice breasts, long dark hair and full bow-shaped lips with brown eyes. The woman who stared back at her was someone many would find incredibly sexy and irresistible. Nathan most certainly did. She loved Nathan very deeply as it turned out, and he loved her though it seemed more casually. The spanking seemed, to her, to have perhaps brought them closer somehow. It had also made her feel more assertive and less of a pushover. She was the provider, and she should be calling the shots. Up until the moment she had had him over her knee she had never felt empowered. Now she certainly did.

Cassandra had a shower, got dressed, and decided what to do with her day. A lady of leisure with more money at her disposal than she probably needed, she could do anything she wanted. She was a loner, and had few female friends. She spent most of her time with Nathan or alone painting, reading, or writing poetry. She dressed in jeans and a t-shirt, put the sandals away in her cupboard and went downstairs to eat.

The morning post was on the counter unopened. Cassandra set down to her freshly made avocado, pepperoni, cheese, pickle and mayo sandwich on a plate on the breakfast bar, alongside a cup of tea. She picked up the letters and looked them over. It was the usual bills, and correspondence about insurance, but one caught her eye. A letter from her credit card company. She opened it to find it was an over-limit notification which they wanted immediately rectified. The account was in her name, but Nathan was an authorised user. It had a generous limit and, as far as she knew, he never abused it. However, it seemed as if there had been some unwarranted expenses.

Cassandra became annoyed. She didn't like wasteful spending and she managed her affairs very well. She had a good reputation with the banks and finance companies and did not want that ruined. Determined to get to the bottom of what had happened, she finished her sandwich and pulled up the credit card account on the computer. There had been a large payment to a tyre company, for car tyres, she presumed for the Mazda sports car which she had bought him. She paid for the servicing and maintenance. It seemed very odd the tyres had needed to be replaced so soon, but Cassandra imagined it must have been for a good reason. After all, Nathan might be wayward, but he wasn't a wastrel, or so she thought.

Cassandra dealt with the over-limit and made a payment. However, she was still upset. Nathan should have told her about the purchase. It was a loose agreement that he would consult her if there was going to be a big expense. She was also very cross he'd gone over the limit and she had to find out from the credit card company. It was true he might not know, but had he mentioned it she could have checked. She sat stewing on it for a while sipping her tea and then she came to a decision. The sandals would be coming out that evening and Nathan would learn another lesson. His mobile spending had been much reduced since his spanking and she had been checking up on it, so to that degree, the last spanking had worked. He undoubtedly needed another one and she was going to give it to him as soon as he got home.

As her ire cooled, she felt a new sensation. A thrill. The thrill of the idea of once more having Nathan's naked bottom across her lap. She couldn't deny the sexual feelings which arose from this once more. It made her almost instantly wet. The spanking wasn't just about payback, although she wasn't ready to admit it to herself completely. She enjoyed giving him a spanking and was looking forward to giving him another now she had a reason to justify it. The feelings were too new to her to examine it closely. Perhaps that reflection might come in time.

***

Cassandra was sitting on the sofa wearing a short red dress at Nathan's home time. She had made dinner which was a beef stew in the slow cooker. Feeling quite naughty she wasn't wearing anything under the dress at all. She had the sandals on her feet and wondered if he would notice, and what he would do if he did. She wasn't going to say anything at first, but she had her strategy planned out. The letter from the credit card company was sitting open on the breakfast bar, along with a statement and the offending purchase underlined. The tyres for the Mazda were not cheap and it wasn't a small amount.

On the table beside her was a glass of her favourite Merlot and an open bottle. She felt the need to fortify herself, although it was going to be far easier than the first time she had spanked him.

As she took another sip, Cassandra heard his car pull up in the drive. She lived in a detached but quite modern house at the end of a very long drive. It was quite close to the town but far enough from other houses to be secluded. Her husband had installed an alarm and all kinds of security systems when he was alive as for some reason, he was paranoid about security. They had a big garden which sported a nice gazebo, beds and lawns. She had a man who came and mowed it, and also did some of the hedge trimming although Nathan was pretty handy in that department when he could be persuaded. Cassandra liked the garden and pottered around in it particularly in summer. She would grow vegetables and nurture her flowers. The garden had nice borders too due to her ministrations.

The front door opened and closed. Nathan would have taken off his shoes, and hung up his jacket. There was a hook for the keys. Cassandra believed in being tidy.

Shortly afterwards he came into the living room. He smiled as soon as he saw her. Nathan was well built, and looked it in his jeans and t-shirt. He kept his dark blonde hair in the contemporary style, had a nice line of stubble, and blue eyes. He was undeniably handsome, incredibly good looking in fact. Cassandra would even go so far as to say he was drop-dead gorgeous. When he got his clothes off, she loved his sexy twenty-five-year-old body. Even more, she loved his thick hard cock. It seemed big to her although she had no idea or anything to compare it to except Leonard's and his was OK, as in, it did the job. But Nathan's cock inside her was an experience she couldn't get enough of.

"Hi, baby," he said leaning down to kiss her. He called her that even though he was nearly ten years younger. A toy boy to some but she loved him just the same.

"Hi," she said, kissing him back and feeling the flames start to ignite inside her. She wanted him almost at once and had to fight with her resolve to teach him a lesson.

"So, how was your day?" he said, helping himself to her wine and sitting down cradling it in his hand.

"It was OK, how was yours?" she said in a non-committal tone.

"Yeah, you know. Lectures, study, lectures, I've got a paper to write…" he stopped tailing off.

While he was talking Cassandra had crossed one leg over the other. She had begun to rhythmically tap the sole of her sandal against her foot using her toes. All the while she was watching him innocently as if it wasn't a deliberate act of provocation.

"You were saying?" she prompted.

"Yes, the paper…" he stopped staring at her foot and the sandal slapping up and down as if mesmerised.

"The paper?"

"Is that?" he said. "Are those?"

"My sandals? Yes, darling, yes they are."

"Oh." It was clear he was searching through his memory to see if he could figure out what he'd done with a slightly furrowed brow.

"Let me put you out of your misery," she said interrupting his train of thought. "What did I say to you about these sandals?"

"I…" he stopped. It was clear he didn't want to repeat it.

"Come with me," she said getting up, "Come on." She held out her hand.

He took and let her pull him up regarding her quizzically.

"Where are we going?"

"You'll see," she smiled, led him into the kitchen and up to the breakfast bar. "What is that you see on there?"

"I err…" he picked up the letter and read it, and then the statement. "Oh!" He flashed her a guilty look. "I can explain."

"Well, go on," she said standing with her arms folded but still perfectly affable.

"I mean I was going to explain, and it slipped my mind."

"I see." She pursed her lips not happy with this.

"Look the tyres got worn down, I noticed them the other day, I'm not sure how, maybe they weren't that good quality. The guy at the tyre place said they might not be, and I mean you want me to be safe, don't you?

So, I got them changed. He did me a great deal on four tyres. I used my credit card, and I was meaning to tell you…" once more he stopped.

Cassandra was regarding him a little more sceptically, "Four tyres, Nathan, how could *all* four tyres get worn down?"

"Like I said, I've been driving it just as normal. I mean it's a lot of mileage to and from uni and stuff."

It didn't sound right to her, but she passed over it and tackled the other offences she felt he had committed. "Didn't we talk about you asking me first if it was going to be a big amount?"

"Well, yeah but it was an emergency, I mean once I saw the tyres were worn, it had to be fixed."

"You could have rung me. Texted me. Talked to me, darling, and you didn't."

"I'm sorry, babe," he ventured.

"On top of which if you had at least told me afterwards I would have been saved the embarrassment of this letter." She picked it up and dropped it back onto the counter.

"Yes, I know, I should have. Like I said, it kind of slipped my mind." It sounded lame even to him.

"How could it slip your mind? We are supposed to be truthful with each other, not hide things… well not like this."

"I'm sorry, really…"

Cassandra looked at him. She could easily let it slide, as she had always done in the past. He stood there like a big kid being told off and hoping she wouldn't be mad at him for long. He was endearing and so beautiful. It was hard to be angry with him. However, that was the old Cassie, and she had changed. She knew she needed to continue to change or go back to the old ways. If she let this pass, he'd do it again for sure and they would be back here again a month or six with another missed expense. No, she decided firmly, it was not going to happen.

"Sorry isn't good enough, Nathan," she said quietly.

He didn't reply.

"What did I say would be happening if I wore these sandals again?"

"I... I don't like to say," he hesitated.

"Well, I want you to say, so tell me what I said." Her voice was a little more assertive, firmer now.

"Fine, you said I should remember the spanking I got and the one I was going to get." He sighed.

"Exactly. Do you remember the spanking you got?"

He nodded slowly. She imagined he could hardly forget. It was all too memorable for her and she hadn't been on the receiving end of the sandal. His backside would surely remember it, if nothing else.

"Good, because now you're going to get another one."

"Do we have to…" he began.

"Yes, darling, we do!" she said in even more assertive tones. "For my sanity and for you. I was very upset today with what you did, and I want you to understand how it feels for me. This is my way of showing you and getting you to remember in future."

He regarded her a little morosely for a moment although he seemed also apprehensive. The spanking probably had stung his ego as much as his backside, she thought.

"OK, what do you want me to do?" Having realised there was no getting out of it, he seemed almost to want to get it over with.

Cassandra didn't want to go quite so fast, but she was certainly in the mood now to give him a sound spanking.

"Come back into the living room," she said.

"Not upstairs?"

"No."

"OK," he shrugged.

Cassandra returned to the living room and sat down on the sofa. It seemed as good a place as any, and she could get him comfortably over her lap. He stood waiting for her to tell him what to do.

"Take your clothes off, honey, all of them."

This time she didn't ask him to do it slowly or sensuously. She felt sexy but on reflection wanted him to see it less in that light.

"OK." He looked askance at her remembering the slow striptease she'd wanted before.

"Just take them off, come on!"

He stripped a little perfunctorily, perhaps realising this was less of a game than he thought. He stood naked in a very short space of time. She raked a glance over his body, not daring to linger. It was arousing. He had been working out at the gym even more and his six-pack was well defined. He had a few tattoos which gave him a bad boy image, even though he was very far removed from that.

Slowly and deliberately, she reached down and took off her right sandal. She held it by the heel just like before and tapped it lightly in her other hand.

"Come here and get over my knee."

"OK."

He walked towards her and she could see his cock begin to harden. Once more she suspected there was something about it, he liked. He knelt down and settled across her lap quite readily. She didn't have to order him this time.

"Do you remember the rules?" she said softly, placing the sole of the sandal against his arse, "Or must I remind you."

"I have to do what you tell me," he said at once.

"*When* I tell you and what else?"

She began to lightly run the sole of the sandal over his bottom. His cock was fully erect now between her legs. Part of him was enjoying this, she could swear to it.

"Erm…"

"Really, Nathan, how could you forget?"

She lifted the sandal and brought it down with a resounding SMACK and then on the other cheek SMACK.

"I don't know, what?" he said frustrated.

"You SMACK are SMACK to SMACK call SMACK me SMACK Mistress SMACK!"

She punctuated what she was saying with sharp spanks of the sandal, lifting it off on impact knowing this would sting. Red marks appeared on his buttocks where the sandal had made contact.

"OW! Fuck… yes Mistress!" he managed.

"Good."

She paused, the spanking had to be effective, and she wanted to make sure he understood why he was getting it too, like last time. Last time she had worked up to it. She had kissed him beforehand and seduced him almost, rubbing his cock and making it hard before taking him upstairs to spank him. This time she had dispensed with the preamble as if the spanking took on a new importance, it was the priority. The seduction would come later, when he'd had his lesson.

"So, darling, tell me why you are back over my knee for another spanking," she said to him. This time he knew better than to beat around the bush.

"I spent money on the credit card, and it went over the limit and I didn't tell you about it," he said to her all in a rush. Perhaps he was hoping this would mitigate his fate.

She raised the sandal once more, this was good, but it wasn't going to change anything about the spanking.

"Yes, SMACK that SMACK is SMACK exactly SMACK correct SMACK good boy SMACK."

"OW," he said after each spank, "I'm sorry, I've learned my lesson, I won't do it again."

Perhaps he felt this would get him off lightly, but he was wrong, as Cassandra was determined to show him

"No! SMACK you SMACK have SMACK not SMACK learned SMACK anything SMACK you little shit!"

She did not know where that last bit had come from. There must be something inside her which was emerging like a butterfly from a chrysalis. A dominant streak she never knew she had.

"I have, honestly…" he protested.

"No, Nathan. You're going to learn a lesson but my way. I'm the one giving you the spanking and like I told you before I will say when it's over."

She paused, adjusted herself a little.

"Now SMACK in future SMACK you will never SMACK spend anything like that amount SMACK again without asking me SMACK will you? SMACK."

"OW, fuck… no…"

"No SMACK what?"

"No, Mistress."

"Better." SMACK SMACK.

"You SMACK will consult me SMACK about big amounts SMACK or otherwise SMACK you will be getting SMACK another spanking SMACK understood?"

"Yes, Mistress."

She smiled to herself. He was sounding far more contrite and compliant. Time to test his understanding, she felt.

"What SMACK did SMACK I say SMACK you are SMACK to do? SMACK"

He hesitated a little too long.

"I SMACK can't SMACK hear SMACK you SMACK."

"I… I must speak to you about spending big amounts in future and if I don't, I'll get a spanking, Mistress," he said quickly.

"Good SMACK boy SMACK."

Cassandra was happy so far, and his backside was certainly getting very red just like before. She could feel the wetness building between her thighs and part of her couldn't wait until the spanking was over. However, she wanted to be sure she reinforced the lesson.

"Very good, darling, and now I'm going to make very sure you remember what I've said."

"Oh… but…" he got no further because she began a volley of smacks on his backside, peppering it with the sandal each getting harder than the last.

SMACK "Ohhh" SMACK "OWWW" SMACK "Fuck" SMACK "Ahhh"

SMACK "God Cassie" SMACK "Fuckkk" SMACK "wowowow" SMACK "ooohhh"

SMACK "OWWW" SMACK "Shittt" SMACK "AHHH" SMACK "OWW"

SMACK "Nooo" SMACK "Fuck" SMACK "Ouchhh" SMACK "Ahhh"

SMACK "God fuck fuck" SMACK "Owww" SMACK "Shittt" SMACK "Ahhhh"

SMACK "Nooo" SMACK "Ow ouch" SMACK "OW OW OW" SMACK "OWWWWW"

She stopped for a moment. His bottom was a nice shade of crimson.

"So, do you promise never to do that again, Nathan?" she said softly.

"Yes, yes I do, Mistress."

"Good, very good."

He stayed silent hoping it was gone. Cassandra had other ideas, and she wanted, once more to end his spanking with some final very hard spanks.

"You're getting another ten of the very best spanks before I let you up. I want to make sure you understand what I will and won't accept from you. I love you, darling, but you need to understand my limits."

"Yes, Mistress," he whispered.

She began the final spanks waiting between each one and smacking them very hard.

"One" SMACK, "OW"

"Two" SMACK "Ouchhh"

"Three" SMACK "Ahhhh"

"Four" SMACK "Shit oh fucking shit"

"Five" SMACK "OWWWW"

"Six" SMACK "OUCH OWW"

"Seven" SMACK "OWWWWWW"

"Eight" SMACK "Fuckkkkkk"

"Nine" SMACK "OHHHHHH"

"Ten" SMACK "OW OW OW OW OWWWWW"

She stopped.

"Have you learned your lesson?" she asked him.

"Yes, Mistress.

"And are you sorry for what you did?"

"Yes, Mistress."

She listened to the inflexion in his voice. He sounded as if he genuinely meant it.

"OK, then you can get up now," she said. She put the sandal down beside her.

Nathan pulled himself up onto her knees and stretched a little. She could see his cock was standing well to attention. Seeing him like that, an idea suddenly occurred to her.

She opened her legs wider and pulled her skirt up. He saw her pussy was exposed, and he couldn't take his eyes off it.

"I'm not wearing any knickers, and I am wet as fuck," she whispered.

"Oh God," was his response.

"Lick me, I want you to lick me." Her eyes locked with his which became lustful, hungry. He loved to go down on her and needed no encouragement to do so.

He swiftly moved around kneeling between her thighs and lay forward so that his mouth could access her pussy. His strong arms came behind her and pulled her in while his tongue began to work its magic.

"Fuck, oh Nathan, oh my God, I just love it when you do that, oh, oh, oh darling, oh!" she started to moan, and cry out laying back against the squabs on the sofa. He pulled her in harder tighter, increasing the intensity with his tongue.

"Oh, oh my, oh fuck, oh fuck, oh, oh, oh, oh God, oh, I'm going to…" she let out a long sigh and the orgasm which had been building inside of her unleashed and she screamed out, "oh, oh, ohhhh, ohhhh, ohhhh, ohhhh." Over and over again while his tongue relentlessly teased her until she couldn't take anymore and pushed his head away.

"Oh fuck, you are so fucking good at that, so good," she gasped.

He was looking up at her and smiling, seemingly no worse for wear for his spanking. She wanted to fuck him, but it could wait. Seeing his cock like that as he sat up on his knees, she said, "Stand up, I want to suck you, darling."

He obliged with alacrity as she took the hard shaft in her mouth, teasing her lips around the head. She worked him with her tongue, lips and fingers. She used her fingers to wank his shaft, while her tongue and lips took his head in and out.

He gasped and moaned in pleasure.

"Oh, oh, fuck, Cassie, you bitch, you bitch, oh, oh, fuck."

She continued pushing him harder feeling his cock start to pulse. She could tell by the sound of his moans he was close and began to move faster.

"Ow, fuck, shit, yeah… oh my fucking God, Cassie, ow, fuck, ow, oh, oh, ohhhhhhhhhhhhhhhhhhhhhhhhhhhhh!" he climaxed his cock pumping hard, and she took his cum into her mouth, and savoured it before swallowing it in enjoyment at the taste. Somehow, she had always liked the flavour from him.

When he finished, she stood up and started to kiss him hard and passionately. Her hands roving over his body, and his hands running over hers under her skirt. After a while, she stopped.

"Would you like some dinner?" she asked smiling.

"Yes, please, but what's for dessert?" It was a little bit of a growl, but she knew what he wanted.

"Me of course. You can take me upstairs and fuck me."

"Oh, I intend to, you little bitch, I fully intend to."

"Am I such a bitch?" her eyes teased.

"Yes, yes you are, and I love you for it, God help me."

"Did you really learn your lesson?" she whispered moving in for one more kiss.

"Yes, I did. I really did."

"I enjoyed giving it to you."

"I know, and that's why you are a bitch." He let out a low laugh.

She kissed him. Things were changing between them, almost becoming more visceral. There was something quite macho in him which was coming to the fore, and he was right, there was a lot of bitch in her too. She loved it, the power play. That seemed to be part of it. As yet she didn't fully understand it, but she knew she would.

***

A day or so passed since the second spanking. Cassandra had indulged herself with the vibrator thinking of it. She had also begun to google words like dominatrix and other interesting things. One thing she liked was the corset and high heels get up that some of them wore. She thought it would suit her very well, and she wanted one for herself.

There was also still something bothering her about the tyres. She couldn't understand how they had worn out so quickly. Nathan's explanation wasn't quite good enough for her.

Whilst on an outing to purchase a corset from Ann Summers, she happened to drive past the tyre place where Nathan had had the tyres changed. She remembered the name, *Maximum Tyres*, from the credit card statement. On impulse she pulled into the forecourt left her own car and headed for the reception.

"Hello, how can I help?" asked a man at the counter whose name tag said his name was 'Mike'.

"Hello, Mike, is it? I just wondered… my boyfriend came in a while back to get all four tyres changed on his red Mazda."

Mike thought for a moment, and then said, "Oh, yeah. I do remember it, yes."

"I just wondered, I mean," she fluttered her eyes at him a little, playing the slightly helpless woman, "I just couldn't figure out why the tyres were so worn, erm, they weren't *that* old, it seems odd. He said you told him the tyres were substandard or something."

She knew how to play the part of being naïve, something she was far from in actuality. She had a degree and had studied Fine Art at university. That was one of the few times she had mixed with others. By the time she went to uni, she was married to Leonard, he had funded her studies. She hadn't done the usual student stuff and certainly not the promiscuity of other students. There was no extramarital fucking for Cassandra. Though she had studied Art History as part of her degree and was very literate, she could easily appear otherwise when she wanted.

"Oh, did he?" Mike looked a bit put out at this intelligence. "Well, no, that's not the reason at all. The tyres were top of the range."

"Goodness, really? I had no idea, I bought the car for him, I had assumed he'd been looking after it. I mean I just pay the bills."

He regarded her with newfound respect. She was the paymaster this much was clear to him. Apart from which she was looking very attractive in a summery floral dress and a pair of thong sandals (one of her older but favourite pairs) with narrow straps and kitten heels.

"Your, erm, boyfriend, wore the tyres out I'm afraid," he said frankly.

"What?" She raised an eyebrow in surprise.

"Yes, he came in, in a bit of a panic actually."

"Oh?"

"Yes. He's young your boyfriend, yes?"

"Yes, he is."

He could see she was older and more mature than he would have remembered Nathan to be.

"Anyway, you know these young blokes getting up to larks."

"What kind of larks exactly?" she said more sweetly than the bitterness welling up inside.

"Burnouts, it's all the rage. They go on an aerodrome and then they do handbrake turns to see who can make the most smoke. A burnout. The trouble is it wears the tyres out like nobody's business."

"Really?" she pursed her lips on hearing this but kept her tone more level than she felt.

"Yes. Apparently, he'd been in a burnout contest. He won but the tyres were shot. They post this stuff on YouTube, by the way, he showed me on the phone."

"Do they indeed?"

"They do," he gave a short hollow laugh, "I've still got the tyres if you want to see them? You can look for yourself."

"Yes, I would very much like to, if it's not too much trouble."

"Not at all." He had warmed to her attitude which was friendly and open. Cassandra was a very cordial person although shy of others. She was easy to like.

He led her out to a pile of used tyres at the back and pointed to four which were sat one on top of each other. As she got closer, she examined the tyres and saw that not only were they bald but almost shredded to the wire in some places."

"Good God isn't that dangerous?" she asked him quite shocked.

"Absolutely, I'm surprised he wasn't pulled over by the cops, to be honest. It would be a hefty fine. Also stopping would be difficult with those."

"I would imagine. Surely he can't have driven far with those?"

He screwed up his face, "I think he said it was a fair distance, to be honest. About a thirty-minute drive to here."

"Thirty minutes?" Her mind was racing at the risks he would have taken driving for that amount of time. She took out her phone. "Do you mind if I?"

"Be my guest."

She took several photos of the tyres including closeups of the worst bits and then put her phone away.

"Thank you, Mike, you've been more than helpful."

"My pleasure," he said as they walked back, "Don't be too hard on him. Boys will be boys. As they say."

"Oh sure, of course," she said absently.

"Is there anything else?" He resumed his position behind the counter.

"No, but thank you again, I will definitely come here when I need some tyres," she told him.

He flicked a glance out to her four by four. She hated it. Leonard had insisted she drive it to keep her safe. Something in her couldn't get rid of it now he was gone.

"Those don't come cheap when you do want some replacements."

"I don't drive it much." She smiled.

"Ah."

"Anyway, I won't take any more of your time, thank you."

"My pleasure."

He watched her walk away before turning to his computer.

Cassandra remained perfectly composed until she got into her car. She drove it a little way down the road and then burst into tears. She parked up and indulged in a hearty bout of weeping. Nathan had lied to her and she was very upset. This was aside from the fact he'd done something very dangerous and stupid. He had indulged in an activity which was incredibly childish to her and it had cost a lot of unnecessary money. It felt like a dreadful betrayal. The tears subsided, to be replaced by anger. Not be hard on him? Oh, no. Nathan was going to pay very dearly for his bad behaviour and his lies. This merited something far more than just an ordinary spanking.

In a determined and grim mood, she headed for Ann Summers. She was looking for something which would transform her into Cassandra the Mistress. They didn't really have any corsets, but she decided she could get one online at a later date. It didn't take long, however, to find the most appropriate item they had. A black faux leather stretchy cami suspender with a halter neck which created a plunging neckline. At the back, it dipped halfway down her back. The ensemble zipped up at the front. She bought herself a pair of lacy knickers to go with it, although she had not decided whether to wear those or not. It might be good for him to see what he wasn't going to get until she had dealt with him properly. She went to the shoe shop and picked out a pair of high heeled black shiny patent mules. Disappointingly Peyton wasn't there. Perhaps it was her day off. In any case, she had other things on her mind than flirtatious shop assistants. Whatever her thoughts were regarding Peyton, they could wait for another day.

Cassandra returned home feeling a bit better after shopping. It had calmed her down, but inside she was still very angry and emotionally bruised. One thing she would never do was lie to Nathan. She might not tell him things, like her masturbation sessions at home but if he asked her outright, she would tell him the truth. She made herself some lunch while she planned Nathan's fate.

She took a nap after lunch and then a long bath. Then she painted her nails bright red, and put on some light makeup. She was going to wear some very glossy red lipstick just like the dominatrixes she had seen on the internet. She tied her hair back into a ponytail which made her look very severe. This time she did not need a glass of wine. She was hyped up enough as it was. Looking in the mirror, the outfit made her look hot, and the stretchy fabric hugged her curves. She had decided to leave the knickers off. Her nicely shaved pussy was on view, but this was all to the good, he would want it and not be able to have it. On the bed, Cassandra placed the black leather riding crop brought from an equestrian store, and the pink thong sandals. Both would be used that evening when Nathan returned home. She did not have long to wait.

She sat in the living room as it neared the time for Nathan to return. As usual, she heard the front door open and shut, he took off his shoes, and wandered into the living room. He stopped dead.

"Cassie?" he said his eyes almost popping out of his head.

"Nathan," she said smoothly.

"What the…" he was bereft of speech never having seen her look like *that*. "I mean not that I don't like it, I mean fuck, Cassie, Jesus. That's fucking hot as fuck."

"Sit down, Nathan," she said not cracking a smile.

"OK." He looked at her uncertainly.

His appearance had brought back her anger at what he'd done.

"Do you know what I did today?" she asked him.

"I'm thinking you got the outfit maybe, for one thing…"

"I did, it's true but on the way to get it, I did something else. I happened to pass the tyre place. You know the one you changed the tyres at?"

"Oh yes." He looked at her with great affability, not catching on at all.

"So, I went inside and spoke to a nice guy called Mike, about your tyres. It's just I couldn't quite understand why they had worn out so fast."

"Oh? Oh!" His face fell a little ludicrously, like a schoolboy caught out on a prank.

"Do you know what he told me? Hmm?" she got up and paced the floor a little, her eyes beginning to flash. "No, don't answer me. He told me you had stripped the thread off the tyres doing burnouts at a competition. And then you drove to the tyre place for thirty minutes with the tyres in shreds." She raised her voice a little as she let go of the tight control on her fury.

"Now, it wasn't really so bad, babe," he began.

"Wasn't it? Wasn't it?" she picked up her phone and held it up showing him the photos. "I've seen the tyres. Nathan and you are lucky you didn't have an accident or worse!"

Her tone made him flinch just a little. She had never been so angry as she was now, and he was certainly feeling her wrath.

"OK, you got me, I didn't tell you because I thought you'd be mad, and that's exactly what you are," he said sounding defensive.

"Didn't tell me, no, you outright lied to me. You lied to my face. How could you?" Her voice cracked a little.

"Shit," he said noticing her eyes start to glisten. "Babe, look I'm sorry."

"Sorry, you're sorry. That's what you always say, Nathan, but sorry doesn't cut it for me, not this time."

"OK, so what do you want me to say or do?" His voice took on a sulky tone.

"Don't! Not today. Don't you dare start to sulk, not after what you've done." Cassie surprised herself and Nathan. She had become so much more assertive, almost as if it came naturally to her.

He bit his lip, rather like a child.

"Fine, but what do you want to do, Cassie? Tell me and I'll do it."

Cassandra pulled herself together with an effort.

"You need to be punished, Nathan. That's what I want to do."

"Punished?" he looked at her sharply.

"Yes, punished for your lies and your deception," she retorted.

"Oh no, this was a game, and I accepted it," he stood up angrily. "But punished, like a child? How dare you expect me to submit to *that*, Cassie?"

"How dare I?" Angry tears sprang to her eyes. "How dare *you*? I cried for half an hour in the car after I heard about what you'd done. I love you so much, and you hurt me, with lies. You lied to me, and I'm upset. I'm so upset." The tears flowed unbidden down her cheeks as she said it. She hadn't meant to get so emotional, but his flat-out rebuttal and his attitude got to her.

It also got to him, as he wasn't used to seeing her cry either.

"Now, Cassie, darling, Cassie, Cassie," he stepped towards her to try and take her in his arms.

"Don't touch me! I'm so angry with you right now. I'm disappointed and I'm very hurt. I love you so much, but you've wounded my heart. I'm going upstairs now, and you can think about what you've done. You deserve something, don't you? I think you do, and getting punished seems to be the only thing which improves your behaviour. But if it's not what you want then please come up with an alternative which is going to work and make me feel better too. Look you've made me cry all over again. Anyway, I can't talk to you anymore about this, not at the moment."

"Cassie, Cassie, I'm really sorry," he tried to say.

She was crying openly now, and dashed the tears of rage away from her face. Her voice was full of emotion. She left the room abruptly and ran upstairs to the bedroom shutting the door a little more forcefully than necessary.

She sat on the bed sobbing angrily for a while, before coming to her senses. She dried her eyes, fixed her makeup, and lipstick again which made her feel better. There was no sound from downstairs but at least she had not heard the front door slam, so he must still be at home.

She began to feel a bit more rational. Raising her voice to him and telling her how she felt had got quite a bit of it off her chest. When she thought about it objectively, perhaps the punishment bit was a bridge too far for both of them. After all, he was a grown man and the spanking had been fun. This was crossing lines maybe which should not be crossed. Perhaps it was too much. As she was contemplating going down and telling him she would accept his apology, there came a knock at the door.

"Cassie?" Nathan's tone was very tentative.

She sat up straight suddenly on the bed, thinking she might as well hear what he had got to say first.

"Come on in, Nathan." She was calmer now, and her voice was quite neutral.

He entered very quietly, came and sat down on the bed beside her.

"Cassie, I'm sorry. I'm sorry about the lying. I've been a fool and it was stupid of me and idiotic. I don't know what I was thinking."

"OK." She sniffed.

"It was very bad of me, and I feel terrible I made you cry like that. I never want to make you cry. I love you. I really do. You know that don't you?" His voice was coaxing looking for a positive sign from her, perhaps relenting a little.

"OK."

He reached out and held her hand, she didn't resist.

"I want to make it up to you, Cassie, I do," he said. He paused and then continued. "If it will make you feel any better then I'll accept your punishment, if that's what you want to call it."

She looked at him with a question in her eyes. Hesitated for a moment.

"But will it do any good? If I do?" she asked him.

"I… you said yourself I was better behaved after the first spanking. So maybe," he shrugged. "Maybe it's what I need."

It seemed strange to her he was ready to agree to it, having been so dead against it. Perhaps there was something in him which wanted to relinquish control, to her.

"The second one didn't seem to help though did it?" She was feeling a little more the thing now they were talking reasonably.

"I won't be using the card for a big purchase like that again, I can assure you, not after what you did yesterday," he said half-serious.

"OK. But the lying, Nathan, it was unforgivable. I'm not such a bad person, am I? That you can't tell me the truth?"

"You're not bad, Cassie, not at all. You're kind to me, generous. So many things. I shouldn't have lied to you, I know that."

"You're a bastard sometimes, don't you know? I love you so much. You went and did childish burnouts like someone out of kindergarten. I can't believe you did it." She leaned her head on his shoulder and he put his arm around her.

"So, then do whatever you want to do."

"Are you sure?"

"Yes. I'm pretty sure I deserve it so… do your worst."

She put her hand in his and squeezed it. This was quite a turnaround. It made her happy somehow, but the argument had killed the mood.

"OK," she said with a sigh, "But not today. Let's have some dinner, maybe watch a movie."

"If it's what you want."

"Yes, I've had enough emotion for one day. Tomorrow when you come home, that's when you'll be getting your punishment." She smiled at him mischievously.

"OK. What will I have to do?"

"You'll find out. But you have to promise to follow my rules, do what I say, without any argument."

"Yes, Mistress Cassandra, I will. Are you going to wear that outfit for dinner?" he enquired with interest.

"No, but you'll see it again tomorrow, I promise you that."

"OK." He dropped a kiss on her lips, and she kissed him full on. She became aroused and almost threw everything to the winds to fuck him there and then. It would be a release.

Instead, she stood up, removed the cami and put it in her wardrobe along with the shoes. Then she put on a satin robe and tied it fast. He watched her smiling all along. She took his hand, and they went downstairs together. If he had noticed the riding crop and sandals on the bed, he didn't say.

Tomorrow would be a better day, when she was ready to exact her retribution and it would be more fitting for him to wait, until then. What was it they said? Revenge is a dish best served cold? This wasn't revenge. She wasn't a vindictive bitch. But perhaps punishment was also better served cold, and considered, like a mistress should. She chased the thought around her brain. Like a mistress should. What was she becoming? In any case, she was glad he had come around, although she had been ready to capitulate. On balance it was going to be better for their relationship, she reflected, that she had not.

***

They had fucked that night after dinner and a movie on Netflix with a passion. Cassandra had been ready for his cock and it seemed he couldn't wait to plunge it hard into her either. As soon as they had got into the bedroom, she had virtually ripped his clothes off him while he pushed her roughly down onto the bed. She liked to be manhandled somehow, it was arousing. He locked her hands down with his arms, and slid his hard cock into her pussy with ease.

"Oh fuck, Nathan," her eyes widened. Somehow it felt thicker, bigger. Perhaps the whole thing in the afternoon had been arousing.

"I'm going to fuck you," he said beginning to move slowly at first going deep and then pulling almost out, before going in again.

"Oh… fuck!" She gasped as he did so, again and again.

"Oh, Cassie, Cassie," he breathed, unable to contain himself and moving faster. His cock went deep each time and she gasped at the feeling of it.

"Nathan, oh fuck me, fuck me, fuck meeee…"

Needing no second bidding he began to use the full force of his hips almost ramming it home, hard, fast, panting with exertion, neither of them able to hold on they both hit their climax at almost exactly the same time.

"Oh, oh, oh, oh, ohh!" she cried out.

"Ah, fuck, Cassie, I love youu!" he shouted.

She felt his cum shooting inside her and smiled. This was perfect, he was perfect when he did that. She never wanted anything more in those moments, than him. Nathan was a considerate lover, but he also could be rough. Cassandra enjoyed both sides of it. She liked to be nurtured but she also liked to be taken and fucked hard. It just depended on her mood. He was a turn on for her and she revelled in him. Perhaps Nathan didn't know how lucky he was to be with her. She wondered it sometimes, because in spite of everything she adored him and doted on him. The spanking was adding some spice to an already spiced up sex life.

The next day once he had gone to university, she put on her pink sandals and took a photograph of her foot dangling one of them. She sent it to Nathan with the message "These are waiting for your bottom tonight. Mistress Cassie. xxxx"

This would make sure he was thinking about it all day. She didn't know where the ideas were coming from, but they seemed to flow from within her. To take her mind off it she went out into the garden and did some weeding. She was preparing for the spring planting season and so she sorted out the greenhouse. Cassandra had green fingers, Leonard had always said so and indulged her. He enjoyed the fruits of her labour with summer salads that she made. For her, it was therapeutic, meditative. She came inside refreshed and had some lunch. There was no answering text from Nathan, but she knew from the read receipt he had read it. Cassandra smiled to herself. She texted him and asked him what time he would be home. He texted back he'd be there around five p.m. and added several kisses. This reassured her he was still on board with her plan.

Eschewing her vibrator, she read for a little while instead. She wanted to leave herself in a state of high arousal, and it was building with every hour which went by. Nearer the time, she went for a bath and wanted to touch herself so badly, but she didn't. This was going to be a special session. She was going to be christening the riding crop on his backside and she didn't want to spoil it for herself. When she finally had his cock inside her, afterwards, it was going to be explosive.

After her bath, she got out the riding crop, and examined it. Having never used one, Cassandra placed a pillow on the bed for practice. The crop made a deliciously naughty sound when she swung it through the air, and she was sure when it connected with his bottom it would make a nice thwack. The pillow wasn't quite the same, but she figured out with a few experimental shots, the best way of delivering a stroke. Thus prepared, she put the pillow back and replaced the crop on the bed along with the sandals. She touched up her nails, and put on her lip gloss. She tied her hair back into a ponytail because it was quite sexy. The cami felt good once she had it on again, as did the mules. She loved the way they arched her feet, and spent a while looking at herself in the mirror. This wasn't the Cassie she knew, it almost seemed like someone else.

In order to catch Nathan before he left uni, she sent him a text.

"Nathan, when you get home, you are to come straight upstairs, take off your clothes and knock on the bedroom door. Enter when I tell you and then you must do everything you are told without question. I hope you understand that. I love you but you are going to be properly punished like we agreed. Mistress Cassie. xxxx."

After a few moments, she received a reply "Yes Mistress xxx."

This was enough for her. She was sure now he had not changed his mind and all she would have to do was wait. She moved the chair into the centre of the room and sat down clearing her mind of the thoughts chasing around it. Her heart was making wild flutters at the anticipation of this new game. In a short while, she heard his car in the driveway and the front door open and close. She wondered what he would be thinking as she heard him moving about. Was he wondering about the spanking he was about to receive? He climbed the stairs and then he was outside the door. After a few moments, he knocked.

"Come in," she said remaining seated.

Nathan opened the door and closed it behind him. He was naked as instructed which pleased her no end. His cock was half erect and as he drank her in with his eyes, it began to harden even more.

Cassandra stood up.

"Nathan, thank you for obeying my instructions. It's time for your punishment. You know what you did, and we agreed that you would pay a price for it, didn't we?" She spoke quietly but her voice was somehow different, as if it did not belong to her.

He nodded, still looking at her with lustful eyes. She could tell he wanted her. It was a very familiar expression.

On impulse, she went to the bed and picked up the crop. His eyes widened slightly on seeing her with it. Perhaps he was thinking about what it was going to feel like on his bottom.

"I said I would punish you didn't I, Nathan? And I'm going to." She advanced on him and without thinking started to tease the end of the crop along the shaft of his penis.

He gasped.

"Do you like that?" she smiled. "You're going to be getting this across your backside very shortly."

"Oh fuck!" he breathed as his cock was standing proud, while she ran the tip of the crop lightly up and down it.

"You mean, oh fuck, Mistress, don't you?" she tapped the head of his cock very lightly.

He groaned.

"Yes… yes, Mistress."

"Better," she told him, "Don't forget your manners, or I shall have to remind you of them."

She teased the crop over his naked skin. He closed his eyes as the sensations became quite intense.

Abruptly she pulled the crop away, not wanting to push him over the edge. It was time to begin.

"Go over to the chair and bend over putting your hands on the seat," she ordered him peremptorily.

He opened his eyes which held hers for a moment but then he did as she had bid him. The sight of his backside so nicely presented made her wet, as did the idea of him submitting to her will. This had not occurred to her before but in that precise moment, she thought of it and liked it. She walked over to him slowly.

"Keep your hands on the seat, understand?" she said teasing his skin once more.

"Yes, Mistress."

"Good."

Cassandra moved into a better position to take a swing on his left-hand side. She lined up the crop on his buttocks making sure to place the tip on the centre of his buttock cheek.

"You are going to be punished, Nathan. But tell me, why are you being punished?" she asked tapping the tip lightly a couple of times.

"I… because of the tyres."

"Yes, that's one thing, but there is more."

She took lifted the crop, brought it back and let fly. It made a beautiful thwacking noise as it landed on his naked skin.

SWISH CRACK!

"Fuck!" he gasped as the crop left a red line across his buttocks. She had lifted it off swiftly to make it sting, just like with the sandal.

"Let's start again, why are you being punished?"

"I didn't tell you about the tyres, what I did to the tyres."

SWISH CRACK! "OW!"

This wasn't good enough. She needed him to fully acknowledge his faults.

"No Nathan, you lied."

SWISH CRACK! "OW!"

Two more lines appeared, and his bottom began to turn a satisfying pink.

"You SWISH CRACK lied SWISH CRACK, didn't you? SWISH CRACK."

Cassandra was determined to drive the message home.

"Ow, fuck… shit… yes, I lied and that fucking hurts," he complained.

Cassandra smiled at this. At least the crop seemed to be hitting the right spot, where perhaps her words had not.

"It's meant to SWISH CRACK. That's why it's a punishment SWISH CRACK."

"Ow… you bitch."

Her response to this was swift.

"Mistress Bitch Cassandra SWISH CRACK to you! SWISH CRACK."

"Yes, Mistress. Sorry, Mistress."

He still hadn't told the whole story and she wanted him to spell it out.

"What SWISH CRACK else SWISH CRACK did SWISH CRACK you SWISH CRACK do?"

"I lied. I did a burnout competition which was a stupid thing. I drove recklessly on the shredded tyres and I didn't tell you about spending the money or what I'd done."

He must have figured if he said everything at once she might spare him a little. Cassandra wasn't minded to do so and lifted the crop again. She alternated her target each time making sure the tongue hit the centre of one cheek and then the other for maximum effect.

"Which was lying SWISH CRACK wasn't it? SWISH CRACK."

"Oww, ow, fuck. Yes, Mistress. I'm sorry."

"Yes and SWISH CRACK you will be sorry SWISH CRACK when I've finished."

He'd had about eighteen strokes so far and his bottom was crisscrossed with red lines. She was careful to go easy, so it didn't break the skin. But she was whipping him hard enough for him to certainly feel a good sting.

"I'm sorry already, Mistress…" he said again.

"Your punishment isn't over until I say it is. I want you to learn this lesson well before we end it."

She decided to give the crop a rest for the moment and went over to the bed. She put down the crop and picked up the sandal, returning to her position. This would give her more of a chance to swing with it and she could smack harder standing up. The sandal would do less damage than the crop and give him something more the think about.

She decided to remind him of her text.

"Remember how I promised you this? I sent you a picture of my sandal?"

"Yes, Mistress."

"Good, because now you are going to get the spanking of your life."

He was silent. She placed the sole against his arse and pulled it back. She didn't know where these words were coming from, it was almost as if she turned into a different person once she started spanking. She was going to spell out his faults to him and reinforce the message with a hard spanking.

"Let me be clear, so you understand properly what you did. You lied to me and you made me cry."

SMACK, "Ohhh", SMACK "OWWWW", SMACK "Noooo", SMACK "Ouchhh"

"You did a stupid childish thing with your car."

SMACK, "Ahhh", SMACK "Oh God", SMACK "Fuck that hurt", SMACK "Fuckkkk"

"You drove recklessly and put yourself in danger."

SMACK, "OWW", SMACK "Ahhhh", SMACK "Ohhhh", SMACK "OW"

"You are being spanked for all these things."

SMACK, "Ohhh", SMACK "Nooo", SMACK "ooohhh", SMACK "shit fuck"

"You've been very bad. Incredibly childish and immature. I hate that! And maybe this will help you understand how much."

SMACK, "OH GOD", SMACK "FUCK", SMACK "OW OW OW", SMACK "OWWWWW"

"Yes, Mistress, I do, honestly," he gasped. He almost involuntarily lifted his hands off the seat as if to rub his burning behind.

"Put SMACK your SMACK hands SMACK down SMACK and keep them there SMACK until I say SMACK you can move SMACK!"

She saw him wince, but he pushed his hands back hard into the seat.

She continued the lesson, having hit her stride. Her attention was solely on the spanking as if she was almost mesmerised by the action of it. At the same time, the pull on her loins was unmistakable, as was the wetness she felt there.

"You are never to lie to me again."

SMACK, "Ahhh", SMACK "Ohhh", SMACK "ooohhh", SMACK "shit shit shit"

"Is that understood?"

SMACK, "Ahh", SMACK "Fuckk", SMACK "Oh FUCK", SMACK "OWWWW"

"Yes, Mistress," he said when he could get a word in edgeways.

"What will happen if you do?"

SMACK, "AHHH", SMACK "NOOO", SMACK "Oh oh oh", SMACK "Ahhhh"

"Punished… I'll be punished."

"Yes, you will!"

SMACK, "OWWW", SMACK "Noooo", SMACK "Ooohhhh", SMACK "Aaahhh"

"I'll spank you so hard you won't sit down for a week."

SMACK, "OWOWOWOW", SMACK "Fuck that's sore", SMACK "Fuck it", SMACK "FUCK IT!"

"Do you understand?"

SMACK, "Ouch", SMACK "OW Shit", SMACK "OW OWWW", SMACK "OW fuckkkk"

Cassandra smiled at herself, and her mistress talk. She had never realised how assertive she could really be.

"Yes, Mistress, please, Mistress. Isn't that enough?" he pleaded.

His bottom looked as if it was on fire, it had gone a deep shade of red.

"No!"

SMACK, "Nooo", SMACK "pleaseeee", SMACK "Ahhhh", SMACK "Shit shit fuck"

"You deserve every bit of this spanking, darling."

SMACK, "OWWW", SMACK "OW OH OWW", SMACK "Ohhhh", SMACK "fuck that was just owwww"

SMACK, "Fuckkkk", SMACK "shit", SMACK "ahhhh", SMACK "OWWW"

SMACK, "FUCKK", SMACK "NOOO", SMACK "OWW WWW", SMACK "Ohhhhh"

Cassandra paused. She had certainly spent any residual ire and she hadn't held back at all with the sandal. He must have felt every one of those spanks, for sure. Perhaps it was time to finish, but like the last two spankings, she wanted to leave a lasting impression before she stopped. She went back to the bed and picked up the riding crop.

"Now then," she said resuming her position. "You are to promise me, never to lie to me again."

"I promise, Mistress," he said breathlessly.

SWISH, CRACK! "OW FUCK!"

"Promise what?"

"I promise never to lie to you again, Mistress."

"Good Boy!"

SWISH, CRACK! "OW SHITTT!"

"Now. Have you learned your lesson?"

"Yes, Mistress."

SWISH, CRACK! "OW OW OW OW!"

"And are you sorry for what you've done?"

SWISH, CRACK! "OWWWWW!"

"Yes, Mistress, I am."

SWISH, CRACK! "FUCKKKK!"

"Let me hear you say it."

SWISH, CRACK! "JESUS CHRIST!"

"I'm sorry, Mistress, really sorry for what I did."

SWISH, CRACK! "OWWWWW FUCK!"

"Good boy and you'll never do burnouts again?"

SWISH, CRACK! "OW OW OW OW!"

"No, Mistress."

SWISH, CRACK! "Fuck it fuck fuck fuck!"

"Good boy."

She paused contemplating what to do next and decided six of the best was appropriate.

"I believe you're sorry and I believe you won't do it again, or lie to me. Just so you remember the whipping you'll get if you break your promise, I'm going to give you six more." She announced.

He sighed a little but said nothing.

"One" SWISH, CRACK! "OWW!"

"Two" SWISH, CRACK! "OW FUCK! OWWW"

"Three" SWISH, CRACK! "OW OWWWWWWWW!"

"Four" SWISH, CRACK! "FUCKKKKKKK!"

"Five" SWISH, CRACK! "SHITTTTTT!"

"Six" SWISH, CRACK! "AHHHHHHHHHHH OWWWW!"

She considered giving him one more for luck but decided against it. She let her arm relax and giving in to temptation she reached down between her legs with her other hand. She was soaking wet and as her fingers found her clit, she gasped and moaned. Nathan started to try to look around with curiosity.

"Stay down, and don't look, oh, fuck, oh, fuck, oh, oh, oh, oh, ohh!" she let out little moans frigging herself hard and fast, and she came in a rush. The sight of Nathan's red bottom and everything about it had turned her on. She was unable to stop herself once she started.

When her head cleared a little, Nathan was still there, and his cock was straining at the leash.

"Stand up!" she said. On the spur of the moment, a new game occurred to her.

"Is my punishment over, Mistress?" he asked hopefully. He had heard what she was doing, and his head would be focused on one thing only and that was fucking her as hard as he could.

Cassandra moved the chair until it was facing the bed.

"Sit there, and put your arms behind the back of the chair. Don't move them until I say!" she ordered.

He obeyed, possibly expecting a blow job. She wasn't intending that at all. Instead, she went over to her bedside table and retrieved her rabbit. His eyes widened as she sat on the end of the bed facing him and turned it on.

"When the fuck did you…"

"Hush, darling, don't speak, just watch." She smiled and inserted the dildo into her pussy with a gasp. "Oh, fuck, oh, oh." She flicked it onto half continuous pulse crying out, "Oh, oh, oh God, oh."

As she lay back, she saw him watching her with fascination and something more, a visceral and guttural longing. Then she was too far gone.

"Oh, fuck, fuck, oh, oh, oh, oh," she was so close, she moved it rapidly to the maximum setting and almost at once, the orgasmic wave crashed through her. "Oh, fuck, fuck, fuck, ohh!" She squirmed and gasped with pleasure.

Removing the vibrator, she turned it off and laid it aside. It was time to put Nathan out of his misery. She stood and approached the chair. His cock looked like it was ready to explode. Without a second thought, she straddled him and lowered herself sliding the shaft inside her.

"Oh, fuck, Cassie!" he moaned.

"I'm going to fuck you, Nathan, yes I am!" she told him and started to ride him.

"Oh, fuck, oh, fuck, fuck, oh," he moaned.

Cassandra began to go harder, rising and falling faster.

"Oh, Cassie, Cassie, fuck me, fuck me, fuck meee, ahh, ahh, ahh, ahh!" He shouted out spurting inside her as she continued riding until his hands came around to still her. His cocked was pulsing, his head was laid back and his mouth drawn out in a grin.

"Oh, Nathan, Nathan," she said softly taking hold of his head, seeking out his mouth with her own. She kissed him then, softly, and then more passionately. The kiss made her dizzy, just like it always did.

"I love you, Cassie," he breathed, "I love you so much."

"I love you too, Nathan, I burn with love for you. You just don't know."

"I do, oh yes, I do."

He pulled in tight, and she laid her head on his shoulder. They stayed like that for a long time, exhausted from the intensity of their session. Later she would take a bath with him, wash him down affectionately, feed him the casserole she'd made. They would make love again, and all would be forgiven. One thing she knew, was their world and their relationship had irrevocably changed. She was changing too, into a new Cassandra, a different Cassandra. She had no idea where it was taking her, but she felt ready for the ride of her life.

Cassie's spanking playmate (Book Three)

Cassandra lay back on the bed, as Nathan spread her legs. She smiled as he looked her over appreciatively. His cock was standing proud as his gaze raked over her breasts. Wordlessly he raised her pelvis and slid into her. He filled her up as always and she gasped as he entered.

"Oh, fuck, Nathan, fuck me, darling, fuck me," she breathed waiting for him to move.

He began with a grunt, slowly at first looking into her eyes, and pinning her hands to the bed with his own. Her own eyes flicked glances at his abs and when he freed her, her hands came up to feel his tight arse. The arse she had spanked and whipped only a few days ago. Her nails dug into it and he hissed in appreciation.

"You're a bitch do you know that?" he growled.

"But I'm your bitch."

"Yes, a fucking bitch who needs to be fucked." Somehow, he would often turn into a bit of a caveman in bed. She didn't object as he began to move faster and harder.

"Oh, Nathan, oh God, oh my, fuck, fuck, oh fucking fuck, my God, oh, oh, oh," she squealed and moaned in delight as the shaft moved deliciously in her wet slick pussy. She loved the way he filled her up and how good it felt as he fucked her.

"Oh, God, Cassie, I love to fuck you," he said in guttural tones, grunting now with exertion as he began to pound into her almost mercilessly.

"Oh, my, GOD!" she shouted lost in the sensation of his cock thrusting within her and feeling a wave building inside her, her head began to go fuzzy as a precursor to her climax. "Oh, God, Nathan, Nathan, Nathan, oh, Nathan, Oh fuck, ohhh!" The wave crested and broke.

He must have felt her tensing and clenching around him as he hit his own orgasm. She felt his cock begin to pulse and then heard him cum, in a loud roar, "Oh, fuckkkk, ohhh, ahhh, fuckkk, ahhhh, ahhh!" He shouted filling the room with the sound as he drove himself home deep inside her.

She felt him shooting his load within her, enjoying the sensation before he lowered himself gently onto her chest. Her arms came around him and held him tight.

"I love you, you big growly fucking bear," she laughed.

He rolled off her and regarded her quizzically.

"A big growly bear. It's what you sound like sometimes when you fuck me."

"I'll have you know I'm perfectly refined." He put on a posh accent and the two of them dissolved into giggles.

After a while, she turned to him, "Do you really have to go away?" she pouted.

He was due to leave on a field trip for his course. He was studying geological formations or something like that. Although it seemed to her the most unlikely thing for him to be doing just from his appearance. Cassandra imaged geologists to all wear be socks and sandals while sporting long beards. However, Nathan assured her this was not the case, lots of them were like him and the postgrad degree he was studying would land him a very lucrative role probably with an oil company. He was a highflier and had gained a first with honours for his bachelor's degree. He went on to do a master's because he said it would get him places. He was even hinting at a doctorate. Cassandra hoped not but it was very likely he would get the funding if he did. He already landed a full scholarship for his master's.

"Yes, yes I do, I'm sorry, baby, but it's only for a week."

She said nothing for a moment, considering it. He had not been away from her very often since they got together, and he moved in. She would miss him for sure.

"Are you going to behave while you're away?" she asked him.

"What?"

"It's a serious question. You've shown yourself to be childish at times, you know you have. We had to have a conversation about *that* didn't we."

"I'd say it was more than a conversation." He gave a hollow laugh.

"Well let's say, me, my sandal and my riding crop had a conversation with you and your bottom, is that better?" She smiled sweetly.

"Don't remind me." He made a face at her.

"I am reminding you, Nathan, and you know why."

He rolled his eyes as if she was being silly. This slightly irritated her, but she let it pass.

"Do you really think I'm going to cross any lines, sweetheart, after *that*? Not a chance. I'll be as good as gold."

"What would you regard as crossing lines?" she said with interest, now he'd brought it up.

"You know, not spending on the card, asking you before on big purchases, those sorts of things."

"Telling me the truth, not lying?"

"Of course."

One thing she wanted to ask him, but she wasn't sure he'd like the question.

"Would you sleeping with another woman be crossing a line?" It certainly crossed her mind sometimes that he might. He was younger than her by nearly ten years, wouldn't he be tempted?

He wasn't fazed at all, and became serious too.

"God, Cassie, you do come up with things. Of course, it would. I wouldn't do that to you."

"That's the right answer," she smiled and so did he.

However, she hadn't quite finished.

"What if *I* slept with another man?"

He frowned, "I'd want to punch his fucking lights out most probably."

"So, you wouldn't approve?"

"No! Why are you asking me these things?"

"I like to test you sometimes, you know." It was true, she and most women set traps for their partners. It was nothing new.

He shook his head in mock resignation.

"Fuck, Cassie, I'll never understand you."

She gave him a look like the cat who got the cream. She liked to tease him. It kept him on his toes.

"What if I slept with another woman?" her eyes twinkled.

He paused, wondering if she was serious and then said, "Well, that would be different."

"Really?" her eyes widened a little. "How is it different? Isn't it still unfaithful?"

"Ah come on, Cassie. It's every man's fantasy, plus if I got to join in…" he left the sentence unfinished.

"Ah, so you *do* want me to sleep with another woman." She pounced on this like a tiger.

"That's not what I meant. I mean if you slept with her, then I'd want to as well, it's only fair. I mean apart from anything I've always fancied a threesome, to be honest. What man hasn't?"

This part was true, from what she knew of her limited experience. Other girls at uni had certainly mentioned it to her then naïve ears. Some of them had even done it. Cassandra couldn't imagine what it felt like, or rather she could but pushed the thoughts away before they became too arousing.

"Two girls, doing your bidding? Is that what you mean?" she laughed.

"I suppose. But we're talking hypothetical, aren't we?" There was nevertheless a hopeful tone in his voice.

"Sure of course. Though hypothetically I get a free pass with another woman, as long as you can fuck her too, right?" But she was thinking of Peyton.

"Hypothetically, yes. I don't how we get round to these topics of conversation."

He gave her a searching look, as if he thought there was something more to what she was asking. She returned it quite blandly. What was in her head were thoughts, desires not yet formed, but they were there, nevertheless.

"What if I punished you and part of the punishment was watching me fuck her?" she wondered where these ideas came from, it was bizarre.

"And then I get to fuck her too?" was all he wanted to know.

"Hypothetically, yes. But she would have seen you getting a spanking first, just so you know."

He shrugged as if this was not an issue, and Cassandra noticed his cock was starting to harden again as the conversation had progressed. Some wheels were being set in motion in her head. She didn't know if she could carry it through, but the thoughts were definitely there.

"Anyway," she said changing the subject, "I want to make sure you behave when you are away, so turn over."

"Why?" he said suspiciously.

"Just do it, Nathan. I'm the Mistress remember?"

"OK, but…" he rolled onto his stomach.

Cassie reached under her side of the bed and retrieved one of her pink thong and tan sandals. She was keeping them handy and glad she'd thought of doing so. She knelt down beside him and placed the sole on his buttocks.

"What you doing?" he said but he didn't move. He knew exactly what was coming. On the spur of the moment, the devil had unleashed itself inside her.

"This."

She raised the sandal and brought it down in rapid succession on each buttock cheek, lifting it off right after each smack. A now-familiar routine to her. She was a fair way to becoming an excellent spanker.

SMACK, SMACK, SMACK, SMACK

"Owww, Cassie, what the fuck?"

"I'm making sure, Nathan, you remember this in case you think of misbehaving."

"Cassie?"

She paid his half-hearted protest no mind, a few spanks wouldn't go amiss, she thought.

"You won't engage in any childish pranks, will you?"

SMACK, SMACK, SMACK, SMACK

"Owww, fuck! No, I won't, can you stop?"

Cassandra ignored this too.

"And you will behave yourself and not do anything stupid?"

SMACK, SMACK, SMACK, SMACK

"Owww, no I won't, please."

She continued relentlessly to drive the message home.

"And if you do then you know you'll be getting a spanking when you get back, don't you?"

SMACK, SMACK, SMACK, SMACK

"Owwww, yes for sure, but Cassie please can you…"

"Yes, Nathan, that is just a taster of what's to come if you do misbehave, OK?"

"But, Cassie, I won't." It was clear he wanted her to stop. She smiled. It was strange how much of a kick she got out of it.

"Promise?"

SMACK, SMACK, SMACK, SMACK

"Oww, yes I promise."

"Good, now turn over."

He did so and was glaring at her a little, but his cock was rigid.

"I think you enjoyed that, didn't you, Nathan, I did," she said slyly.

He didn't answer, not wanting to admit to any predilection for spanking.

"A pity to waste it though," she murmured, straddling him at once and inserting his cock into her pussy which was once more wet. The act of spanking aroused her, she knew it now, and it was like a sexual trigger when she did it.

"Oh, Nathan, oh, that's so good," she gasped beginning to fuck him.

She put her hands on his chest and started to ride his cock in earnest, bouncing up and down like a yoyo in fast motion.

"Oh, Nathan, oh fuck, oh, oh, oh, oh, oh, fuck."

"Ah, Cassie, you are such a horny fucking bitch, oh God, oh fuck, fuck fuck, oh, ohhh!"

He passed the point of no return very rapidly and pushed up into her, she felt him cum copiously inside her. She kept going, however, until her climax took her too. She pitched forward onto his chest, screaming his name.

"Oh, Nathan, Nathan, Nathannnn!" she cried out.

He held her tight, and she fell into a pleasure-filled sleep on top of him.

***

Nathan had headed out on his field trip a day later and Cassandra was left to her own devices. After he had gone, the rabbit had come out to play, just like it did every day when he was at university. She had kissed him passionately and reminded him to be a good boy. It was surprising how Nathan had submitted to her spankings so easily. He must really love her to allow it and perhaps inside of him was a need perhaps to be controlled. She didn't really understand a lot about what she had discovered to be called BDSM, or domination and submission. She had a desire to dominate, however, this much was clear from what she had experienced so far. The thwack of her sandal on his bare bottom was also a massive turn on and even thinking of it made her wet.

Cassandra had been so naïve about sex, and suddenly she had blossomed into this sexual creature she was only just coming to know. Nathan had quizzed her about the rabbit after she had masturbated with it in front of him as part of the last spanking session. She admitted to him she had bought it at Ann Summers. He was disappointed she hadn't taken him, and she promised to do so one day. For her, it was, however, a very personal journey of self-discovery. She needed the time to find out for herself what she liked and didn't like. So far, she'd liked the things she had tried an awful lot. She promised him she might use the rabbit during sex, and she wanted to try it out on his cock, to see the effect of the fronds, would it make him cum harder? There was so much she didn't know.

She mused over this as she ate her lunch, a ham, cheese and salad roll with mayo. Cassandra thought about a takeaway for dinner, since cooking for one wasn't so exciting. Nathan also cooked quite often, and she enjoyed the luxury of that. Cooking had also often turned into fucking and he'd had her naked on the worktop more than once. She was wearing a pair of tightfitting shorts, and a t-shirt which curved nicely around her breasts. He liked her wearing things like that and she did it sometimes to turn him on, as much as anything.

She was also barefoot because she liked it, and because she liked her feet. They were sexy to her, she kept them in good condition. She liked the feel of walking barefoot and did so whenever she could. The idea of feet being something sexual though was new to her, it would have to be a woman's feet to turn her on.

On this thought, her mind turned to their recent discussion. Apparently, fucking another woman wasn't off limits in Nathan's book, as long as he got to fuck her too. This was almost like a free pass. Cassandra was old fashioned perhaps in believing in being faithful, and monogamous. She hadn't any reality on other kinds of sexuality, like, for example, someone being polyamorous. She had seen the word when browsing the internet but had no idea what it meant. What if she did, really fuck another woman? Her mind turned to the shoe shop, and Peyton. Something had stirred when she saw Peyton, and the assistant had put her number on the receipt which Cassandra still had in her drawer upstairs.

On impulse, she pondered whether she might visit the shoe shop. After all, what harm could it do? She wanted another pair of sandals anyway or maybe two. Red ones perhaps or black, to wear around the house. Perhaps another pair to spank with. What if she wore the pink one's out? Cassandra laughed. That would be a lot of spankings. Her focus shifted to Nathan. Would he behave on his week away? She hoped so, part of her hoped he didn't.

After finishing her tea and her sandwich, Cassandra had decided. She was going to visit the shoe shop. It was almost a compulsion. What she would do when she got there and saw Peyton, she did not know.

She parked the black four by four at the mall and wondered once more why she didn't change it for something smaller. Leonard had bought it and it was something she felt she had to keep in memory of him. After all, he had given her the lifestyle she had, albeit mainly in his death. He had always been kind to her and generous. She had wanted for nothing. She jumped down from the driver's seat, locked the door and headed for the shop. She wondered if Peyton would be there.

When she entered the shop, her eyes met and locked briefly on those blue ones. Peyton smiled and came forward from around the counter.

"Hi," she said.

"Oh, Hi." Cassandra was mesmerised all of a sudden, almost bereft of speech.

"You came back."

"Yes, yes I did."

They stood there looking at each other, blue eyes meeting brown as if time stood still. What's happening to me? Cassandra shook herself out of the mental stupor.

"I err... I'd like some more of those sandals, a different colour maybe."

"Sure, did you like the last ones?" Peyton led her to the rack where she had found the pink pair.

"Yes. Yes, I did."

"Were they... suitable?" a smile was playing on Peyton's lips. It was as if Peyton was reading her mind and knew about the spanking. Surely not. If Peyton did think that, then it was pure speculation.

"Very, actually." Cassandra's expression gave nothing away.

She ran her hands over the sandals and selected several pairs.

"I'd like to try these," she said, "And I think I'll try some mules too."

"Oh, OK, splashing out?" Peyton lifted a quizzical eyebrow.

In her mind, Cassandra was trying to rid herself of the notion that she simply wanted to kiss her.

"It's just I can't decide, perhaps you can help me?" This was quite mendacious, and Cassandra knew it.

Peyton fetched several pairs in the right size, and set them down for Cassandra. She put on the first pair of sandals and walked up and down parading herself in front of Peyton. She noticed Peyton could not take her eyes off her feet. It was a good job she had put on her favourite pink nail polish she thought, selecting another pair.

The sexual tension became palpable between them as Cassandra tried pair after pair, turning her feet this way and that, asking Peyton's opinion. Peyton's cheeks were flushed by the time Cassandra had finished. She picked a red thonged pair and a black thonged one to match her pink sandals. She decided to purchase a pair of shiny patent red mules to go with the black pair. The mules in particular seemed to take Peyton's fancy, almost as if she was mesmerised by Cassandra's ankles and the way the mules arched her feet.

"I'll take all these," she smiled handing them to Peyton. The other's hands were trembling slightly, as she took them.

"OK, do you mind if I just put these other ones away?" Peyton asked.

"Sure, let me help."

Cassandra gathered up the unwanted pairs with Peyton and helped her stack them behind the counter. Then she stood waiting to pay. She suddenly felt bereft of words. She wasn't sure what to say after all. She wasn't used to opening the bidding. She had met Leonard at a party, and Nathan had come up to her and talked to her in a coffee shop. Starting the conversation was not her forte.

Peyton took her credit card and Cassandra entered the pin number. She was struck dumb as she accepted the bag from Peyton with sandals and shoes. Something in her head was urging her to speak. She found herself completely bereft of the right words.

"Thank you." Cassandra turned away, disappointed in herself.

"Wait," said Peyton suddenly.

"Yes?" Cassandra turned back eagerly.

"You forgot your receipt." Peyton was holding it out.

"Thanks." Cassandra reached out to take it, but Peyton did not let go willing her to say something. Wanting her not to leave. Suddenly Cassandra found her voice. "Would you like to have coffee with me?" It came out in a rush.

The blue eyes broke out in a smile. "Sure, I'd love to, I'm due a break anyway, hang on."

Cassandra's heart started to beat faster, and she tried to calm herself thinking it's just a coffee. But she knew it was more than that, or eventually, it was going to be.

Peyton spoke to another assistant and then came towards her smiling.

"Let's go."

In few moments, they were sat on the opposite sides of a table at a coffee place in the mall. Cassandra had a latte which was rare for her, and Peyton a cappuccino. They introduced themselves more formerly as Peyton didn't know her name. Cassandra had the leisure to look at Peyton more closely and admire her very sensual kissable bow-shaped lips. Peyton's face was heart-shaped, and she had beautiful big blue eyes, with long lashes. Her blonde hair was tied up, but Cassandra could imagine it flowing free and how sexy it must look. Her eyes strayed lightly over Peyton's breasts and she wondered when they might feel like. She closed her eyes on the image of running her tongue over Peyton's nipples. Where were these ideas coming from? She felt wet and hoped it wouldn't soak down to her knickers.

"So," said Peyton, "You like shoes? I mean obviously." She laughed.

"Yes, I do. Very much."

"You have beautiful feet."

"Thank you."

"What do you do, I mean for a living."

"Not, much, I don't have to."

"Nice."

This was too much small talk. Peyton sipped her coffee and waited. Someone had to break the ice.

"Why did you write your number on my receipt?" Cassandra suddenly demanded.

Peyton looked taken aback, "Did I?" she teased.

"You know you did."

"OK, I did, sorry… I just… well… because I wanted… hoped… to see you again." Peyton blushed.

"Why?"

"Because you're beautiful and sexy. I just thought maybe…"

Cassandra's heart was in her mouth, she drank half the cup of coffee and her hand was shaking. Peyton reached out and gently guided her hand to the saucer to replace the cup. Then Peyton's other hand came around and clasped Cassandra's tightly.

"I thought maybe you liked me. I think you do. I like you. Sorry, is that so forward of me?"

Cassandra's hand went up to her mouth. "Oh, shit, fuck. I have a boyfriend. No, I can't. I shouldn't. I mustn't. I can't do this."

She stood up abruptly and picked up her bag. "I'm sorry, Peyton, I've got to go."

"Cassandra, wait!" Peyton called after her, but Cassandra rushed away terrified of the sexual feelings which were threatening to be unleashed within her.

"I can't," she said to herself. "I can't."

In the refuge of her car she sat breathing fast, heavily, until her sudden anxiety subsided, and she began to feel calmer. She drove home, put the sandals away and thought about dinner. She tried to put Peyton out of her mind, but Peyton refused to leave it.

Cassandra had a phone call with Nathan who was cheerful and babbled on about his day climbing around rocks at a well-known geological site. He seemed very happy to be away and not sounding as if he missed her at all. She said goodnight, told him she loved him, and couldn't wait to feel his cock inside her again. That would get him thinking, she smiled.

Then inexorably, after resisting the impulse for as long as she could, she found herself sitting at her bedside table. She pulled open the drawer, found the receipt with Peyton's number and dialled it.

"Hello? Who's this?" Peyton answered.

"It's me, Cassie," said Cassandra.

"Oh!"

"I'm sorry, I'm really sorry about earlier, I don't know what came over me."

"It's OK." Peyton laughed.

"You're not… upset?"

"No, look. I sort of came on to you a bit strong and I shouldn't have done that, it's my fault. I don't blame you. I'm just glad you called."

"Would you like to have dinner?" Cassandra asked suddenly.

"Sure, where did you have in mind?"

This seemed so easy, far easier than Cassandra had imagined. There was definitely chemistry. Wasn't it supposed to be harder? Dating someone? But this wasn't dating. She only had one thing on her mind with Peyton and that wasn't just a date.

"My house? As long as you're not… a serial killer." It was Cassandra's attempt at humour.

"How do I know you're not one? Asking me to your house." The teasing tone was back but Peyton sounded pleased.

"I'm not, I just… I just prefer it, at home. I'm a good cook. I'm not one for going out much."

"OK, if you give me your address?"

"I can pick you up."

"OK, I'll text you my address then."

"Good. Tomorrow then."

"Sure, sounds great."

"You're not a vegetarian or anything are you?" Cassandra said as an afterthought.

"No, you're safe enough there."

"Bye. I'll see you tomorrow."

"I'm looking forward to it."

Cassandra reluctantly disconnected the call, she wished to talk longer but they could do that over dinner. She lay back on the bed. What the fuck was she doing? She didn't know but she couldn't stop herself. The thought of what Peyton might look like naked had taken hold of her imagination. She took off the robe she was wearing and began to play with her breasts and nipples. She imagined another mouth on them, Peyton's, sucking, biting. A soft pliable bow-shaped mouth.

"Oh fuck!" Cassandra gasped as she reached down to her wet pussy and found her clit. She began to play with herself moaning softly. In her head Peyton's tongue was flicking and caressing her pussy, finding her clit and beginning to make sensations run through her. "Fuck, oh, oh, oh."

Cassandra reached for the drawer, pulled out the rabbit and turned it on. Would Peyton use it on her, or better still would she use it on Peyton? "Oh, God, fuck, oh, oh, oh, oh, God, fuck, oh, fuck."

She flicked it onto full speed. Images going through her head. Soft smooth skin, kissing her, licking her.

"Oh, oh, oh, oh, oh, ohhhh!" Cassandra climaxed quickly and hard pushing up against the rabbit fronds while the dildo pulsed inside her, just like Nathan. As the waves subsided, she began to think of Nathan. What would he say? A free pass is one thing but wasn't this just as bad as he was? Not telling, lying?

She lay back. It wouldn't be too late to cancel but Cassandra knew she wasn't going to do it. It would work out. Nathan wouldn't mind, he said, if he could fuck Peyton too. Cassandra would have to find a way to make him put his money where his mouth was. It would not be so hard. Nathan was bound to need a spanking sooner or later. Probably sooner if the past few weeks was anything to go by. Calmed by the thought she put the rabbit to one side and rolled over to sleep.

***

The following day, Cassandra was in a tizzy. She was once more tingling with anticipation but this time not for Nathan. She put him firmly from her mind to concentrate on getting ready for the evening. There was no doubt in her mind that she was going to fuck Peyton.

She had read it in those clear blue eyes and the message was unmistakable. They both wanted it. Peyton had accepted an invitation to her house to dinner, it was only going to end one way. It seemed strange that she hardly knew Peyton and yet she felt she did know her. She knew she wanted her. It was a visceral unyielding desire. The same desire she felt for Nathan. What did it all mean? Cassandra didn't know.

The whole day was about preparing for Peyton. She went to her favourite nail parlour and had her nails done. She had her hair cut and styled a little more. It wasn't much different but slightly more layered. Cassandra liked her long hair, Nathan liked it too and said it was sexy. The pampering made her feel good. She decided to make coq au vin, with rice and sauteed vegetables. There would be ice cream for dessert, although her mind was on a desert of quite a different variety. Once the dinner was in the slow cooker, there was nothing further to do cooking wise. The rice would be made once she had picked Peyton up. Although she fancied gardening, it might spoil her pedicure, as Cassandra liked to garden barefoot or in sandals quite often.

Instead, she did some drawing. She was very good at figure drawing and she had lately started to draw more female nudes. She ended up sketching Peyton from memory but naked. It was a turn on. Her hand strayed between her legs and she lifted up her skirt.

"Oh, fuck, oh, God." Once more her imagination ran riot. Peyton was licking her wet pussy while she laid back. What was that going to feel like? "Fuck, oh, God, God, oh, fuck, I... ohh!" Cassandra climaxed quickly. Without thinking she took her wet finger and wiped it on the drawing. Now her drawing had cum juice on it. It seemed quite naughty to her. Maybe she'd give it to Peyton.

What was this evening going to end up being anyway, she wondered? A quick fuck? Something more? How could it be when she was with Nathan? Thoughts crowded her brain making her anxious. It would soon be time to go. She went and had a hot bath, luxuriating in the water and restraining herself from masturbating again. She needed to save it for later. When she'd finished, she brushed her hair leaving it loose, and put on the red dress she'd worn when she had spanked Nathan. Was that prophetic? She didn't know. She eschewed knickers but wore a bra this time. On impulse, she selected the red thong sandals to wear. Would these also be spanking sandals? Cassandra tried to still her unruly mind.

Leaving the red sandals at the door, she put on some others to go out with. She didn't want to dirty the soles, especially if they might be used for spanking. She arrived at what was probably Peyton's house or rather a block of flats. As she pulled up, Peyton came running out down the pathway and jumped into the car.

"Hey." Peyton smiled. "I'm glad you came."

"Did you think I wouldn't?"

"I did wonder after yesterday."

"I wouldn't do *that* to you."

Impulsively Cassandra reached out a hand and touched Peyton's bare shoulder. It was like an electric shock. She gasped and pulled her hand away. Peyton felt it too. She was wearing a loose and short summer shift, and thong sandals like Cassandra. A glance at Peyton's feet told her they were very pretty.

"Shall we go?"

"By all means."

***

Dinner was fun. Peyton sat chatting while Cassandra made the rice, and the vegetables. When she served it up, Peyton ate it with a good appetite and said it was delicious. They talked about this and that. Peyton had also finished university but ended up working in the shoe store. It seemed although she'd enjoyed her psychology degree, he had no real calling to use it. In fact, Peyton seemed without much ambition barring having a happy life. Cassandra could hardly criticise her for it, as she felt much the same, the difference being Cassandra had the money to facilitate it more easily. When they had arrived at her house, Cassandra had put on the red thong sandals and she noticed Peyton stealing glances at her feet when she could.

"So," said Peyton pushing her plate away. "That was lovely. Thank you so much for the beautiful meal."

"You're welcome. I'll make some coffee."

"No, let me. Tell me where all the stuff is," said Peyton getting up.

Cassandra told her and then moved her chair out from the table. She crossed her legs and began to rhythmically slap the bottom of the sandal against her right foot using her toes. She knew the effect it had on

Nathan and she could see the effect it was having on Peyton. Peyton was seeing to the coffee, but her attention was completely on the sandal and the sound it was making. Peyton poured the milk into the cups and brought them to the table.

"Thank you," said Cassandra smiled, but not stopping what she was doing.

"Oh God," said Peyton unable to bear it any longer, "That's so horny."

"This?" Cassandra did it even more.

"Yes, fuck, sorry but I had to tell you because… Because it's turning me on and…" Peyton stopped, gasped and then said quickly, "And I can't stand it much longer, Cassie, I want you. I want you so badly, and if I don't tell you, I'll never tell you and…"

She got no further, Cassie left her coffee untouched, got up from her seat and pulled Peyton up onto her feet. There was no thinking anymore, or speculating. She put her arms around Peyton and pulled her in for a kiss.

Peyton's lips were like velvet and roses all in one. So different from Nathan's. They felt soft and pliable. The kiss sent her into a spin, her brain was mush. Her arousal levels went through the roof. She half dragged Peyton into the living room and down onto the sofa. They were kissing all the while.

Without a second thought, Cassandra's hand slipped under Peyton's dress and found she wasn't wearing any knickers either. Without any preamble, her fingers found Peyton's very wet pussy. It felt strange to feel it instead of a cock, but she began to move her fingers with the precision she had learned through masturbation.

"Oh, oh, oh, Cassie!" Peyton cried out at the touch. "Oh, God, God, how I've wanted you, so much, oh."

Cassandra kissed her then as they sat together awkwardly while her fingers continued with little movements she knew. It seemed to be working on Peyton who pulled out of the kiss and laid her head back.

"Oh, fuck, Cassie, oh, oh, oh, oh, oh, oh, God, more, more, I'm so close, I'm so... ohhh!" Peyton screamed and her body began to convulse, tensing and untensing as she climaxed. The build-up to this had been almost endless from the moment they had met, and Cassandra found it unsurprising she had cum so quickly.

Cassandra smiled all the while as she watched her orgasm. She had just finger fucked another woman. It felt amazing.

"Oh, Cassie," said Peyton, opening her eyes. "God, that was so good, so fucking good."

Without more ado, Peyton pushed her back onto the sofa and lifted up Cassandra's dress.

"God you are one horny bitch," Peyton exclaimed. "You're not wearing knickers either."

"I know."

"I love your pussy, it's beautiful."

"Really?"

"And now I'm going to lick you…" Peyton's voice became a husky wanton rasp.

Cassandra gasped as she heard that. Her fantasy had come true. Peyton's head went down between her legs, and she felt the flick of her tongue.

"Oh, oh, oh, oh!" Cassandra cried out. It felt so good, and deliciously different to Nathan's.

Peyton continued, expertly finding her clit and making delicate flicks and licks which started to increase in intensity and speed. Her tongue felt so good, Cassandra couldn't get enough of it.

"Oh fuck, fuck, fuck, fuck, oh, shit, oh, God, don't stop, I'm going to, I'm going to, I'm going to cummmm, fuckkkkkkkkk! Oh, Godddddddd! Ohhhhh!" Cassandra cried out at the top of her voice, as the waves which had been building inside her crashed through her.

All the tension and anticipation was released in her climax and she was lost, taken to dizzy heights by Peyton's relentless tongue. Eventually, she stilled Peyton's head with her hands pushing her gently away unable to stand it.

Peyton lay down beside her on the amply sized sofa and held her tight.

"Thank you," said Cassandra.

"You don't have to thank me," Peyton laughed, "I've been wanting to do that for ages, ever since I first saw you."

"Really?"

"Yes, really."

Peyton kissed her softly and then a little more passionately. After a while, she stopped, and moved apart a little.

"Can I ask you something?" Peyton said quietly.

"Sure."

"What is it you really did with those sandals?"

Cassandra looked at her quizzically.

"Don't you know?"

"I sort of think I could guess but could you tell me?"

"I wore them why?"

"Sure, but come on, what else?" Peyton smiled mischievously.

"I thought you guessed, haven't you?"

"I think so, but I want you to tell me."

"Why?"

"Because… humour me?"

"OK, well I gave my boyfriend, Nathan, a good spanking. In fact, he's had about two proper spankings now with those sandals and I also used the riding crop."

"Oh, God, wow. Oh fuck! That's so…"." Peyton flushed a little and her eyes went a little rounder.

"Horny? Does it turn you on?" Cassandra smiled.

"Yes, it does."

"It turns me on too, when I spank him."

Peyton was silent for a while.

"We didn't drink our coffee, and it's probably cold. I'll make some more." Cassandra got up.

She could see Peyton had become very pensive. She wondered if something was amiss.

She made fresh coffee, brought it into the living room and sat down next to Peyton, handing her a cup. Peyton took it and sipped it but still said nothing.

"Is something the matter? Did I do something wrong?" said Cassandra at length, after a few sips of her own beverage.

"No, nothing like *that*," said Peyton hastily.

"Then what?" Cassandra could see something was bothering her new friend. She didn't know what else to think of Peyton as. A fuck buddy maybe? She'd heard that term before.

"Could I ask you something?" Peyton's eyes were now full of apprehension.

"Of course, I mean, we sort of know each other now somewhat intimately. You just ate my pussy…" Cassandra laughed lightly.

"I did, didn't I."

"I loved it by the way."

"I'm glad."

"So, what did you want to ask me?" Cassandra could see Peyton was avoiding the issue.

"I wanted… I mean I wondered… I just… would you… would you spank me too, please, Cassie?" Peyton seemed to have trouble getting the words out.

This was unexpected.

"You want me to spank you?" Cassandra felt a sudden catch in her breath and rush to her loins.

"I… yes… sorry… I'm just shy asking you it seems so lame, so silly." Peyton looked away.

"No, not it's not. But why, why do you want to be spanked?" Cassandra put her hand out to lightly touch Peyton's arm in reassurance. Peyton smiled back gratefully.

"Because… I've fantasised about it ever since you bought those sandals, that first time. God this seems so terrible asking you that, we hardly know each other."

"What have you fantasised?" Cassandra asked very interested now.

"You know, just being put over your knee, and then spanked with the sandal, and stuff like that…" Peyton tailed off.

"Have you been spanked before?"

"No, I was always too shy to ask like now. But I… well I've watched a lot of spanking porn and read stories and so on. So, I know about it. I've just never experienced it and I want to… I thought you might… maybe… because it's you… and because we had like a connection and… you're special somehow… you really are… I'm sorry… God… such a fool… I just felt… you were the right one to… oh God I'm making a mess of this." Peyton stopped and regarded her a little apprehensively.

Cassandra was silent for a while sipping her drink. Peyton watched her without saying anything, perhaps wondering what she was going to say. The idea was more than just appealing to Cassandra. She hadn't thought about it before. Her fantasies were all about fucking Peyton, kissing her, making love. But now, the thought of Peyton's bottom turning crimson with her sandal was almost too much to bear, it made her so horny. Peyton still didn't speak, and Cassandra decided to stop keeping her in suspense. As Peyton had brought it up, the idea of spanking Peyton took hold with a vengeance, and why wait? Now was as good a time as any to fulfil Peyton's fantasy. She put down her empty cup.

"Well, it sounds as if you've been very naughty to me, Peyton. Watching porn, things like that."

Peyton swallowed and flushed pink. Perhaps she had expected some indication that Cassandra was going to acquiesce, rather than being plunged straight into it.

"Spanking porn too, that's very very naughty indeed."

Peyton was staring at her wide-eyed. Cassandra's whole demeanour had changed. She suddenly seemed a little severe. Cassandra hoped it was what she wanted. She continued on with her role.

"What do you think should happen to a naughty girl like you?" Cassandra asked casually.

"I…"

"Tongue-tied? You weren't so tongue-tied just now. In fact, I think you asked me to spank you, didn't you?" Cassandra was surprising herself, how easily she was starting to slip into this dominant frame of mind.

"I…" Peyton seemed bereft of words.

"Well," said Cassandra a little more firmly. "I can answer the question for you. Naughty girls deserve a spanking, and that's exactly what you're going to get, Peyton. You're going to come upstairs to my bedroom, and you are to do exactly as you are told, understood?"

Peyton nodded and bit her lip in the most endearing way, her eyes now brimful of anticipation. Cassandra seeing her suddenly make herself so vulnerable wanted to kiss her, but she also wanted to spank her. This was the dichotomy she found herself also with Nathan just before the spanking. The spanking won, however. She knew the sex would be so much better afterwards.

"You will call me Mistress, or Mistress Cassandra while you are being punished, understood?"

Peyton nodded again.

"What did I say?"

"I must do everything you tell me, Mistress Cassandra," said Peyton in a voice which was almost a whisper it was so quiet.

"Good girl, now, let's go, shall we?"

Cassandra stood up, put her red thong sandals back on, and held her hand out to Peyton. Peyton took it and Peyton's hand was trembling. Cassandra pulled her close and kissed her. Her hand went down to Peyton's pussy and found it was incredibly wet. Peyton gasped at the touch.

"You *do* want a spanking, don't you? I can tell." She smiled pulling out of the kiss.

She withdrew her hand, licked her fingers with a smile, then made Peyton taste her fingers too. After which she took hold of Peyton's hand once more and led her upstairs.

***

Cassandra closed the bedroom door and turned to Peyton. She was wet herself in anticipation of giving Peyton a spanking. It was all they were both thinking about, she was sure. Everything else had left her head.

"Stand there until I say," said Cassandra walking over to her dressing table and picking up her chair. The chair with no arms and padded seat had proven to be ideal for spanking although no conscious thought had ever entered her head when she'd bought it. She placed the chair in its familiar spot in the centre of the room facing Peyton. Cassandra took a seat with Peyton watching her all the while.

"Take off your dress," said Cassandra.

Peyton hesitated. She'd asked for this but perhaps she was a little reticent after all.

"When I tell you to do something, you do it! Now… take… off… your… dress. Peyton… don't make me tell you again." Cassandra made her voice more assertive.

Peyton did so all in a rush. She wasn't wearing a bra, but the dress had been slightly fitted at the bust, so it kept her breasts in place. Cassandra looked her over and particularly Peyton's almost perfectly shaped breasts which were quite nicely pert. Her pink nipples were standing out indicating a high state of arousal. Peyton had a good figure and youthful smooth skin. Cassandra looked forward to running her hands over it very soon. But first, she had to deliver the spanking Peyton wanted, and she was very keen to give it to her too.

Cassandra leaned down, slowly and deliberately removed the right sandal from her foot. She brought it up to her lap and began to tap it in her left palm as she had done before with Nathan. Peyton's eyes widened at this and her tongue ran around her lips involuntarily.

"Come here, Peyton and stand beside me."

Cassandra pointed to her right-hand side.

Instead of moving, Peyton dropped to her knees.

"What on earth are you…" Cassandra began but Peyton was starting to crawl on hands and knees towards her in the most submissive way possible.

"Fuck!" Cassandra gasped finding this incredibly erotic and wishing she had thought of it herself.

Peyton stopped as if she wasn't sure or whether Cassandra didn't like it.

"Don't stop, I love it, so horny, you dirty little bitch." Cassandra bit her lips. The most awful things came out of her mouth when she was aroused.

Peyton seemed to like being called a 'dirty bitch' because she gave slight smile and continued on her hands and knees until she was kneeling beside Cassandra's right hand.

"Good girl," said Cassandra approvingly, "Get over my knee for your spanking."

Peyton slid across Cassandra's knee and settled herself in. Cassandra had hitched up her dress a little and could feel the skin-to-skin contact. It felt soft and tingly.

She began to run the sole of the sandal lightly across Peyton's pert bottom as a precursor to the spanking. Peyton let out a little moan of pleasure as she felt it.

"Do you like that do you? Well, I can assure you you're going to like it much less very shortly," said Cassandra. "You know what you're going to get now, don't you?"

"Yes," said Peyton a little breathless.

Cassandra raised the sandal and began.

SMACK SMACK

Peyton let out a gasp as the first two spanks left red marks on her buttocks.

"What SMACK did I say SMACK you were SMACK to call me? SMACK."

Cassandra punctuated her speech with spanks, as was becoming her spanking style. She smacked down and lifted off the sandal at once knowing it was going to sting that way much more.

"OW! Mistress, you said I should call you, Mistress." Peyton yelped.

Perhaps she had not been expecting the sandal to hurt so much, but she was in for a shock in that respect, Cassandra thought.

"Good girl, now don't forget!"

SMACK SMACK "Ouch"

Cassandra resumed running the sandal over Peyton's buttocks. She found them rather enticing, shapely and so squeezable. However, for now, the spanking was her focus.

"You're going to get a spanking, Peyton. Tell me, why *are* you being spanked?" she said. She followed this by a volley of spanks to emphasise her point.

SMACK "Owww" SMACK "Ohhhh" SMACK "oh God" SMACK "Fuckkk"

"I… I was naughty, Mistress." Peyton was much less quiet now. She was yelling at each spank as it stung her pretty backside. Her voice was louder when she answered too.

"That's not good enough, what *exactly* did you do?"

This was Cassandra's modus operandi. She liked to be sure that Nathan reiterated his offence to her when being spanked and Peyton should be no different.

SMACK "Oh shit" SMACK "OW that stings" SMACK "oooohhh" SMACK "ow ow ow ow ow"

"I watched porn, Mistress."

"Really? Though what kind of porn?"

SMACK "OWWW" SMACK "Oh ow ow ow" SMACK "Fuck fuck owww" SMACK "Ohhh that's hard"

"I… spanking porn, it was spanking porn, Mistress."

"Good girl. Ironic isn't it? Being spanked for watching spanking porn."

SMACK "Ahhhh" SMACK "my bottom" SMACK "Ouchhh" SMACK "eeeeehhh"

Cassandra was relentless with the sandal. Experienced now at picking her target so that the bottom being spanked was pink all over. Peyton's was certainly turning a nice shade of pink by now. However, the spanking wasn't going to be over so quickly.

"Did you masturbate afterwards? Tell the truth!"

SMACK "Ow ow ow" SMACK "Oh God please" SMACK "that stingsss" SMACK "Ouchhh"

"Yes, yes I did, Mistress."

SMACK "ooooooh" SMACK "ahhhhh" SMACK "OW OW OW" SMACK "Oh Godddd"

"And did you enjoy it?"

SMACK "Eeeee" SMACK "ooooooo" SMACK "Ow ow ow ow oh ow" SMACK "my bottommmmm"

"Yes, Mistress, I did."

Cassandra decided to up the ante, words came unbidden to her lips.

"You are a dirty little bitch, aren't you? A dirty naughty little girl."

SMACK "Ah fuckkk" SMACK "shittt" SMACK "FUCKK" SMACK "OWWW"

"Oww, oww, God, yes, Mistress I am, I am a dirty little bitch," Peyton cried out.

"Does it hurt?"

"Yes, Mistress, it stings like fuck!" Peyton said.

"Good because it's supposed to!"

SMACK "Ahhhhh" SMACK "Oh please please" SMACK "Owww it hurts" SMACK "So sore owwww"

"Owww, owww, owwww," Peyton cried out again and it sounded as if it was a little tearfully.

Cassandra looked down and Peyton turned her head up to meet her gaze.

"Are you crying?" said Cassandra suddenly concerned.

"Yes, Mistress," Peyton nodded, tears were squeezing from the corners of her eyes.

Cassandra became worried, it was meant to be a game.

"Do you want me to stop?" She genuinely meant it. It was one thing to have some horny fun, another to make Peyton cry.

"No, no please don't stop, I want it, I need it, I need it, please spank me, really hard, please," said Peyton almost choking with emotion.

"Are you sure?" said Cassandra tentatively, still unsure, "Last chance to say no."

"I want it, please. This is my way of enjoying it, it's part of it, please, Cassie, I've wanted this for so long, so long." Peyton was crying a little, but it seemed this was something she wanted to go through. "These are kind of happy tears, Cassie, really, please spank me and don't hold back."

"OK," said Cassandra. She put the sandal down for a moment on Peyton's back, and reached down between her legs.

"Oh! Oh, ohhh!" Peyton cried. She was soaking wet.

"You are enjoying it aren't you," said Cassandra, "I'm going to enjoying licking that wet pussy very soon."

"Yes, oh, yes," Peyton whispered.

Cassandra wondered for a moment how to proceed. She was unused to any of this. Spanking was still relatively new to her and she'd only spanked Nathan before. He had never reacted this way being so much more macho. She stroked Peyton's back absently and let her rest a little. Her bottom was starting to turn red, but it was clear Peyton wanted a lot more. Cassandra picked up the sandal again after a few moments and placed the sole once more lightly against Peyton's buttock cheek.

"Very well. You want a proper spanking, Peyton, then that is exactly what you are going to get. You're a dirty little bitch. You've been watching spanking porn and wanking yourself off. Well, now you're going to find out what a real spanking is, my girl. I'm going to give you the soundest spanking you've ever had."

Peyton went very quiet. Cassandra had spoken firmly and in her best assertive voice. She was honing it every time and it became less like her and more like someone else when she did so. There were two Cassandra's one of them was turning into a right bitch. She smiled and raised the sandal.

SMACK "OWWW" SMACK "OW OW OW" SMACK "Oh Goddd" SMACK "Ahhhh"

SMACK "Oh oww oww oww" SMACK "Oooh hooo" SMACK "Noooo" SMACK "owowowowowow"

SMACK "Ouchhh" SMACK "Ahhhh" SMACK "oh noooo" SMACK "Fuck that stings"

SMACK "It stingggs" SMACK "Ouch" SMACK "Ohhhhh" SMACK "Oh my God"

SMACK "Shitttt" SMACK "ow ow ow ow" SMACK "ahhhhh" SMACK "fuck fuck fuck"

"Oww, oh God, oh my God," Peyton gasped.

"See Peyton? Be careful what you wish for. Otherwise, you'll find yourself across the knee of a bitch like me."

SMACK "Ahhhh" SMACK "Ouchhhh" SMACK "OWWWW" SMACK "Nooooo"

SMACK "Eeeeee" SMACK "ow my poor bottom" SMACK "God oh God oh God" SMACK "ow how"

SMACK "ow how how" SMACK "ow how how" SMACK "oooh hoooo" SMACK "OW WOW WOW OW"

SMACK "Oh God my bottom" SMACK "OWWW my bottom" SMACK "Please my bottom" SMACK "oh ho hoo it hurts"

SMACK "It hurts Mistress" SMACK "Owwww" SMACK "Oh OWWW" SMACK "Ouchhhhh"

Peyton's bottom started to turn a deeper shade of red and she squirmed a little in Cassandra's lap.

"Stay still, you naughty girl, until the spanking is over."

SMACK "Ahhhh" SMACK "Fuckk I'm trying" SMACK "God it's so sore" SMACK "Ow how how how"

SMACK "ow Mistress" SMACK "Ahhhh" SMACK "owwww" SMACK "Oh oh oh oh"

SMACK "Ahhhh" SMACK "owwww" SMACK "ohhhhhh" SMACK "ouchhhh"

Cassandra paused. She wondered if it was enough. Peyton had stopped wriggling and crying too.

"Have you learned your lesson?" she asked Peyton.

"I think so, Mistress," said Peyton quietly, she sniffed a little.

Cassandra thought her bottom must surely be burning but she wasn't letting her off so easily.

"You think so?"

SMACK "Ohhhhh" SMACK "I meant yesss" SMACK "Pleaseeee" SMACK "I have I have have have"

Cassandra was well into it now and felt she should reinforce the lesson. Peyton wanted a good hard spanking and she was getting her wish.

"That's not good enough. Let's see if we can make sure, shall we?"

SMACK "Ohhhhh" SMACK "OWWW" SMACK "OHHHH" SMACK "AHHHH"

SMACK "Oh my God" SMACK "OW OW OW" SMACK "FUCK" SMACK "FUCKKK"

SMACK "SHITTT" SMACK "OW OW OW" SMACK "Oh OWWW" SMACK "Oh no no no OW OW"

This time Cassandra had made the spanks much harder. Peyton had been yelling at the top of her lungs after every smack.

"Owww oh owwww, owwww owwwww," said Peyton tearfully, "Yes, yes I've learned my lesson, I have, Mistress."

Cassandra smiled. Peyton had obviously had enough.

"Good, girl, and are you sorry for what you did?"

SMACK "OWWW" SMACK "Sorry" SMACK "I'm sorry" SMACK "OWWW"

"Yes, yes Mistress, please, I'm sorry, really I am." There was a pleading note in Peyton's voice.

"Good, then we're just going to make sure. You're going to be getting another six hard spanks."

"No, please, please, Mistress. No, I don't want it, no!"

This was definitely the wrong thing to do, now Cassandra was in the zone. She wasn't having any of it.

"What did you say?"

SMACK "OWWW" SMACK "OH OWWW" SMACK "AHHHHH" SMACK "OOUCHHH"

"Did you just say no to me?"

SMACK "I didn't" SMACK "Didn't mean it ohhhhh" SMACK "Oh please I didn't" SMACK "OWWWWWW"

"I decide when the spanking is over, you little brat, not you, how dare you?"

SMACK "AHHHH" SMACK "OWWWW" SMACK "OUCHHH" SMACK "OHHHH"

"Oh, God, God, sorry, so sorry, Mistress," said Peyton.

"Good, see how you got many more that time then if you had said nothing. Now you're getting twelve more hard spanks, twice more than I just told you for being a little brat. Have you anything to say about it?"

"No, Mistress. Thank you, Mistress. Whatever you say, Mistress." Peyton obviously didn't want more spanks than necessary.

"Better."

Cassandra lined up the sandal on Peyton's right cheek. She tended to alternate cheeks with each spank or sometimes do two or four on one and then the same on the other. For these last twelve, she would do one on each cheek at a time and make each spank a little harder than the last. The last two would be the hardest.

She began the spanking and Peyton got more vocal after each spank.

"One" SMACK "Ow"

"Two" SMACK "Oww"

"Three" SMACK "OWW"

"Four" SMACK "OWWW"

"Five" SMACK "OWW WOW"

"Six" SMACK "OW WOW OW"

"Seven" SMACK "OW OW OWOOW"

"Eight" SMACK "OW WOWOWOWOW"

"Nine" SMACK "OW OW OW OW OW OWW"

"Ten" SMACK "OW OWOWOOWOW WOW"

"Eleven" SMACK "OWWWWWWWWWWWW"

"Twelve" SMACK "OW WOOWWWW OWWWWWWW"

"Owww," Peyton cried, "My bottom, my poor bottom, oh, oh, oh, ohh!"

This wasn't quite the reaction Cassandra had been expecting but it was gratifying, nevertheless. The spanking had had quite an effect. She had obviously done a good job of it. She tossed the sandal aside.

"You can get up now, your spanking is over. I'm pretty sure you've learned your lesson."

Cassandra waited patiently while Peyton burst into tears.

"Ooooh hoo hoo, oooh hooo hoo, oooh hooo hoo," Peyton cried.

It seemed as if the spanking was somehow cathartic. She stroked Peyton's back gently once more, and rubbed her bottom lightly which was a deep shade of red. She wondered if she had become too carried away with the spanking, but Peyton had seemed to want it. It was too late now in any case, she would ask her later, just to make sure. After a little while, Peyton stopped crying and eased herself off her lap. She knelt in front of Cassandra.

"Thank you, Mistress," said Peyton with eyes still full of tears, "Thank you, so much. I deserved all of that and more."

"You're welcome." Cassandra smiled, leaned forward and kissed her on the lips for a long moment.

"May I, may I kiss your feet? Mistress?" Peyton asked, now a little bolder since they had somehow perhaps bonded through the spanking.

"If you want to, yes."

It seemed an odd request to Cassandra, but she also quite liked the idea.

Peyton shuffled back and lay on her stomach almost prostrating herself. This was a turn on in itself for Cassandra. Peyton gently took off Cassandra's other sandal, and then began to plant butterfly kisses on Cassandra's toes.

"Oh, oh my," Cassandra breathed feeling the new sensations. Peyton began to lick her feet on the underside, up the arches and suck her toes one by one. "Oh, fuck, oh my God, that's so good, oh, oh."

"I love your feet, Mistress, I love them so much, I want to worship your beautiful feet," Peyton said continuing the passage of her tongue around each foot in turn.

"Oh, fuck, fuck, fuck," Cassandra gasped.

Peyton's tongue was running up the inside of her calf, up her leg, and then suddenly Peyton was spreading Cassandra's legs and once more her tongue was on her clit.

"Oh, oh, ohhh!" Cassandra screamed. The feeling was so intense, and she was so worked up with giving the spanking, that within almost a few seconds, her orgasm rushed over her. "oh, oh my God, oh my God, oh my God, my God, my Godddd, ohhhh, ohhhhh, ohhhhh!" Cassandra let out a high-pitched squeal pushing her pelvis hard into Peyton's mouth bucking and writhing as Peyton lapped up her juices with relish. Cassandra gripped the side of the chair seat hard and eventually, the sensations subsided. She came down from her high to see Peyton looking at her with something akin to adoration in her eyes.

Cassandra stood up, led Peyton to the bed and lay her down on her back. She dipped her head down and between Peyton's legs to find her sweet shaven pussy. It was incredibly wet. Cassandra put her mouth close and reached out with her tongue to the wet softness. It tasted good and she began to lick in and out little flicks paying attention to Peyton's response.

"Oh, fuck, Mistress, oh my Mistress, oh, oh fuck, that's so good, so good!" Peyton cried out.

Cassandra went a little faster and, on a whim, put one then two fingers inside Peyton while she was licking, reaching for what she'd read might be her G spot or at least a sensitive spot. It worked, Peyton started to shout loudly, her voice rising to a scream.

"Oh, oh, Cassie, Cassie, Cassie, Cassieeeeeeeeeeeeeeee! Oh, my fucking Godddd! I'm cummminnnnnnnnnnnnnnnngggggggggggggggg! Ahhhhhhhhhhhhhhhhhhhhhhhhhhhhhh!" Peyton filled the room with her cries of pleasure while Cassandra continued to lick her for as long as she could stand it. Finally, Peyton was frantically pushing her head away as the sensitivity was just too much.

Cassandra eased herself up with Peyton to the top of the bed, so they were lying with their heads on the pillows, and under the quilt. She held Peyton close. Peyton said nothing but she was smiling, then she closed her eyes with a contented sigh and went to sleep.

Cassandra lay holding her and thinking for a while about everything which had just happened. The spanking was quite incredible, so different to spanking Nathan. Peyton's pussy was every bit as good as she had imagined it, the taste the feel, compared to a cock. She still wanted Nathan's cock for sure, but this new experience was something else. Peyton had taken her to heights she had not imagined perhaps because she was also a woman. Then there had been the foot kissing and licking. What had Peyton called it, foot worship? That had felt wonderful, and Cassandra wanted it again, in fact, she wanted it all again and soon. She closed her eyes too, for a while.

A little later Peyton woke up and Cassandra was looking at her smiling

"Hi, Mistress," said Peyton.

"Hi," said Cassandra, "But you can call me Cassie now, the spanking is over. Did you enjoy it? Was it as good as your fantasies?"

"It was better, so much better than I ever imagined. You're so good at it too, as being a mistress."

"Did I..." Cassandra left the question hanging.

"You were everything I wanted and more," said Peyton. "You didn't spank me too hard, so don't worry about *that*. I wanted it and I wanted it to hurt, to really feel it. And before you ask, I cried because it was so good. I don't know what happened really. All my life I've fantasised about exactly this and I suppose it was just something of a joyous occasion to get it and from someone so lovely as you."

"Really? Thank you," said Cassandra very surprised by this speech.

"Yes, honestly. I couldn't ask for a better spanking. I mean I can't compare it anything, but it lived up to all my expectations."

"I'm only just learning, so that's a compliment." Cassandra laughed.

"Well, you're very good at it, so fucking erotic, horny, such a turn on. I also really loved making love to you, Cassie, you know, before that, just so you know."

"Wow, well you're a turn on yourself. I loved how you licked me and when you licked my feet. I loved making love to you too."

"That's foot worship like I said, didn't you know?" Peyton smiled.

"No, there's a lot I don't know."

"I could teach you," said Peyton tentatively.

"I'd like that but…" Cassandra stopped. She didn't want to upset her.

"But?"

"I have a boyfriend, and I can't really be your girlfriend as well, at least, I don't think so."

"I understand," said Peyton and she was silent for a while.

Cassandra looked at her wondering if she was offended, but Peyton didn't look as if she was. In a little bit, she spoke.

"I don't want you to be my girlfriend."

"Oh?"

"But I'd like it if you would be my Mistress."

"Mistress, you mean like an affair?" Cassandra looked at her strangely.

"No, not like *that*!" Peyton laughed. "My *Mistress*. Who will take me in hand, and punish me when I need it?"

"Oh!" Cassandra thought about this. "So, what does that mean exactly?"

"It means, that when I'm naughty I will contact you and come to you so you can punish me. And… other things…"

"Other things?" Cassandra's eyes twinkled.

"I want to lick your pussy again, worship your feet… and…"

"I want to lick you and finger you too, and fuck you." Cassandra breathed thinking of it.

"So, will you?" Peyton looked at her hopefully.

"No strings?"

"No."

One thing Cassandra knew, she wanted to see Peyton again, and she wanted to fuck her again.

"OK. We can try it, see how it goes. I will keep the red sandals just for your bottom then, how's that?"

"Thank you." Peyton smiled and moved close to kiss Cassandra.

This was a strange request but somehow a compromise between Peyton becoming a girlfriend outright. Cassandra had no clue what this new relationship really entailed. However, over time it would become clear, she was sure. There was much to learn. Also, she just liked having sex with Peyton, and hoped they would be able to do that too sometimes, which would perhaps make Peyton a fuck buddy of sorts. Cassandra decided not to think on it too deeply. It would work out, one way or another.

"You're welcome," said Cassandra after they had kissed for some time, "Would you, like to stay the night? Make love to me, again, if you want to?"

"Yes, yes please, I really do, but can I ask you one more thing?" Peyton looked hopeful once more.

"What?"

"I want to watch you spank Nathan."

Cassandra laughed out loud, little did Peyton know about what Nathan and she had talked about., "Oh, I think that can be arranged."

Cassie spanks while Peyton watches (Book Four)

Cassandra half eagerly awaited Nathan's return from his field trip, and half with trepidation. Even though they'd talked about how she could sleep with another woman, she didn't really know how he might actually react when he found out. Also, how to tell him? That was another thing. She felt it was disingenuous of her to spank him for keeping secrets and this would be the biggest secret of all. The best way, of course, would be to introduce Peyton into a spanking session which where he would hardly question it. He would want to fuck Peyton and Cassandra wasn't sure how she felt about that either although it would be hypocritical not to let him.

The spanking session with Peyton had been incredibly horny and sexually charged. Peyton had stayed the night, they had sex several times, and then in the morning after breakfast, Cassandra drove her home. She was now Peyton's Mistress according to their agreement which meant Peyton would be wanting a spanking again. The thought of this definitely made Cassandra wet. She was sitting alone in the living room but could not help her hand stealing down to her pussy. She began to finger herself gently the images of turning Peyton's bottom scarlet with her sandal playing through her mind.

"Oh, fuck, fuck, oh, oh," Cassandra gasped as her fingers moved faster, in and out, and deeper, "Oh, fuck, fuck, oh my God!"

Peyton had kissed and licked Cassandra's bare feet. She has sucked Cassandra's toes. The recollections drove her wild. Her fingers were rapidly bringing her to her climax.

"Oh God, God, oh fuck, God, oh shit, shit, shit, fuck, oh, oh, ohhh!" Cassandra laid her head back and bit her lip. The orgasm rushed through her like a wave, her toes curled, and she let out a long moan of pleasure. She left her fingers in her pussy for a little while as the delicious shivers subsided.

On impulse, she took a photograph of her wet fingers and sent them to Peyton with the words. "I just finger fucked myself thinking of what we did. xxx"

The response was not long in coming, "Oh fuck! xxx"

Cassie smiled to herself.

Peyton sent another text, "So, when are you going to spank me again?"

Cassie replied, "When I want to and when you need it. Also, you are to call me Mistress when you talk to me about spanking!"

"Yes, Mistress, sorry, Mistress," came the hasty reply.

Cassie laughed. That would get Peyton going for sure. In the meantime, she got up and laid aside the book she had been reading. She went to prepare dinner and for Nathan's return. He would be rampant, at least she hoped so. She put thoughts of Peyton out of her head. The time would come to reveal her existence. Who knew what Nathan had been up to anyway? He might have done something deserving of a spanking after all. On that note, she went to the kitchen. She wanted to have a bath, look her best on his return, wear accessible clothing to entice him.

***

When Nathan arrived home, Cassandra was bathed and fragrant as she intended. She was wearing a very short, pleated skirt and a crop top which just about covered her breasts. She had no underwear on and bare feet. Her hair hung shiny and loose down her back, her nails were painted her favourite pink. She was wearing a scent which Nathan liked, and all of this was a deliberate effort to arouse him. She was pretty confident it would work.

Cassandra was in the kitchen when the front door opened and shut. The sound of a bag and rucksack being put down was followed by him evidently divesting himself of his boots.

"Cassie?" he called out.

"In the kitchen, darling," she replied.

She was gratified by the sight of his broad smile, and tousled blonde hair. His stubble and grown into a beard which she rather liked the look of. She was standing by the counter having just been in the act of checking the lasagne through the glass door of the cooker.

"Oh fuck!" he exclaimed checking her out in the most gratifying way.

"Did you have a nice time, my darling," she said walking over to him slowly so her could take her all in, and then kissing him soundly.

"Mmm, I did, very much," he replied when their lips finally parted.

She enjoyed the kiss. It was different to Peyton whose lips were softer but there was no mistaking the electricity which flew between her and Nathan when they kissed. Even better was the hard bulge in his pants which told her he was pleased to see her.

"Oh, Nathan, what's this?" she cooed softly rubbing her hand on the front of his trousers.

"Oh, fuck, Cassie, God, I've missed you," he said, "And my cock has certainly missed you, you horny fucking bitch!"

"You say the nicest things," she laughed.

"Let me do something even nicer," he growled.

She squealed as he unceremoniously bodily lifted her up and onto the kitchen counter, pushing her legs open. She willingly let him as her pussy was melting in anticipation of his cock.

She wasn't disappointed to see him rapidly undo his belt and release his organ which was hard as a rock. It was wet with precum.

"Oh, Nathan! Oh God, I want *that* inside me, now!" she gasped when she saw it.

"And you're going to get it!" he pulled her to the edge and slipped into her without preamble. His hands moved up to her breasts making her gasp as his fingers caressed them and her nipples grew erect under his circling thumbs.

"Oh, fuck, oh," she gasped.

"I've been wanting to fuck you all week," he said beginning to thrust. She moved her legs up to circle his buttocks and keep her in tight.

"Oh, Nathan, Oh, yes, Nathan, fuck me, fuck me, so fucking hard, I want it, oh God," she cried out as his cock began to move inside her filling her up.

"As you wish!" he said thrusting harder and faster, unable to contain himself.

"Oh, fuck, Nathan, oh, fuck, fuck, oh, oh, oh, oh," her voice went up an octave as he picked up speed. Her orgasm was close, her head went back, she closed her eyes.

"Oh, Cassie, oh, fuck, oh, God, I'm going to, oh, God, I'm going to," Nathan was shouting.

"Yes, yes, yes, oh, God, yes," Cassandra was lost in the sensation, edging ever closer to release, listening to his voice was also turning her on so much.

"Ahh, Cassie, I'm going to, cummmmmmmmmm, Ahhhhhhhh!"

Nathan thrust in hard. She felt his pulsing cock spurting his hot spunk into her. She loved the sensation and it sent her over the edge.

"Oh, Nathan, oh, oh, oh, ohhh, oohhhhhhhhh!" she screamed out as she climaxed, feeling wave after wave of pleasure crashing through her.

Eventually, the sensations subsided for them both and she gave him a smile. He grinned.

"Mmm, I enjoyed *that* homecoming," she said.

"Certainly, a lot of cumming," he quipped.

Cassandra laughed, threw her arms around and kissed him.

"Would you like some dinner now? It's lasagne. Your favourite."

"I'm starved, yes please."

Nathan pulled up his boxers and trousers, then did them up. Cassandra busied herself steaming broccoli and tossing it in a salad with parmesan shavings. She took the lasagne out of the oven and served him up a healthy portion, before getting a more modest one for herself.

"You wore that getup on purpose," Nathan observed while she was doing this.

"Maybe." Cassandra shot him a saucy smile.

"You did, don't deny it."

"It worked didn't it?" She laughed putting his plate in front of him. She poured him a glass of Merlot and then one for herself. Then she sat down with her food.

"I think you know the answer to *that*. This is delicious, I missed home cooking," he said having consumed half of it in the blink of an eye.

"Glad you like it, darling." She consumed hers a little more sedately

"I'm doing the cooking for the rest of this week though," he told her.

"OK." She looked at him meekly. He was a good cook, and this was a way to contribute to the household. She liked him to cook for her. It made her feel pampered and loved.

"Did you have fun?" Cassandra gave him a second helping which he started to eat a little more slowly.

"Yes, I did."

"Looking at rocks?" Her eyes teased him.

"For the most part, though we went out in the evenings, for a drink and stuff, you know, dinner that sort of thing."

"Who's we?" she said, curious.

"Oh, me and the boys, and well girls too." He gave her a sheepish grin.

Cassandra ran her foot lightly up his calf.

"Did you behave yourself?" she said trying to keep her voice neutral.

He didn't answer for a moment, and pretended to be intent on his food.

"Nathan?" she said at length beginning to suspect something might be amiss.

He put down his fork and sighed. "I was going to tell you, but not now, I mean I've only just got back and..."

"Tell me what?" she said, her tone a little more concerned.

"I did something I shouldn't, and I don't want you to be mad, and..."

Now he definitely had her attention. What had he done?

"Nathan, just tell, me, OK?" she gave him a smile of reassurance. First, she needed to know what it was before deciding if she wanted to do anything about it.

"Well, fine. We got drunk, very drunk one night and there was this girl. I think she was a local girl or something. I was missing you and she was there, and I... well... I kissed her... that's all." He regarded her apprehensively.

Cassandra digested her information and in her mind were pictures of her kissing Peyton, and more.

"Oh, I see. Was it a full-on kiss? Or..." It would still be good to know.

"It was a bit of a snog to be fair." He shrugged.

"OK, and did you fuck her?" This was blunt but she needed an answer. The thought of him kissing another woman stung her, but not as much as she imagined it would.

"No!" he exclaimed. "Just a kiss. I know it was wrong and if you want to…"

She stopped him, moving her chair closer and putting a finger on his lips.

"It's OK."

"What?" he looked surprised.

"I forgive you," she said simply.

"But you said…"

"I know what I said but you were drunk like you said, and you didn't fuck her, and I'm OK with it."

"Really?"

"Yes, really."

"OK, if you say so." He looked doubtful.

"Was she pretty?" She couldn't help asking this, of course.

"Yes, she was, well I was drunk so, you know my judgement was probably flawed." He gave self-deprecating laugh.

She moved closer so that her lips were almost on his.

"Was kissing her better than kissing me?" she breathed softly

"No!"

"That's OK then."

She kissed him, and made it a long slow kiss. He pulled her hard into his embrace and kissed her back with a passion.

"It could never compare to your kiss, Cassie, because I love you," he said fiercely.

"I love you too," she said. "Now let's go upstairs so you can fuck me again."

***

After Nathan had gone to work the following morning. Cassandra thought about what he'd told her. He had kissed another woman. The feelings this aroused in her were quite mixed. She thought she would be more jealous, but she wasn't. Was this to do with her and Peyton, she wondered? Was it because she didn't love Nathan as much as she thought? This wasn't true. All those deep feelings had been aroused when he was fucking her the night before.

He had fucked her hard, she smiled. Three more times after they had had sex in the kitchen, he had risen nobly to the occasion. The final time she had sucked him dry, and he'd licked her pussy until she had screamed the house down. They had finally fallen into a satisfied but exhausted sleep. Cassandra didn't know how she managed to have such a big sexual appetite. She wasn't aware she was probably right in the zone of her sexual peak. Cassandra was ignorant about many things regarding sex, but she was learning very fast.

She had also recently googled 'polyamorous' on the internet and started to wonder if this applied to her because of Peyton. Time would tell as things would or would not develop with Peyton. Currently, it was a loose no-strings relationship where Peyton was going to come to Cassandra for spankings. If feelings started to happen then Cassandra might have to reconsider things between them.

In the meantime, Nathan was back, and Cassandra put Peyton out of her mind. After breakfast she did some painting, and then on impulse over a lunch of homemade chicken Cesar salad with buttered baguette, she flicked on the television. Cassandra hardly ever watched it, other than for movies but it happened to be on the lunchtime news. As she idly chewed on a mouthful of chicken and salad, an item caught her attention.

"It's gone viral," the newscaster was saying, "A silly prank gone wrong. A group of university students on a field trip apparently decided to streak down the high street for a dare."

The picture switched to the footage which was obviously taken on a mobile phone, it showed several men and women running naked screaming wildly.

"However, the locals didn't take kindly to the joke, and the pranksters ended up getting arrested. After some intervention from a university official, in the end, they got off with a warning, and all's well that ended well. However, for some, that's not the end of the story. Footage of them naked has gone all over the world, they probably won't be living it down anytime soon, or at least until the next internet sensation arrives which in this fast-moving world won't be long."

Cassandra almost dropped her fork. She pursed her lips which was one of her traits when she was vexed. One of those streakers looked like Nathan. She wasn't happy. Cassandra finished her salad, trying not to be angry and then went to log onto her computer. It wasn't hard to find the footage. However, there wasn't just one video, there were many from people who obviously had thoughtfully photographed the escapade. She watched some of the videos and pausing them at intervals could very clearly see that it really was Nathan plus his other friends. The local paper ran a story "Geologists get their rocks off in a naked high street dash."

To say she was annoyed was an understatement. Nathan's kissing incident seemed nothing by comparison to *this*. One thing was for certain. Peyton was going to get to watch Nathan getting a spanking much sooner than she had imagined.

Cassandra had seethed over Nathan's behaviour for most of the afternoon. She did some gardening to try and assuage her anger but for some reason, she could not shake it off. Nathan was going to be getting told exactly what to expect from her when he got home. Cassandra wasn't intending to spank him that night, he was going to be made to wait until the following evening and by then she would have arranged for Peyton to come over. Another reason was that she felt she should not punish Nathan when she was in a bad mood, it should be more reasoned and considered.

Cassandra made a casserole for dinner even though Nathan had said he would cook. It helped to take her mind off Nathan's childish behaviour. She could not put her finger on why she was so upset. It was, after all, a prank and university students did get up to silly pranks. But he was a postgraduate and she felt perhaps he should have more common sense. If he had been eighteen, she would have understood it more easily.

In any case, before he came home, she had a shower and put on her red dress. She had started to think of it as her spanking dress, coupled with the pink sandals. It was possible she might not be able to restrain herself in any case, and might need to give him a preliminary spanking, as a precursor, after all. Also, it might help get rid of some of her ire. In her current frame of mind, she didn't feel like letting him fuck her, and she didn't want to end the evening like *that*. It might drive a wedge between them. A spanking would be a better option.

Nathan arrived home and as usual, she heard him divest himself of his shoes and hang up his keys before coming into the living room.

"Hi, baby," he said breezing in. "I was going to cook remember…" Nathan stopped dead.

Cassandra was sitting with one leg over the other so that her foot and the sandal were clearly visible. She was rhythmically slapping the sole of the sandal onto the bottom of her foot by flexing her toes. He'd seen her do this before and he knew exactly what the pink sandals meant.

"Oook," he said sitting down nearby. "What have I done now?"

The sarcastic tone annoyed her. She was already suppressing her anger, but this was the trigger which lit the blue touch paper.

"What have you done? What have you done? You've got the barefaced cheek to ask me that!" she said getting up and coming to stand over him.

"Cassie, I mean, come on, I told you about the drunken kissing," he protested looking up at her.

"This is not about the drunken kissing, Nathan!" Cassandra raised her voice. "It's about something else, let's see if you can figure it out!"

She began to pace the room.

"Cassie…" Nathan began.

"What, Nathan? Don't you know? Are you really telling me you have no idea?" It was unbelievable and his attitude simply made her furious.

"Well, I no… not really." He looked at her blandly.

She was incensed and it was all she could do not to slap his face. She went to her phone, found one of the streaking videos she had saved and held it up for him to see. He looked puzzled for a moment, then his brow cleared.

"Oh *that*," he laughed. "That was just a bit of a lark that's all, what's the big deal?"

"What's the big deal?" Cassandra was unable to believe her ears. "You got arrested, the university had to intervene, Nathan. These videos of you running around naked are all over the internet. You're lucky you didn't end up being prosecuted. How do you think it makes me feel?"

"I don't know." He shrugged as if it was wasn't a major issue, but it was to her and he ought to at least acknowledge it. She was infuriated by his casual attitude to her feelings.

"Don't you shrug at me like that, mister, don't you dare!" she shouted. "I am embarrassed, absolutely embarrassed while you behaved like a child. And what did you agree after the tyres? Hmm? You said no more childish games."

"You said no more burnouts," he retorted.

This was the last straw for Cassandra. Time for talking was over.

"How dare you, Nathan! You know exactly what I meant last time you were punished. But here you are behaving like a child again. If you are going to be so immature about it, you're going to get a childish punishment."

She turned away and went to sit on the sofa. She took off her right sandal and placed it beside her.

"Come over here," she said.

Nathan didn't move.

"I said come over here now! This is your mistress talking!" she said angrily.

Nathan sighed and rolled his eyes before getting up, and walking over to where she was sitting.

"Did you just roll your eyes at me?" she said her own eyes flashing. "You're going to pay for that, Mr and no mistake. Now take down your trousers and boxers."

"Don't you want me to strip?" Nathan asked her.

"No, you're getting a spanking and then we're going to have dinner. Then if I feel in a better mood, you're coming upstairs to fuck me. Tomorrow, however, is a different story, you're going to get a damn good whipping on your bare bottom. I warned you but you didn't listen. So, consider this spanking just a taste of your forthcoming punishment. And you'd better remember to call me Mistress or it will be very much the worse for you."

Nathan looked suddenly contrite, as if her words were hitting home. Faced with the sandal he perhaps dropped his bravado.

"Yes, Mistress," he said as he undid his trousers, and dropped them to his ankles. Followed by his knickers.

"Bend over my knee, you know what to do," said Cassandra ignoring his half-erect penis. She was interested in only one thing and that was giving him a red bottom.

Nathan did so and Cassandra picked up the sandal. She placed the sole against his left buttock cheek as she selected her first target.

"I'm very disappointed in you Nathan, I cannot believe you can be so childish. I'm even more upset that you can't even see what you did was wrong. I hope the two spankings you're going to get will give you pause for thought."

Cassie lifted the sandal with precision and brought it down on his buttocks, alternating cheeks and lifting it straight off. She hoped very much it would sting him into reflection of his stupid behaviour.

SMACK SMACK SMACK SMACK

"How dare you break your promise, Nathan!"

SMACK SMACK SMACK SMACK "Owww"

"I hope this hurts you. It's meant to because the sandal seems to be the only thing getting through to you."

SMACK SMACK SMACK SMACK

"Also, you rolled your eyes at me!"

SMACK SMACK SMACK SMACK

SMACK SMACK SMACK SMACK

She was spanking quite hard to teach him a lesson. Angry red marks sprang up on his backside.

"Owww, fuck, fuck, fuck, fuck," he said.

"You may well say ow, you little bastard. I'm so fucking angry with you Nathan."

SMACK SMACK SMACK SMACK

SMACK SMACK SMACK SMACK

SMACK SMACK SMACK SMACK

"Ow, ow, ow, ow, fuck, fuck, ow, ow, ow"

Nathan was crying out after each spank because Cassandra wasn't holding back.

"Let this be a lesson to you, you little shit. Coming home pretending it was all fine, telling me you kissed a girl when you'd done something far worse."

She changed the pace of the spanks making each one more deliberate.

SMACK "Oh fuck" SMACK "ahhhh" SMACK "oww fuck it Cassie" SMACK "Ow that fucking hurts"

SMACK "OWWWW" SMACK "OUCH" SMACK "OW" SMACK "OWW"

SMACK "Oh fuckkk" SMACK "oooohhh" SMACK "SHIT" SMACK "ow ow ow ow"

SMACK "Cassieeee" SMACK "Ahhhhhh" SMACK "ouchhhhh" SMACK "wow fuck me that stings"

His vocalisation to the spanking was a testament to the fact it was having an effect. In a perverse way she was pleased.

"Do you understand now why I'm so upset? Do you have any idea?" she demanded as his bottom began to turn from pink to red.

"Yes, Mistress, I think so."

This was the wrong thing to say.

"You SMACK think SMACK so? Well SMACK let's see SMACK if you can get more certain SMACK."

SMACK "Ahhh fuckk" SMACK "ooowwww" SMACK "wow fucking helll" SMACK "Ahhhhhhh"

SMACK "OWW" SMACK "shit oh God" SMACK "Fuckkk" SMACK "Ah I think I do ow ow ow"

SMACK "I mean owwww" SMACK "nooo fucking helll" SMACK "shittttt" SMACK "OWWWW"

Nathan tried again to mitigate things, perhaps hoping she would stop. Cassie wasn't in the mood for conciliation just yet.

"Fuck, Mistress, I mean, yes, I get why you are angry."

Cassandra began to calm down a little. The spanking had started to assuage some of her fury. The sandal was also finally making an impression on Nathan it seemed.

"Good, well that's something at any rate."

SMACK "AHHH" SMACK "fuckkk" SMACK "isn't it enough?" SMACK "oooooh that fucking hurt"

SMACK "shiiittt" SMACK "ahhhhhh" SMACK "ouch fuck" SMACK "owwwww"

SMACK "fuck fuck fuck" SMACK "Oh God" SMACK "Jesusssss" SMACK "Ahhhhhhhh"

Cassandra paused. She was feeling a lot better after the last volley of spanks. He was going to be getting another spanking the next day and so she didn't want to overdo it.

"You're going to be properly punished tomorrow, when you come home from work. Then we'll see if you're sorry or not, Nathan. You'll be getting the sandal and the riding crop just so you know. Is that understood?"

"I guess so," he said in a resigned voice.

"You SMACK guess so SMACK? Where SMACK are SMACK your manners?"

SMACK "owwwww" SMACK "sorrieeee" SMACK "fuckkkkk" SMACK "OWWWW OWW OWWW"

"Oww, sorry, Mistress, I mean yes, I understand."

"Good, you will text me to tell me what time you're going to be home. When you come home, you are to come upstairs like before, take off your clothes and knock on the door. You can expect a very hard spanking, my darling, so you can think about *that*, have you got it?"

"Yes, Mistress," he said.

"Good, just so you remember what I told you."

SMACK "oh Jesus" SMACK "Jesus fucking Christ" SMACK "fuckkkkk" SMACK "holy shit fuck"

SMACK "owwwww" SMACK "oh pleaseeee" SMACK "no more pleaseeee" SMACK "owwwwwww Cassie pleaseeee"

His bottom was a deep fiery red. She hoped maybe he'd feel it for a while. She would be making it an even deeper shade of red the next evening. She put the sandal aside. Cassandra was beginning to feel somewhat horny now, and was pretty sure once dinner was over, she would be ready for sex. This was a good thing. Even through her anger, she could also feel her arousal and the wetness between her thighs.

"You can get up now, and pull up your boxers and trousers. We'll have dinner, then you can take me upstairs because I want you to fuck me. Consider yourself lucky I don't make you stand in the corner like a naughty child."

"Thank you, Mistress," Nathan said getting up, rubbing his sore backside and then pulling up his underwear. He did his trousers up and gave her a tentative smile.

Cassandra smiled back. The idea of putting him in the corner had just occurred to her. She was on the brink of trying it but held back from doing so. Perhaps next time. She stood up, took her foot out of the other sandal. She slid her arms around his neck and kissed him.

"I love you, Nathan, but you really do try my patience."

"I can tell, and I'm sorry," he said quietly.

"You'll be even more sorry tomorrow if I have anything to do with it, but let's have dinner sweetheart."

She had temporarily forgiven him and took his hand to lead him to the dining room. She would remember all of her annoyance when she spanked him again, she was sure and then she would make sure to do a proper job.

***

They had incredibly intense sex that night, something Cassandra noticed happened after he had received a spanking. His cock seemed harder, and he fucked her vigorously. The orgasms were certainly worth it. Unwittingly he did not realise he was simply making a case for more spankings with these sexual performances.

Cassandra texted Peyton that morning after Nathan went to university. She said, "Peyton, you are to come to my house after work. Nathan is going to be getting a spanking and you're going to watch."

The text back was almost instantaneous. "Really? Oh God! Count me in, what should I bring, wear?"

Cassandra told her and it seemed Peyton possessed the items she suggested. As for Cassandra, she had recently acquired a red and black satin corset. It looked fabulous on and she would be pairing it with her red stiletto mules. Nathan would probably cream his jeans when he saw her in them, at least metaphorically.

She picked up Peyton after work and brought her home. Peyton had left early with a promise to her boss to make up the time. It seemed she didn't want to miss any part of the evening's events. Cassandra suggested they have a shower together, and they slipped naked under the hot water. The walk-in shower was quite large and well able to accommodate two people as Cassandra knew only too well. She and Nathan quite often had a shower, and more.

Cassandra began to soap Peyton gently, and inevitably they began to kiss. The flame lit up in her loins and Peyton's hand was soon between Cassandra's legs. Peyton turned her around and Cassandra put her hands on the glass while Peyton began to finger her.

"Oh fuck, Peyton, oh God, fuck, oh, oh, oh, oh," Cassandra cried out as Peyton relentlessly took her closer to the edge. The rushing water made it all the hornier, and Cassandra soon felt the wave about to burst over her. "Oh, Peyton, oh God, God, fuck, oh God, God, oh my God, oh, oh, ohhh!" She climaxed pushing her arse hard into Peyton who pulled her in tight, and was biting her neck. This drove Cassandra wild intensifying her climax, until eventually, it subsided.

She turned to do the same to Peyton but found a finger on her lips.

"Later," Peyton smiled. "It's my job to serve my Mistress, not for my Mistress to serve me."

"Really?" Cassandra looked surprised, but Peyton had already moved into her role. She collected herself and replied more appropriately. "Yes, absolutely."

She turned Peyton around and delivered half a dozen well-placed smacks to her arse.

SMACK SMACK SMACK SMACK SMACK SMACK

The sound echoed around the shower cubicle and Peyton blushed, "Thank you, Mistress."

"Very good, good you know your place. Those were just to make sure you remember it too." Cassandra affectionately flicked Peyton's cheek.

They dried each other, and then Peyton insisted on doing her Mistress' nails, and makeup. Cassandra did not demur. Then Peyton did her own. They opted for red nails and lipstick. They both straightened their hair before putting on the corsets and mules. It was getting on for time for Nathan to be home.

"Now, remember, I'm the Mistress when Nathan comes upstairs, and you are to do exactly what you're told. Understood?"

"Yes, Mistress," said Peyton meekly.

The way Peyton was subservient to her was making Cassandra horny, and it was only set to get more arousing once Nathan arrived. Her anger had subsided since the previous night, but she still wanted to punish him severely. He had to learn a lesson and yesterday's taster spanking was insufficient to the offence to her mind.

"Mistress, may I say you look ravishing in that outfit and I want desperately to put my mouth on your beautifully shaved pussy."

"You may say so, Peyton, and you look very sexy yourself. I'd like to fuck you and I'm going to be doing so."

"Will Nathan be fucking me too?" Peyton wanted to know, but she kept her eyes on the ground perhaps feeling it was how she should behave.

"That's up to me, but I'm sure he's going to want to, my darling."

Peyton flashed a look of surprise at the endearment. She gave Cassandra a shy smile and then looked at the floor again. This was beginning to bother Cassandra and she said so.

"You can look me in the eyes, Peyton, in fact, I want you to, so stop that at once."

"Yes, Mistress," Peyton replied.

"Behave yourself or you'll be bent over for the sandal before I even get started on Nathan!" Cassandra was saying things she felt Peyton wanted to hear rather than how she really felt. The Mistress persona was new to her, but Peyton evidently needed her to be dominant and she had agreed to do so. Now she had to live up to. Cassandra wasn't really sure how she felt about it.

However, she found herself more and more attracted to Peyton and enjoying having her around. Was she getting feelings? Cassandra pushed the thoughts away for the moment. As Peyton was here, she might as well be of use.

"Peyton, go to that cupboard, get my pink thong sandals and the riding crop you'll find in there."

"Yes, Mistress," said Peyton and hurried to do her bidding. She extracted the items and placed them reverently on the bed. "Mistress…"

"Yes, Peyton?"

"I think you should get some more things, for spanking."

"Do you now? And did I ask for your opinion?" Cassandra said putting on a severe sounding voice.

"No, Mistress, sorry, Mistress," said Peyton.

"Bring me that sandal."

Peyton's cheeks went a little pink, but she did and handed it to Cassandra.

"Now turn around, bend over and put your hands on your knees."

Cassandra decided if she was going to play the part, it was best she played it.

Peyton was bending over, Cassandra lined up the sandal on Peyton's creamy bottom.

"When SMACK I SMACK want SMACK your opinion SMACK I will SMACK ask for it SMACK."

The spanks rang out as she left several red marks on the previously pristine buttocks.

"Yes, Mistress, sorry, Mistress."

"You will be if you try my patience again, now stand up and put the sandal back. Don't you dare be so impertinent again. You will wait without speaking until I ask you to."

Peyton took the sandal from her and curtsied clumsily. She hurried and replaced it carefully on the bed. Then she stood with her arms by her sides waiting for further instructions. Cassandra nodded her approval. A glance at the bedroom clock told her Nathan was due to arrive shortly. She had texted Nathan not to be late or face the consequences.

Right on cue, she heard his car pulling up at the house. The door front door banged open and shut, and in a few short minutes, he came up the stairs. There was a knock at the door.

"Come in, Nathan," said Cassandra trying not to smile.

Nathan entered and closed the bedroom door behind him. He was buck naked and stood staring as soon as he saw Peyton. In fact, his jaw almost hit the floor. It was all Cassandra could do not to laugh. Peyton was likewise looking Nathan over, and it was fair to say he was a sight for sore eyes. Well-muscled, tattooed and a six-pack. His hair had an undercut and his beard had been trimmed nicely. He'd obviously been to the barber. Cassandra appreciated the fact he had. His cock was already standing to attention taking in not only Cassandra but Peyton both in corsets and stiletto mules.

"Nathan, this is Peyton. She is going to watch you being punished. Then you're going to watch me fuck her, and if you take your punishment like a good boy, then it will be your turn."

He said nothing but licked his lips like a tiger contemplating a fine meal. Well, he, might, Cassandra thought, two fine meals in fact. She was suddenly feeling the sexual charge in the room and her pussy was becoming very wet. They hadn't even started.

"Peyton, fetch me the riding crop, there's a good girl," said Cassandra.

"Yes, Mistress." Peyton hurried to obey, picked up the riding crop and handed it to Cassandra

"Very good, Peyton, back to your place."

Peyton obeyed. Nathan watched this exchange with interest, the wheels turning in his head. He was evidently wondering where Peyton had come from and how long Cassandra had known her.

"All in due, course, Nathan. I can see what you're thinking," said Cassandra approaching him with the crop.

Just like the last time she began to run the tip lightly over his skin, and then along the shaft of his cock.

"You're wondering about Peyton, I know, and I'll tell you, later. For now, you're mine and you're in here to be punished. So, don't forget it."

He hissed in a breath as the tip of the leather crop touched the head of his penis, which was now fully erect and hard.

"Excuse me, Mistress," said Peyton.

Cassandra's head whipped round as this impinged on her thoughts, she was just getting into the session.

"What?" she said impatiently.

"Shouldn't you milk him first, when he's like that?"

"Milk him?" said Cassandra puzzled.

"Yes, get his spunk out, Mistress, that way he'll feel the punishment more."

"Really!" Cassandra said sceptically.

"Yes, Mistress, I read it on a spanking site."

"Did you?"

"Yes, Mistress."

"Well," said Cassandra advancing on her, "Thank you for the suggestion, but what did I tell you?"

"To not speak unless you asked me to, Mistress." Peyton hung her head.

"And what did you do?"

"I spoke, without being asked."

"Fetch that chair over here and place it in the centre of the room, Peyton," said Cassandra pointing at what she now thought of as her spanking chair.

Peyton did so and set it down, so the seat was facing Cassandra.

"Good girl, now bend over and put your hands on the seat."

As Peyton obeyed presenting her bottom once more, Cassandra took her place to Peyton's left side. She levelled the whip on Peyton's cheeks. If Peyton wanted her to be a strict Mistress, then she was going to get it.

"It seems you don't understand instructions, do you!"

SWISH CRACK "owwwwww"

"No, Mistress."

"When I say you are to do something, you do it"

SWISH CRACK "owww oooh Mistresss"

"Do you understand?"

SWISH CRACK "oww howwww"

"Owww, yes, Mistress."

SWISH CRACK "oooh hooooo"

Cassandra paused for a moment and then, on a whim, decided to administer several more strokes.

"Good, now this might help you to remember it."

SWISH CRACK "oww how how"

SWISH CRACK "oh God owww owwww"

SWISH CRACK "ooooohhhhhhh"

SWISH CRACK "Ahhhhhhhhhh"

SWISH CRACK "oh Mistresssssss"

SWISH CRACK "OWWWWWWWWW"

"Owww, owww, owwww, oh, oh, oh!" Peyton howled as the crop stung her buttocks again and again.

"That's better," said Cassandra surveying the crisscross lines on Peyton's backside, which was also now a nice shade of pink.

She noticed Nathan had been watching this with a high state of arousal. There was precum on the tip of his cock.

"Get up Peyton."

Peyton did so and turned to face her, looking suitably chastened and subservient.

"Go and stand in front of Nathan.

"Yes, Mistress."

As Peyton did so, Cassandra could see Nathan was looking at her with a hunger in his eyes, like a wolf eyeing up his prey. He was going to enjoy the next part then. It had occurred to her on the spur of the moment while she was punishing Peyton.

"On your knees, Peyton."

"Mistress."

Peyton sunk to her knees level with Nathan's engorged cock.

"Since you're so keen on milking him, you can suck his cock."

Peyton hesitated.

"Go on, do as you are told, you know you want to," Cassandra said lightly.

Peyton took his cock in her hand and put her lips around the head.

"Oh, fuck," Nathan groaned, "Fuck."

Peyton's head began to move expertly up and down his shaft, taking him in and out of her mouth, manipulating it with her hand. Cassandra could tell she'd done this before. Oddly she didn't feel jealous but instead incredibly aroused.

Peyton began to move faster, at the same time wanking him harder with her hand.

"Oh, fuck, fuck, fuck, shit, oh, oh, oh, oh, oh, fuck, ohhhhhhhhhh!" Nathan grabbed Peyton's head and started to fuck her mouth, hard and fast. He suddenly let out a long guttural moan as he came inside her mouth. His head laid back and his lips stretched out in a grin. Cassandra put a finger down to her pussy, it was wet and all she wanted to do was frig herself. She didn't want to lose control however and withdrew her hand from the danger zone with reluctance.

Nathan had finished his orgasm and his cock was now flaccid though still large. It never got *that* small Cassandra reflected. Peyton smiled as she swallowed his cum and licked her lips. Cassandra could tell she'd enjoyed it.

"You can get up now, Peyton, very well done. A good tip for the future, thank you."

Peyton did so.

"Stand over there so you can see," said Cassandra pointing to the right of where Nathan would be bending over. Then she turned to Nathan. "I hope you enjoyed your blow job, Nathan, because I don't think you are going to like the next part. Go to the chair, bend over and put your hands on the seat. Do not remove them until I say."

Cassandra went and took up her position on Nathan's left. She teased the crop over Nathan's buttocks. He winced slightly anticipating what was to come.

"Now, Nathan, you can save yourself a few strokes by explaining in detail why you are being punished, I'll give you one chance before I begin." Cassandra spoke quietly, almost gently.

Her behaviour in the spanking session so far was quite unprecedented for her. She couldn't imagine where this persona came from, or some of the words. Perhaps it had been somehow deeply repressed in her psyche. But Cassandra's parents never laid a hand on her. It was very strange.

"I streaked naked down the high street where we were staying as a prank with the other students, and then we got arrested. We got off because of the university intervening, otherwise, we would have been charged," he said.

"Yes, that's part of it for sure. But not all of it."

She raised the whip and began.

SWISH CRACK "OWW"

SWISH CRACK "Fuckkkkkkkk"

"Well, I don't know what else you want me to say," he complained.

"Manners, Nathan!"

SWISH CRACK "Owwwwww God"

He had to be reminded she was the Mistress when he didn't use that title to speak to her.

"Peyton tell Nathan how he's supposed to address me."

"He's to call you Mistress, Mistress," Peyton said watching the rise and fall of the whip intently.

SWISH CRACK "OOOUCH"

"Yes, did you hear that, Nathan?"

SWISH CRACK "OWWW FUCK!"

"Yes, Mistress, sorry, Mistress."

Evidently, he decided discretion was the better part of valour.

"Good boy, now don't forget!"

SWISH CRACK "Oh God owwww"

"So, what was so bad about what you did, Nathan? Come on."

SWISH CRACK "ooooohhhh"

He hesitated trying to think it through, but he didn't say anything.

SWISH CRACK "OWWWWWWWWWW

"I can't hear you!"

SWISH CRACK "FUCKKKK!!"

"I don't know, Mistress," he said sounding annoyed.

"You don't know. Even after the spanking, I gave you yesterday. Let me spell it out to you."

She didn't like his attitude and was determined to whip it out of him.

SWISH CRACK "shit fuck that hurt"

"You came home without telling me about what you'd done, and instead told me a story about kissing a girl when you were drunk."

SWISH CRACK "fuckkkkk OK yesss"

"I had to find out from the TV news, and videos of you naked are all over the internet."

SWISH CRACK "owwwww oh owwwww"

"I'm embarrassed, Nathan. You broke your promise not to do any more childish pranks and you engaged in yet another childish prank."

SWISH CRACK "FUCKKK oh God owwww"

"You disobeyed me. You were untruthful. You made me feel like a fucking idiot."

SWISH CRACK "Shitttt"

SWISH CRACK "oouchhhh"

SWISH CRACK "Fuckkk"

"Now do you understand?"

SWISH CRACK "oh God fuck fuck fuck"

"Yes, Mistress."

"Do you?"

SWISH CRACK "OWWWW YESSSS!"

"Yes, yes, yes, I do."

"Then you understand why you are going to be properly punished."

"Haven't I been punished already, Mistress?" he asked hopefully.

"Not enough, Nathan, no. I shouldn't have to spell it out to you like this, but it seems that the riding crop and the sandal are the things which make you listen the most. I want to leave a lasting impression on your bottom and perhaps it will finally get through to you." She turned to Peyton. "Peyton, take the riding crop and bring me the sandal."

"Yes, Mistress." Peyton took the crop and placed it carefully on the bed, before taking the sandal for the right foot and handing it to Cassandra.

"I promised you a spanking, Nathan, and a spanking you are going to get."

She lined the sandal up on his backside and began to spank, deliberately and making each spank count.

SMACK "ouchhhh" SMACK "owwwww" SMACK "wow oh woww" SMACK "shitttt"

SMACK "fuckkkk" SMACK "ahhhhhhh" SMACK "fucking hellll" SMACK "oh God fuck me that fucking stings"

SMACK "Oh Cassie owwww" SMACK "Cassieeee" SMACK "ouchhhhh" SMACK "isn't it enoughhhhhh"

SMACK "AHHHHH" SMACK "OWWWWWW" SMACK "JESUSSSSS" SMACK "FUCKKKKK"

SMACK "GODDDDD" SMACK "CHRISTTTTTT" SMACK "oh FUCKKKKK" SMACK "SHITTTT"

SMACK "ow ow ow ow ow" SMACK "fucking hellfire" SMACK "fuck meeeeee" SMACK "ahhhhhhh"

SMACK "OWWW Fuckkk" SMACK "fuck itttttt" SMACK "AHHHHH" SMACK "ow fuck that fuck owwww"

SMACK "shittt" SMACK "Ahhhhhh" SMACK "fuckkkkk" SMACK "OWWWWW"

"Jesus fucking Christ!" Nathan shouted at the end of this volley of spanks. Cassandra smiled at his reddening behind. He had certainly been vocal during this part of his spanking. She had simply ignored it and continued.

"Is that not to your liking?" she asked him with a slight smile playing around her mouth.

"No, Mistress."

"Too bad, because you certainly deserve it."

It seemed quite harsh of her, but she felt it was warranted. Besides when she began spanking, something of a bitch took over her persona.

She glanced down at his cock and saw it was straining and hard. Taking a leaf out of Peyton's book she decided he should perhaps be milked again, although she didn't want him to be unable to fuck her and Peyton later. Nathan's recycle time, was, however, pretty fast, so she felt in the grand scheme of things it wouldn't hurt.

"Come here Peyton and take the sandal," said Cassandra with a mischievous smile.

"Yes, Mistress."

Cassandra moved around to the right side of Nathan and took hold of his cock.

"Now Peyton, I want you to spank Nathan, nice and hard, OK?"

"Yes, Mistress, but…" Peyton bit her lip.

"But?"

"I'm left-handed, Mistress."

"Ah, OK."

Cassandra reversed positions and took hold of Nathan's cock again. He gasped as her hand began to move slowly.

"Spank him, Peyton, until I tell you to stop."

"Yes, Mistress."

While Cassandra began to wank him a little faster, Peyton lined up the sandal on Nathan's arse, and began a spanking copying Cassandra's technique. The enjoyment on her face was obvious.

SMACK "AHHHH" SMACK "Fuck what are you" SMACK "oh Goddddd" SMACK "owww fuckkkkk"

"Harder, Peyton."

"Yes, Mistress."

Peyton took the sandal back further and let fly in unrestrained rhythmic spanks. She certainly appeared to be enjoying the reversal from submissive to dominant.

SMACK "ohhhhhhh" SMACK "fuckking helll" SMACK "shittttt" SMACK "ohhhhhhh"

SMACK "fuckkkk" SMACK "Jesussssss" SMACK "Oh Godddddd" SMACK "fuckkkkkk"

SMACK "ohhhhhhh" SMACK "fuckkkkkk" SMACK "shittttt" SMACK "OWWWW"

SMACK "ahhhhhh" SMACK "fuck God that owwwwwww" SMACK "OW OW OW" SMACK "shit oh shit oh shit oh God"

SMACK "Ooooh" SMACK "oh ohhhhhh" SMACK "oh oh oh oh" SMACK "oh God fuck oh oh oh"

In the meantime, Cassandra was rubbing his cock faster and faster, feeling his shaft getting stiffer, and harder. Nathan was gasping with the spanks and the sensations until his cock began to pulse. Knowing his orgasm was imminent, Cassandra signalled Peyton to stop while she carried on. Cassandra cupped her hand in front of the head of his cock as his spunk began to pump out.

"Oh, oh, oh, fuck, you bitches, you fucking bitches, oh, oh, ohhhhhh!" he cried.

Some of the semen escaped but Cassandra ignored it, she would just have to clean it up, or get Peyton to do so. On impulse, she took her cupped hand and held it up to Peyton. Were things getting out of hand? She didn't know. All she knew was that she was deep into something she could almost no longer control.

"You can lick that up, now, good girl."

Cassandra wondered if Peyton would comply with even this request, but Peyton didn't demur.

"Yes, Mistress."

In fact, she needed no second bidding, and nor did she seem fazed as she licked Cassandra's hand clean. Although Cassandra liked the taste of Nathan's spunk, she wasn't sure she would lick out of her own hand in this fashion.

"Good, girl, very impressive," said Cassandra, "Now get the other sandal and give that one to me."

Peyton did so and Cassandra resumed her position. Another twist in the spanking episode had occurred to her.

"Stand there Peyton," she said indicating Nathan's right-hand side. "Now we're going to spank together, I'll do this cheek and you do the other one. We'll alternate, OK."

"Yes, Mistress," said Peyton eagerly, happy to play the part of the spanker as opposed to the spankee.

"Nathan, you called us a pair of bitches and now we're going to show you how much of a pair of bitches we are."

"Fuck!" he said.

Cassandra raised the sandal and spanked, followed by Peyton, as they took it in turns.

SMACK "FUCKKK" SMACK "fucking bitchhhh" SMACK "owww you bitchhh" SMACK "fuck it"

SMACK "oh GODDD" SMACK "Shitttt" SMACK "oh fuck fuck fuck" SMACK "ow can't you just"

SMACK "OWWWW" SMACK "fucking hellll" SMACK "ow what a bitch" SMACK "God what a fucking bitch"

SMACK "Oh fuck shit" SMACK "shitttttt" SMACK "ohhhhhh" SMACK "Noooooo"

SMACK "AHHHHH" SMACK "OHHHHHHH" SMACK "OUCHHHHH" SMACK "FUCKKKKK"

SMACK "OW OW FUCK" SMACK "SHITTTT" SMACK "OWWWWWW" SMACK "AH GOD YOU FUCKING BITCHESSSSS"

"OWWWWWW FUCK!"

The spanks had been hard, and his backside was turning a dark red. Cassandra gauged it was time to wrap up punishment.

"Put the sandals back Peyton and bring me the crop, then you can watch."

"Yes, Mistress."

Peyton was flushed pink with arousal at what they had done. Cassandra was thinking of Peyton's wet pussy as she once more had the crop in her hand. Not much longer before she could feel that pussy once more with her fingers. Cassandra lined the crop up on Nathan's arse.

"Now then Nathan, I suggest you think carefully when you answer the next questions."

SWISH CRACK "OWWWWW"

"Have you learned your lesson?"

SWISH CRACK "FUCKKKKKK"

"Yes, yes I have, Mistress."

SWISH CRACK "YES OWWW YESSS"

"Good, and will you do it again?"

SWISH CRACK "OWWW NOOO"

"No, Mistress."

SWISH CRACK "OWW OW PLEASE"

"What won't you do again?""

SWISH CRACK "GODDDDDD"

"I won't play stupid pranks again."

SWISH CRACK "AHHHHHHH"

"No, you won't, or you will find yourself bent over for another whipping."

SWISH CRACK "Owww fuck fuck owwwww"

"Are you sorry?"

SWISH CRACK "YES YES OWWWWW"

"Yes, Mistress."

SWISH CRACK "I SAID YESSSSS"

"Truly?"

SWISH CRACK "Oh yes yes OWWWWWW"

"Yes, Mistress."

SWISH   CRACK
"OWWWWWWWWWWWWWWWWWWWW"

She paused, he sounded genuinely contrite, and they had given him quite a spanking overall.

"Good. Well, I hope you have. I really do because I don't want to have to give you another spanking in the near future, as much as I have enjoyed it. Now, here come the last six."

"Fuck!" he muttered although he must have been expecting it. She noticed his buttocks tense just a little.

"One" SWISH CRACK "OWW"

"Two" SWISH CRACK "SHITTTTT"

"Three" SWISH CRACK "OWWWW FUCK"

"Four" SWISH CRACK "OWWWWWWW FUCKKK"

"Five" SWISH CRACK "OWW OWWWWWW FUCKK"

"Six" SWISH CRACK "OWW FUCK FUCK FUCK!"

She stopped and examined her handiwork. His buttocks were crossed with red lines and it was a deep shade of red. She discarded the crop, tossing it aside.

"Now that's what I call a well-spanked bottom. Stand up, Nathan," she said.

He did so, and his eyes looked a little moist. Perhaps it had brought a few tears to them. She felt quite compassionate towards him now. Any residual ire over his offence was well spent in mercilessly tanning his backside. She walked up to him and kissed him full on the lips and held him close.

"My darling, you deserved *that*. It had to be done. You know it did."

He said nothing and his expression was inscrutable. He wasn't going to admit it, even if he agreed. She let him go and turned the chair around to face the bed.

"Sit down, darling, and put your hands behind the back of the chair and keep them there."

He complied, and in his eyes was now a look of expectation. His cock seemed to be recovering well from the second milking, and was starting to harden.

Cassandra threw the sandals onto the floor, stepped out of her mules, and beckoned to Peyton.

"Come here, Peyton, darling, here on the bed."

Peyton blushed once more at the endearment, and came over to her taking off her mules too. Cassandra pulled her into her embrace and began to kiss her passionately. Peyton's hands were running over her skin and her naked buttocks. They were kneeling facing each other, and Nathan was staring at them, his nostrils began to flare like a stallion on heat. Cassandra squeezed Peyton's buttocks and she let out a squeal, her bottom was probably a little tender. Their kisses became more intense. Cassandra's hands went between Peyton's legs to her wet pussy, almost simultaneously Peyton was doing the same to her.

"Oh, fuck, Peyton, oh God, fuck, fuck, oh my God," Cassandra cried out as Peyton's fingers found her clit. She was so wet. She was almost dripping.

"Oh, Mistress, oh fuck, oh my, oh, oh, oh," Peyton cried, as Cassandra's fingers moved faster.

"Oh, oh, God, God, oh, God, oh, oh, I'm going to…"

"Me too, Mistress…"

Neither of them could last too long, the build-up had been so intense. A wave of pleasure broke inside Cassandra, she shouted as she climaxed.

"Oh, fuck, oh, oh, oh, ohhhhhhhhhhhhhhhh!!"

Peyton was climaxing too, almost at the same time, "Ohhhhhhh, Mistressssssss, ohhhhhhh!"

They sat holding each other and kneeling. Pulling each other close. Kissing passionately. A surge of emotion went through Cassandra as she did so. It was similar to how she felt when kissing Nathan. An intensity of passion and something more which perhaps Cassandra was not ready to acknowledge. Deciding this was enough, she pulled away. Nathan was watching with envious greedy eyes. His cock was standing out like a ramrod. It was time to turn him loose.

"Get on all fours, Peyton, with your bottom facing Nathan," Cassandra said softly.

"Yes, Mistress."

Peyton obeyed every command Cassandra gave her as if she'd been born to it. It was gratifying somehow but a strange feeling too, of power over another, in fact, two people.

"Nathan, you can fuck Peyton, go on, and then later you can fuck me."

Nathan needed no second bidding. He was worked up and out of his mind with desire. Looking at Peyton, Cassandra thought, who wouldn't be? He got onto his knees behind her and unceremoniously inserted his cock into her without preamble.

"Ohhhhh!" Peyton squealed. "It's so big."

Cassandra laid back against the headboard to watch, her hand straying to her pussy and beginning to finger herself. Watching Nathan fuck Peyton was a turn on, and she wasn't jealous in the least.

"I'm going to fuck you, you little bitch!" Nathan growled as he began to move.

"Oh, yes, fuck, me Nathan, fuck me, I'm a bitch, I'm a little slut, I'm a whore. Fuck me and use me, please."

"Only too happy to oblige," he said.

"Oh! Oh, oh, oh, oh, oh," Peyton shouted as Nathan's cock began to slide in and out harder and faster.

"Oh, fuck, you bitch, fuck, God, oh my God, you've got a fucking nice tight pussy, you little bitch, fuck, fuck, fuck!" Nathan cried out now unable to stop himself as he built up speed.

"Oh, yes, fuck me, fuck, me harder, harder, oh God, I love it, I love it!" screamed Peyton.

Cassandra's fingers were also working overtime watching them fuck, and she was moaning out loud, trying not to close her eyes on the riveting scene. "Oh, fuck, fuck, fuck, oh God, that's so fucking horny!"

"Fuck, fuck, fuck!" Nathan was shouting going as fast as he could, grabbing Peyton's hips as he prepared for his final thrusts.

"Oh, Nathan, Nathan, Nathan!" Peyton was shouting.

"Jesus fucking Christ!" Nathan shouted ramming his cock home, slamming it into her, his balls slapping on her backside. "Fuck, fuck, fuck, fuck, ah, ah, ah."

"Oh God, Nathan, oh fuck, oh fuck me, oh that's so fucking good!"

"Oh shit, shit, shit," Cassandra cried out frigging herself harder getting closer to her orgasm.

"Fuck, fuck, fuck, oh fuck, fuck, fuckkk! I'm cominggggg you fuckinggg, bitchhhhhhhh, ahhhhhhhhhh!" Nathan was roaring like a lion as he shot his load inside her, pushing hard into her.

"Ooooooohhhhhhh!" Peyton orgasmed at almost the same time screaming at the top of her lungs.

"Oh, shit, shit, shit, shitttttt!" cried Cassandra watching this and unable to resist the waves also crashing through her. The utter debauchery of it all, was so horny she was almost unable to bear it. She had loved every moment of it.

The tableau suddenly slipped into silence, as their orgasms finished. For a few moments, they were still. The sheer energy of what had just happened engulfed them, and took them over. Peyton let out a long sigh of pleasure at last, and Nathan slid out of her pussy. Cassandra opened her eyes and said, "Come here you two, come to me, my darlings, my lovely darlings."

They obliged. Nathan held her close on one side and Peyton on the other.

"You're so fucking beautiful, do you know that?" he said to her quietly.

"And Peyton?" Cassandra wondered.

"She's beautiful too."

Peyton smiled, perhaps unused to compliments.

"Did you enjoy fucking her?" Cassandra said smiling.

"If I did?"

"Then I'm glad, I wanted you to enjoy it. I enjoyed watching you fuck her. I got off on it, didn't you notice?"

Nathan looked at her strangely.

"What?" Cassandra asked. "I'm not jealous."

"You're not?"

"No, and I think we're all going to do a lot more fucking after dinner, all three of us."

"I loved Nathan's cock," Peyton said shyly.

"So, you should, it's a very nice one."

They were silent for a while. Peyton slid her hand into Cassandra's and Nathan put his arm over her and she snuggled into him, enjoying the feeling.

"What is this, what are we doing here?" Nathan asked her at length.

"I don't know, Nathan, don't you like it?"

"It's different, I'll give you that."

Cassandra turned to look at him.

"We talked about this. Don't you remember?"

"I do but I never thought you would…" he left it unfinished.

"But isn't it fun?"

"Yes, but…"

"Then what's the problem?"

"No problem, as long as you're cool with it?" There was still a question in his eyes, as if he couldn't quite believe she would agree to it let alone arrange it.

"And Peyton, she's cool with it too, aren't you, darling?"

"Yes, yes I am, I loved it, every moment," said Peyton with a smile.

"Don't overthink it, Nathan." Cassandra smiled. "Anyway, let's go and have some dinner, hey?"

Nathan shrugged and sat up. He looked gorgeous naked, and so did Peyton. How could Cassandra choose between them, if she was asked to? She hoped Nathan wouldn't want that. She knew she could not. Things had changed, yet again. There was so much more to be explored. The three of them together like this opened up all kinds of sexual possibilities, and she had hardly got started. Whatever the future held, one thing she did know for certain. There was going to be a lot more sex that night, and the thought of it filled her with eager anticipation.

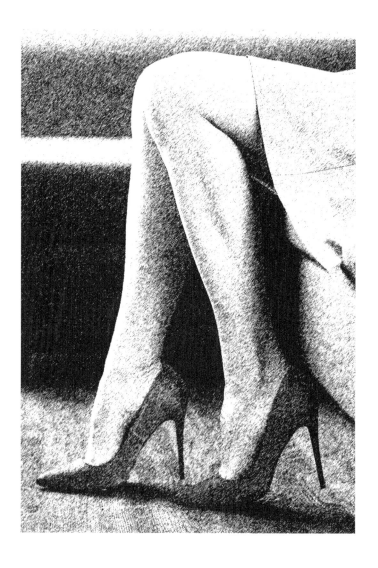

Cassie gives a hairbrush spanking (Book Five)

Cassandra's bottom was raised high in the air, as Nathan took her from behind.

"Oh, Nathan, oh, fuck, fuck, fuck," she cried out her head buried in her pillow. The hard thrusts pushed her forward every time, and Nathan was grunting in guttural pleasure as he filled her up.

"Cassie, oh fuck, Cassie, fuck, oh, oh, oh, oh," he gasped, his hands grasping her thighs to pull her in tighter.

This was her favourite position as it let him go in satisfyingly deep.

"Oh, Jesus Christ, oh, oh, oh, oh, oh." She was nearing her climax as he quickened the pace.

Very shortly he would begin to go as fast as he could, as he reached his own pressure point.

"Oh, Cassie, fuck, you fucking bitch, oh, oh, oh!"

He had recently taken to calling her that when they had sex, and it only turned her on the more he did it. She liked it somehow, and she had been a bitch to him with sandal and the riding crop. Her thoughts strayed to spanking him and the wave which had been building crested over, shudders ran through her.

"Oh, oh, oh, oh, ah, fuck, fuck, ah, ah, ahhhhh!" she was squealing as she climaxed, but Nathan wasn't listening. He was ramming his cock home like a piston which only served to intensify her sensations as he also arrived at the zenith. Cassie felt his cock pulsing and then the warm sensation of cum inside her pussy.

"Oh, fuck, fuck, fuck, ahhhhhhhhhhhhhhhhhhhh!" he shouted at the top of his voice. Nathan had always been very vocal, and this time was no different. There was even the time he had howled like a wolf, Cassandra reflected, as the pleasurable feelings began to subside.

He slid out of her, and lay beside her holding and kissing her softly. She liked this part the best and Nathan was very considerate in this way. He did not just roll over and go to sleep. Although she noticed he had become a tad more aggressive in his lovemaking since the spanking started. Cassandra had a guilty pang and hoped she wasn't damaging him in some way. She didn't know enough about it. It was, however, consensual and he could have simply out and out refused. Some part of him must have wanted it too, even though he never fully admitted it.

After a little while, simply looking into each other's eyes, Cassandra said, "What are you thinking?"

It was a classic female move because she was sure he must be thinking something. Usually, he'd say nothing but this time he spoke.

"So, you met up with Peyton and fucked her while I was away," he said.

Cassandra sighed, "Haven't we talked about this, Nathan?"

"We have," he continued, "But I'm still processing it."

"What are you processing, exactly?"

"That you slept with someone else." This was blunt and perhaps they might be getting to the nub of things. They discussed it before, and it seemed for Nathan it was still an issue.

"Remember though when I asked you about sleeping with another woman, before you went away, and you said as long as you get to fuck her too?"

"We did, but I didn't really think you were serious." He frowned.

"You kissed a girl," she countered.

"But you *fucked* Peyton. You *fucked* her."

"And so did you, and I watched you do it. I let her suck your cock and I didn't say anything. In fact, I enjoyed it and I enjoyed you enjoying it."

"I know," he said and then after a moment, "That's what is bothering me."

Cassandra lay back on the bed, and looked up at the ceiling. After the spanking session, the three of them had had sex several times more, all together. She had licked Peyton while Peyton sucked Nathan's cock. He had fucked Peyton while she licked Cassandra. She had given him a blow job, while he licked Peyton, and many variations thereof. She didn't understand how he could be having qualms after all of that.

"What is bothering you, Nathan, what? I don't understand." She tried to keep the exasperation out of her voice.

"I thought you'd be mine and only mine."

Cassandra was silent. Before Peyton, she would have said she was only Nathan's without hesitation, but now things were different. She didn't think she could give up Peyton.

"Well, maybe I've changed. I'm sorry, darling. I didn't ask to change it just…"

"Happened?" he finished the sentence for her.

"Yes, it did. Maybe I was wrong to start this, but I have, and now here we are." She turned back to him and her eyes flashed a little defiantly. "It doesn't mean I don't love you. I do, just as much as I ever did. I love you so much it hurts, don't you know that?"

"And do you love, Peyton?"

The question hung there like a pall of smoke, almost palpable in its emotional content.

"I don't know," she said at length, "I can't answer that, not just now. If I did, would it make a difference?"

It was his turn to lie on his back. His face was a little troubled and she could see perhaps it was a difficult thing for him after all. However, he deserved the truth, at least, about her feelings.

"I don't know, I don't know how I'd feel about it," he replied, turning his head to see the tears which sprung into her eyes at this statement.

"Do you think I can control this? These feelings? I can't, Nathan, and you can't ask me to. I… why can't you just be happy?" As much as she felt for him, she also felt he was pressuring her into things she didn't fully understand, as yet.

Nathan couldn't bear to see her cry, and he enfolded her in his arms at once.

"I'm sorry, hush, ignore me, I'm just being a big old growly bear. I'll get over it."

She cried a little then, small quiet sobs. He held her tightly feeling her tears wetting his shoulder.

"It's OK, honestly it's OK."

"OK," Cassandra sniffed after a while, recovering a little. They kissed and she felt better. After a bit longer their lips parted.

"Let's just forget it." He smiled disarmingly. Cassandra wasn't fooled. He would bring it up again, she was sure of it.

"How about," she said in a teasing voice to change the subject, "I show you something Peyton suggested."

"Sure, OK," he said looking interested. He knew if Peyton suggested it, it was going to be naughty.

"Lie on the floor then, on your back."

"Why?" he said suspiciously.

"Go on, you'll like it, I promise."

"Fine, I trust you, thousands wouldn't." He laughed back to his old self and lay on the floor beside the bed.

She sat above him and began to stroke his cock with the toes of her right foot. He gasped at once, and started to grow hard. Cassie had beautiful feet, well-shaped ankles, and long well-proportioned toes. Nathan liked her feet, and Peyton loved them.

As his cock began to stand up. She manipulated his cock with the toes of both feet until she was holding it between them. The soles of her feet faced each other.

"What are you?" he began but said no more as she began to wank him gently with her feet on either side of his now bulging organ.

"Oh, fuck, Cassie, where did you, Jesus, oh fuck, fuck, fuck," he lay back and enjoyed the sensation. The soles of her feet were soft and pliable, they would probably feel very sexy on his cock.

She began to move them faster, finding it quite easy to do. It was a little tiring on her legs, but she was getting a kick out of it.

"Fuck, oh, oh, oh, oh, oh, fuck, fuck, fuck." He was hissing in his breath as she picked up speed wanting to finish him. Her legs moved rapidly up and down, and she started to shout, "Oh, fuck, fuck, fuck, oh, God, Cassie, oh, oh, oh, oh, fuck, fuckkkkkk, ahhhhhh!"

His cock pulsed over and over while she held on to it with her toes. Spunk shot out and ran down her feet. It also went onto his belly. She released his shaft and rubbed her feet into his stomach wiping off the sperm. It felt dirty and as horny as fuck. Her hand went down between her legs and she began frigging herself really fast.

"Oh, oh, oh, oh, fuck, fuck, fuck, ah, ah, ah. Ahhhhhhh!" It didn't take long for her to cum. She smiled down at him. He had been watching her the whole time.

"Nice view," he said smiling back, "And nice trick."

"Would you like it again another time?"

"For sure, you can add it to your repertoire, you dirty bitch, but now I'm going to shower and make something to eat. If that's OK?"

"It's fine with me, shall I shower with you?"

"No, Cassie, because then I'll have to fuck you in the shower."

"Is that such a bad thing?" she shot him a saucy smile.

"Later, now I need food."

"Alright, you big caveman!"

"Ug ug!" he mimicked the gait of a chimpanzee and left the room. She watched him go, admiring his well-muscled physique. It was definitely a turn-on for her.

Cassandra was glad he was now in good spirits. This wasn't the end of it, she was sure. Until she got to the bottom of what was bothering him, it wouldn't be.

That was for another day. On the morrow, she was having lunch with Peyton. It was something else to look forward to. She smiled at the thought. Peyton was beautiful, she couldn't wait to fuck her again.

***

Cassandra had lunch with Peyton at an upmarket place she knew. She was paying and Peyton took a longer lunch hour to spend time with her. Peyton worked five days a week, but these could cross over onto weekends, so on her free days would be when they could see each other properly. Such things were still to be arranged, as was the whole Mistress thing and how it would work. Cassandra was still getting to grips with it.

Cassandra let Peyton order anything she wanted. For herself, he had a modest prawn and crab salad with avocado on the side accompanied by buttered wholemeal toast. For mains, she had teriyaki salmon, parsley new potatoes, and mixed stir fry veg. Peyton had more of an appetite, and she started with steamed mussels in a wine sauce. Then she wanted a fillet steak with fries and salad. Cassandra didn't drink as it was lunchtime, so they had diet cokes.

"Thank you, for lunch, Mistress," said Peyton smiling.

"Peyton, you don't need to call me that all the time, just call me Cassie unless you're being punished or unless I tell you otherwise."

They were in a secluded booth and could not be overheard. The conversation could be intimate, and Cassandra had chosen the booth on purpose.

"It's just that I like…"

"I know but I'm asking you not to, there is a time and a place." Cassandra smiled but she was firm. Firmness seemed to be what Peyton wanted.

"OK." Peyton pouted slightly but then seemed to accept the stricture with good grace.

Cassandra took a mouthful of her prawn and crab, and ate it with relish.

"I gave Nathan a foot job like you suggested," she said casually.

"And did he enjoy it?" Peyton's eyes widened.

"He seemed to. I got spunk all over my foot, so I guess so." Cassie laughed.

"I would have licked it off if I was there," said Peyton seriously.

"I know you would." Cassandra was still laughing. Peyton loved her feet, worshipped them in fact. It was a nice feeling.

Peyton laughed too and looked at Cassandra a little shyly. She consumed her mussels with evident satisfaction, licking her fingers after each and Cassandra found it very sexy. She found Peyton entirely alluring overall, and it was often hard to take her eyes off her. Cassandra found her mind straying to Peyton's pink mound and how she wanted to lick her.

"You're making me nervous," said Peyton at last finishing off her mussels.

"Why?"

"Just how you look at me, and I wonder if I've done something wrong."

"Not that I know of, have you?"

"Not, lately, no."

"Well then. I'm looking at you because I fancy the pants off you, darling, don't you know how much I want you?" Cassandra's voice pitched quite low so only Peyton could hear.

"Oh God," Peyton flushed, "You're making me hot."

"That's good."

"What if I was to finger myself?" Peyton said with a saucy smile, pushing away the bowl of empty shells, "Do you think anyone would notice?"

Cassandra glanced around, the restaurant was practically empty, and the waiters were hanging around somewhere out of sight.

"I would notice," she said, "And it would be very horny, but I'd also have to punish you for it."

"Oh!" Peyton flushed.

This brought Cassandra back to the question of being Peyton's Mistress, and what it would or even should entail.

"We haven't really discussed things you should be punished for, have we?"

"No," said Peyton.

"What should you be punished for, do you think?"

"Whatever you think I should be punished for."

This was a smart response. Cassandra gave her a quelling look.

"Don't get sassy with me, missy, unless you want to end up with a red bottom. When we began this agreement, you said you'd tell me when you had done something bad, but so far, I've heard nothing from you. Does it mean you've been very good?" Cassandra treated her to a searching glance.

Peyton shook her head and dropped her eyes.

"So, you *have* been bad, and didn't tell me, that in itself is bad."

"Yes," Peyton whispered.

The waiter arrived just then, and removed the plates. The second course would not be long.

"So, what *have* you done?"

"I, don't specifically remember now."

"That is very bad. I expect you to tell me when you've been naughty in future." Cassandra thought for a moment. She was quite an organised person, and decided perhaps codifying things might help. "I'm going to get a book, and write it down. It will be called Peyton's Infractions. I will give them all a star rating. When you get a certain number of stars you will get a spanking."

Peyton caught her breath. The idea had just suggested itself to Cassandra and she thought it was hot.

"Yes, OK." Peyton nodded.

"Good, that's settled then."

"But what will go into the book?" Peyton wondered after a moment.

"Anything which I feel is naughty, out of line or deserves a spanking. Or which you tell me is let us say… spank worthy."

"Oh…" But Peyton said no more, it was evidently percolating a little.

Cassandra smiled. The idea of being Peyton's Mistress entailed some work, she could see, in order to bring it to fruition. The mains were brought, and Cassandra delicately ate her salmon while Peyton dug into her steak.

"Do you like your food?" she asked Peyton.

"I love it, it's the best thing I've had in ages. I don't get to eat like this, usually."

"Good. It's my pleasure to treat you, my darling."

Peyton bit her lip.

"What's that matter?"

"Nothing, it's just that…"

"Just that?"

"I like it when you call me darling." Peyton blushed fiery red.

"And I like to call you darling. You're very special."

"But you hardly know me."

"I think I know you quite well. I've spanked you, more than once, and fucked you multiple times, darling. I think that qualifies me to know you, don't you?"

"I guess." Peyton blushed again.

Cassandra felt strange. Here was this younger woman treating her as if she had all the sophistication in the world. Here she was living up to that image, almost mysterious in fact. Truthfully, Cassandra felt at sea, naïve. Everything she did was perhaps by instinct. She didn't spend ages reading about it on the internet or watching videos. It was coming from somewhere within. Perhaps this was the real her? She didn't know. She wanted to be authentic somehow, not a sham, an imitation of a dominant woman. Was she? She didn't know that either. Perhaps it would come to her in time, confidence in herself and what she was becoming. Peyton claimed her attention. She had been eating her steak with obvious enjoyment and was nearing the end.

"Miss… I mean Cassie, when are you going to spank Nathan again?"

Cassandra put down her fork, after eating the last piece of salmon. "It depends when he's misbehaved. That's when he gets spanked."

"But I…"

"You *want* to be spanked, Peyton, that's the difference."

Peyton digested this and finished off her plate.

"So, his is for punishment?"

"Mainly, yes. He's not asking me to spank him."

Peyton blushed.

"But you fuck afterwards…"

"Yes, because it's horny, we both get turned on by it. I'm sure you saw that."

"Yes, I did. Doesn't he like being spanked then?"

Cassandra smiled and laughed lightly.

"You ask a lot of questions, young lady. Truthfully, I don't know. He's not about to admit it. He's too much of a macho man for that."

"Oh… but I just like to know."

"It's OK, my darling, really." Cassandra reached over and took Peyton's hand. She squeezed it affectionately. Peyton smiled.

"I've never met anyone like you," Peyton whispered.

"No."

The waiter reappeared as if by magic, and although Cassandra didn't want a dessert, she could see Peyton did. She indulged her and let her order an ice cream sundae. She requested coffees for them both. After the waiter left Peyton spoke again.

"Am I allowed to make a suggestion?"

"Depends, what it is, but for sure."

"Have you thought of buying a hairbrush?"

"Hairbrush?" Cassandra's brows knitted in puzzlement.

"For spanking."

"Oh." The idea had not occurred to Cassandra.

"It's the traditional spanking implement, and it stings very much." Peyton warmed to her theme.

"And you know this because?"

"I've read about it."

"On spanking sites, yes, no doubt. You'll have to be my advisor from now on."

"Really?"

"Yes, but that's enough for one day. I'll think about the hairbrush. You may come to regret the suggestion, when I use it on your bare bottom."

This was calculated to arouse Peyton and it did. She turned scarlet and it was true she flushed very easily. Her hand crept down to her short skirt while Cassandra watched. It slipped under the waistband, and Cassandra knew full well what she was doing.

"Oh, oh, mmm," Peyton whimpered.

"Just imagine," said Cassandra mendaciously, "You'll be over my knee, and the hairbrush will be stinging your arse, smack, smack, smack, nice and hard, wouldn't you like that?"

"Oh, mmm, mmm, mmm, ohhh!" Peyton bit her lip on a scream and had obviously climaxed very quickly. Just in time, she withdrew her hand as the enormous sundae and coffee arrived.

"You've earned yourself at least one star with that little stunt, you are on your way to a hairbrush spanking and no mistake," said Cassandra relentlessly pursuing the theme which she could tell turned Peyton on.

"Yes," Peyton whispered.

"Enjoy your ice cream, my sweet."

Peyton dug into the mass of flavours while Cassandra watched, gratified at how small things could generate such pleasure.

***

After she returned Peyton to work, kissing her softly and soundly before saying goodbye, Cassandra thought about what Peyton had said. On impulse, she stopped off at the mall and visited a few shops. First, she bought a nice leather-bound notebook with designs crafted into the front and a clasp which fastened it. She found a nice fountain pen to write in it. This would be Peyton's book of infractions. It would be like a ritual which is why she bought the special pen. She smiled as she paid for it.

In other shops, there were many hairbrushes and she examined them carefully. Tapping them lightly in her palm. None of them seemed very suitable, however. They were not particularly made of wood and were synthetic. She felt this wouldn't be right. Although taken by a paddle style of brush, she still wasn't satisfied. In her head, she recalled she'd seen somewhere, the picture of an oval brush with a big head. Such a brush seemed much more suitable for spanking for some reason. She left the mall in search of somewhere else to look. The town had a row of antique shops which she liked to browse. She was fascinated by the past, and had, on occasion, bought the odd item.

She parked the four by four, and went into a couple. They had plenty of interesting things but no hairbrushes. Then in the third, she found what she thought perhaps she had been seeking. It was a large ivory or bone handled brush with a big oval head on it, this would give good coverage for sure. It looked quite old and felt solid. One or two light taps of the brush on her hand told her it was likely to be perfect for what she wanted.

"Thinking about spanking someone?" came a voice.

Cassandra almost jumped out of her skin. An older but attractive woman with silver hair cut in a bob had somehow crept up on her. It was the owner of the shop. She was smiling, and wore a blouse, jeans and sandals. Cassandra noticed she had nice feet, full breasts and was pleasantly curvaceous.

"No, why?" Cassandra said recovering her composure and dissembling at once.

"Oh, just the way you were testing it." The woman laughed. "Those hairbrushes had a fearsome reputation you know."

"Really?" Cassandra looked into the woman's sparkling grey eyes with interest.

"Oh yes, my mother had one and I had a few spankings with it I can tell you. It wasn't in the least bit fun, although, I suppose it could be. These days people seem to…" she left it unfinished.

"So, your mother…" Cassandra said.

"I grew up when such things were the fashion. Plenty of my friends got the hairbrush too. That's not unlike the one my mother had though. She could certainly wield it with precision." The woman was laughing at the recollection.

Cassandra couldn't quite tell if there was more to this tale or whether she was just reminiscing.

"Oh, that's interesting, but I was just wanting it for the antique value. Is it ivory?"

"Oh, it's not much value, and it's bone, not ivory. You can hardly get those anymore anyway. But it's a nice piece, if decoration is what you want it for." The expression told her the owner did not believe it. "I'm Faith, by the way." She held out her hand.

"Cassandra." She shook the woman's hand.

"We don't get those very often, so if you really want it…"

"I'll take it, yes."

"Good, good. You won't regret the purchase."

Faith led the way to her desk, and sat down to write an old-fashioned receipt for the brush. As she was doing so, Cassandra's eyes were drawn to a big vase in the corner in which there appeared to be a number of canes protruding with crook handles.

Faith saw the direction of her gaze. "You're looking at the school canes."

"Is that what they are?" said Cassandra.

"Oh yes, they're not used these days, but I collected a few. Nostalgia you know for a bygone era, though again, I've sold some to people who..."

What kind of people she did not say. Though Cassandra felt it was somehow meant personally. Faith got up and pulled one out. She swished it around quite expertly. This certainly made Cassandra start to wonder about her.

"It's all in the wrist action you know."

Faith made a couple of fake strikes as if she was caning an invisible bottom. The sound of the swish was incredibly arousing to Cassandra.

"You've got to pick the target well, so it doesn't wrap around to the side of the bottom being caned, if you see what I mean. It's quite an art, giving a good caning, quite an art."

Faith winked at her, smiled and put it back.

"I see."

"I've got a few other things, a razor strop, old paddles, all instruments of punishment back in the old days. You'd be surprised though what people want these days. Oh, of course, you can get them online, but the old ones have been broken in, well used so to speak."

Cassandra noticed some of these items hanging from a row of hooks near the canes. She began to conjecture onto what exactly she had wandered into. It didn't seem as if it was just about antiques. She forbore to investigate further. Something about the woman's gaze was mesmerising and she started to feel almost as if she was being hypnotised by a serpent. She shook off the uncomfortable feeling, wanting to leave.

"Right." Cassandra got the distinct impression Faith was playing with her, teasing her. She kept her demeanour very straight but inside her heart was doing flutters as, at the same time, these new ideas opened up all sorts of future possibilities with Peyton and Nathan.

"Sorry, I didn't mean to..." said Faith catching her expression, perhaps feeling she had said too much or misread things. She seemed to dial down the intensity almost at once, sat down again and finished the receipt. Then Cassandra paid by card on the machine.

Faith put the brush into a paper bag along with the handwritten receipt.

"I like the old-fashioned things," said Faith handing it to Cassandra, "That's why I handwrite the receipts. There's nothing like the hands-on touch. My number is on the receipt, in case you ever need anything else…" She left the last bit hanging.

What is it about me? Cassandra wondered. Am I sending out signals? Is she coming on to me? Looking at Faith more closely she certainly was attractive though in her fifties. She kept herself well, with red painted nails, a full mouth, nice eyes. Cassandra tore herself away from these invasive ideas.

"Thanks, I certainly will, if I do."

"Well, bye, hope to see you again sometime."

"Yes, indeed, bye."

Cassandra hurried from the shop, and then home. She was in a state of high arousal. Things, naughty things, ideas, were running through her head. She ran upstairs and putting down the paper bag, she went to her bedside drawer and took out the rabbit.

Without preamble, she turned it on, divested herself of her knickers and lay on the bed. She was sopping wet, and the rabbit went in with ease. She turned on the intermittent pulse.

"Oh, oh, oh, oh, fuck, oh." The fronds were teasing her clit. In her mind were inescapable images. Faith giving a caning, giving Cassandra a caning. The thought was delicious, so bad. "Oh God, fuck, fuck, oh, oh, oh." She flicked up pulse to continuous and then maximum. What would it feel like, to be caned? "Oh, fuck, fuck, oh my God, oh, oh, ohhh!" She cried out climaxing fast, feeling the waves of it rushing through her. "Oh, oh, oh, oh, oh, ah, ah, fuckkkkk!" Eventually, she could not stand it and turned the rabbit off.

Conflicting ideas went around in her very active imagination. Wasn't she the dominant one? Why would she want to be caned by an older woman? Cassandra had no idea. These were musings for another day. She got up, and took the brush from its paper bag. She put the receipt in her bedside drawer.

The brush felt good in her hand. She pulled up her skirt and smacked her backside experimentally with the back of it.

"Oh fuck, owww!" It was definitely going to sting.

She took a photo of it and sent it to Peyton with the message.

"Look what is waiting for your bottom, Peyton, next time you are naughty."

There was no response for a while, and then she received a video which was just the sound of Peyton masturbating, presumably in the toilet.

Cassandra texted back. "You are a very bad girl, that is going in the book. I've now bought a naughty book for your, my girl. A few more infractions and you'll be getting the spanking you deserve. Xxxx"

"Yes, Mistress, sorry, Mistress, xxxx."

"It will be too late for sorry, when you are over my knee with a red bottom. Xxxx"

"Yes, Mistress. Xxxx"

Cassandra smiled with satisfaction at this exchange, picked up the rabbit and played the video again.

****

A week passed by without further mention about Peyton from Nathan. Cassandra wondered if he had started to get used to the idea of Peyton being in her life. She also hadn't seen Peyton either, although they had exchanged texts. Instead, she and Nathan settled back into their normal existence with plenty of sex.

It was Wednesday by the time Cassandra was wondering what Peyton might be up to, and whether she should call her and have lunch again. She had taken some time to herself too, as her emotions had been running high since Nathan's last spanking session. Things were bubbling under the surface now there were three of them in the mix. Cassandra wasn't used to having her feelings stirred quite so much. She and Nathan had had a comfortable time of it, until she started the spanking. Then everything escalated emotionally for her and Peyton arrived in her life.

She had started Peyton's book of infractions, and written the two things she had done so far. One was masturbating at the restaurant and the other the video Peyton had sent her. She gave the first one, one star and the second, two stars. She hadn't quite decided how many stars Peyton should get to earn a spanking. The whole Mistress game was something she was playing a little by ear. She was also thinking of the woman in the antique store. Not that she fancied her or felt sexually attracted to her, but there was something about her and the way she had handled that cane. She obviously knew more about spanking than she was letting on. Perhaps she was one of those women who offered services. Cassandra put it out of her mind. It was perhaps horny to think about it, but the actuality would be something different. Besides she had Peyton and Nathan to occupy her thoughts

She had just had lunch and was reading a book when she heard a car in the driveway. A door slammed and the car drove away. Cassandra got up to find out who it was, but the bell rang first. She went to the door and she could see from the CCTV entry phone that Peyton was outside. This was unexpected but not something she was averse to, in fact, she was pleased to see her.

Cassandra opened the door, "Peyton?"

"Cassie, I... I had to see you." Peyton looked quite agitated.

"Come in, I was just thinking about you actually, do you want something to eat?" Cassandra smiled at her and moved casually aside.

Peyton shook her head, she walked past Cassandra and they went into the living room.

"Sit down, darling," said Cassandra smiling, "Would you like a coffee?"

Peyton shook her head once more. Cassandra went to sit beside her. There was evidently something ailing her.

"What's wrong? You seem troubled."

Peyton didn't speak for a moment. Cassandra reached out and took her hand.

"Well, whatever it is, just tell me, it can't be so bad, can it?"

Peyton suddenly started to cry, "It is, it can be. Cassie, oh, Cassie I've done something very bad."

Still wondering what had set this off, Cassandra took Peyton into her arms and held her. Peyton sobbed for a long while and then when she seemed to recover, she sat back up again. Cassandra brushed her tears away with her fingers.

"What did you do, Peyton, which made you cry so much."

"I've been bad and you're going be very angry." Peyton looked scared.

"I won't know, though will I? If you don't tell me."

"OK… well…" Peyton took a deep breath. "I went on Tinder."

"Tinder?" Cassandra frowned.

"It's a dating app, well, sex app, kind of, at least for some people."

"I know what it is, but why?"

It seemed strange Peyton would do such a thing.

Peyton hung her head, she said quietly, "I was horny, and I wanted sex."

"OK." This was a bit of a shock to Cassandra if she was honest. It hit her right between the eyes in fact. Peyton had chosen someone else over her, this point was beginning to register.

"I hooked up with this girl, and I fucked her."

"I see." Cassandra kept her expression neutral while she listened even though her heart was doing flips.

"I enjoyed it, she made me cum so many times and…"

The detail was almost too much.

"Why are you telling me this?" Cassandra interrupted her, some part of her did not want to hear any more.

Peyton let out a wail, "Because I betrayed you, I've been unfaithful and…"

Cassandra pulled herself together. There hadn't been any arrangement between them after all. She put a finger up to Peyton's lips. "Hush, darling. Did I say you couldn't fuck anyone else?"

"No, but…"

"Did I tell you or even ask you to be faithful, or exclusive?"

"No, but…"

"Did anything bad happen to you?"

"No, but…"

"So?"

Cassandra heard herself even though it went against the grain, and she could not help a pang of cold jealousy slicing through her.

"I feel bad, Cassie, I feel bad because I didn't want to sleep with anyone but you. I just couldn't help it." Peyton raised tearful eyes to Cassandra's.

Cassandra found being her confessor a little difficult, given the subject of the confession.

"And you expect me to?"

Peyton's lip trembled, "Punish me?"

"Oh, I see. You expect me to punish you for doing something which you say you couldn't help yourself." Cassandra's tone was a little sardonic.

"Yes."

Having ascertained the full extent of what Peyton had told her. Cassandra had mixed feelings. It wasn't for her to tell Peyton who she could or could not sleep with. At least they had not made such an agreement. However, she was particularly upset Peyton had not called her if she wanted to fuck someone. Why hadn't she? Cassandra wanted to know, and that part made her feel a little deflated, as if she suddenly wasn't desirable.

"I'm not going to punish you for that, Peyton," she said gently.

"You're not?"

"No."

"You're *not* going to punish me?" Peyton looked as if she might cry again.

"I didn't say *that*, but not for fucking someone else."

"Oh."

Cassandra tried to put her feelings into words.

"I didn't say I liked the fact you have fucked someone else, but that's not why I'm upset, and I am upset, Peyton, very upset." Now she had started to articulate it, Cassandra felt more than a little aggrieved.

"I'm sorry…" tears started down Peyton's face.

"Stop it!" said Cassandra a little more severely. She wanted to get things off her chest now she had started.

Peyton wiped her face with her sleeve and bit her lip. She sniffed and stopped crying.

"There'll be plenty of time for tears very shortly, I can assure you."

Peyton said nothing but a tell-tale pink tinge came into her cheeks.

Cassandra got to the nub of it.

"First you can explain to me why you didn't call me if you wanted sex."

"I don't know."

This made no sense to Cassandra.

"You don't know? Did you think I wouldn't *want* to fuck you?"

Peyton shook her head.

"Then what?"

Peyton was silent for a moment. Cassandra waited patiently. She wanted to hear the explanation. After a while, Peyton found her voice.

"I was… afraid."

Cassandra's face softened.

"Of what?"

"That I was bugging you too much, and you would think I was too needy, too clingy, when all I wanted… was you… to fuck you so much… I wanted you, I longed for you and instead…" she tailed off looking at Cassandra with big eyes.

She was so very endearing that Cassandra almost forgot to be cross. It was also exactly what she wanted to hear. Peyton hadn't fucked another woman because she didn't like Cassandra. Just to be clear, she went over it again.

"You thought I would think you were too needy?"

"Yes."

"But really you wanted me."

"Yes."

"Not that other… girl…"

"No. No. I was just… using her."

"But you enjoyed it?"

"Yes… I'm sorry."

"Don't be sorry, I don't blame you for enjoying it."

"But I am…"

"That's alright. Come here, come right over here, darling." Cassandra embraced her and kissed her softly. "You're a silly girl. Very silly to think that I wouldn't want you, my darling, you should never think *that*. You are never to think that again."

The kiss deepened and became more sexual. "Oh Cassie, Cassie, I just wanted you so much, so very much. I do want you."

"I know, my darling and you shall have me." Cassandra pulled apart before they got carried away. "But first…"

"First?"

"I'm going to give you a sound spanking for being such a silly little girl." Cassandra smiled. She was very ready for it.

Peyton nodded.

"You know, if you wanted a spanking, there are easier ways to go about it," said Cassandra in a conversational tone, standing up and taking hold of Peyton's hand. "You don't have to go and fuck another woman to get a spanking, just so you're aware." Cassandra led Peyton up the stairs. "You could just ask me for a spanking, and I would be happy to oblige. But now you're going get properly punished, darling. Yes, indeed."

They arrived at the door to the bedroom. Cassandra let go of Peyton's hand. It was time to become more severe.

"In the bedroom, I'm your Mistress and you will treat me accordingly, OK?"

Cassandra kissed her lightly.

"Yes, Mistress."

"Come on then."

They entered the room together and Cassandra locked the door. There was plenty of time before Nathan got home, more than enough to spank Peyton and fuck her.

"Take off your clothes, Peyton," she said.

"Yes, Mistress." Peyton obliged and Cassandra looked on appreciatively. Peyton's creamy skin was quite alluring, and her blonde hair fell over her shoulders. Her breasts were youthfully firm, and the nipples inviting. Peyton kept her pussy shaved and Cassandra passed her gaze over it, then down to Peyton's feet. She had nice feet, shapely with suckable toes. That was for later.

"Go and get the spanking chair, Peyton and put it in the middle of the room."

Peyton knew exactly what chair it was. It was Cassandra's dressing table chair. It was wooden without arms. She hadn't bought it for spanking but now it had become almost indispensable. Peyton took the chair and placed it where she was instructed. She stepped away and stood waiting for further orders.

Cassandra took her dress off and stood in her underwear. She was wearing a lacy bra and knickers. She would usually put on a corset or her red spanking dress, but as this was a spur of the moment spanking, she decided her undies would do. She was barefoot, as was her usual style around the house. Cassandra had already decided she didn't need her spanking sandals. She kept a pair with red thongs for spanking Peyton, but today, Peyton would be getting the hairbrush.

As Peyton watched her, Cassandra went over to the dressing table where she had left the hairbrush she had recently purchased. She picked it up and felt the smooth sensation of the cold bone handle. She walked purposefully over to the chair and sat down.

"Come here Peyton and stand in front of me," said Cassandra.

"Yes, Mistress." Peyton obeyed unable to take her eyes off the hairbrush.

"On your knees."

Peyton sunk to her knees in supplication, just as Cassandra wanted.

"You're about to get a spanking, Peyton. Is there anything you want to say to me first? Perhaps to explain yourself a bit more or what you've done. Perhaps you want to ask me not to punish you too severely even? Hmm?"

Peyton lowered her eyes. Cassandra put one finger under Peyton's chin and raised it up, so she was looking into her eyes.

"I deserve a spanking, Mistress," said Peyton looking very flushed in expectation, "But can I please ask you one thing, please?"

"OK." Cassandra wondered if Peyton was going to ask her to go easy, although she doubted it.

"Don't spare me, Mistress, please…"

"OK, I wasn't going to…"

Peyton wasn't finished.

"Please, Mistress, looking at that hairbrush I think it might make me cry, and if I do, I don't want you to stop, even if I ask you to stop, I want you to spank me until you feel I've been punished enough." It came out in a rush, but Peyton's expression was sincere.

"Alright, my darling, if you're sure. I mean…"

"Please, Mistress, don't listen to anything I say. Don't hold back. No safe words, Mistress, just spank me as hard you want to, for as long as you want to. I need it, I deserve it and I want it."

Cassandra was silent for a moment. Peyton trusted her implicitly to ask her such a thing. She was certainly planning to spank her hard. If Peyton did cry, then it would probably have swayed her to stop. Now she wouldn't be tempted at all.

"Very well, Peyton, you can get over my knee. It's time for your spanking."

Peyton settled herself across Cassandra's lap, and Cassandra experienced a sudden rush of adrenaline as she ran the back of the brush lightly across Peyton's backside. Peyton's bottom quivered in expectation of what was to follow.

"Peyton, I'm very unhappy with what you've done, do you understand?"

"Yes, Mistress."

"You need to be punished severely."

"Yes, Mistress."

"And you are going to be. Do you know why?"

"Yes, Mistress."

"Good but I'm going to spell it out for you, Peyton. For a start, you didn't call me when you wanted sex."

Cassandra lifted the brush and brought it down on first one and then the other cheek as she started the spanking. She lifted the brush off immediately after each spank, as this was now her technique. She had certainly honed it well enough with the sandal.

SMACK SMACK

"Oww, oh, owww," Peyton cried at once.

Two angry red marks appeared, one on each cheek. The brush must certainly sting more than the sandal, Cassandra thought. She liked to deliver the spanks in groups of four, particularly while she was scolding

"Instead like a little slut you went on Tinder and got yourself a bitch to fuck."

SMACK SMACK SMACK SMACK

"Oww, oh owww, owwww." There was quite a wail already in Peyton's voice.

Cassandra brought up some of the things which were bothering her about what Peyton had done. She was first and foremost human. She was not impervious to insecurities.

"What did she look like, was she pretty?"

SMACK SMACK SMACK SMACK

"Ohh, please, no, oww it hurts, Mistress."

Cassandra ignored this.

"I asked you a question."

SMACK SMACK SMACK SMACK

"Oww, oh owww, Mistress. She was pretty, Mistress."

"Prettier than me?"

SMACK SMACK SMACK SMACK

"Oww howwww... no, Mistress, no you are far prettier."

Cassandra smiled. She was pleased to hear that at least.

"Good and was she a better fuck than me?"

SMACK SMACK SMACK SMACK

"Owww, no, no never, you're the best I've ever had, the very best."

Peyton was saying the right things. It wasn't going to mitigate her spanking, however, and Cassandra was getting into her stride.

"Good to know."

SMACK SMACK SMACK SMACK

"Owww, oowww, owww."

"Does that hurt?"

SMACK SMACK SMACK SMACK

"Yes, oh God, it stings, oh fuckkkk."

"Worse than the sandal?"

SMACK SMACK SMACK SMACK

"Yes, Mistress, it really does."

Cassandra paused. The hairbrush was turning Peyton's pink bottom red in no time. It certainly seemed to be making an impression.

SMACK SMACK SMACK SMACK

"Good because maybe, just maybe you'll learn to pick up the phone in future when you want a fuck and not go on Tinder."

SMACK SMACK SMACK SMACK

"Yes, Mistress, yes…owww, owww, ohhhh, ohhhh, owwww."

"You're a little slut, a brat, a fucking little bitch and I'm going to teach you such a lesson that you're not going to forget it in a hurry."

Cassandra had hit her stride. Her ire was being released. The spanking was cathartic for her as well as Peyton. She decided to up the ante. She changed the rhythm to harder spanks but slower and more deliberate.

SMACK "oww" SMACK "OWW" SMACK "owwhoww" SMACK "OWW"

SMACK "oww" SMACK "owhooo" SMACK "owwhoww" SMACK "OWW"

SMACK "owwww" SMACK "noooo" SMACK "oohhoww" SMACK "OWWW"

Peyton was arching her back a little, and Cassandra pushed it gently flat with her left hand. The spanking wasn't over by any means. She continued to ramp it up, letting her own emotions flow out.

"I cannot believe you went on Tinder, when you've got pussy right here, waiting for you, dripping wet for you, you horny little bitch."

SMACK "owww" SMACK "ohhh" SMACK "oooh" SMACK "OWWW"

SMACK "ow" SMACK "ohh" SMACK "owwhoww" SMACK "OWW"

SMACK "nooo" SMACK "OWW" SMACK "oohhoo" SMACK "OWW"

Cassandra paused for a moment. Inside her anger flowed freely.

"I am furious with you Peyton. How dare you, how dare you!"

SMACK "owww" SMACK "OW" SMACK "oooh" SMACK "OW"

SMACK "ohh" SMACK "ohoo" SMACK "owwhoww" SMACK "OWW"

SMACK "oww" SMACK "OWW" SMACK "ohh" SMACK "OWW"

Peyton began to cry, "ooh hoo hoo, oooh, hoo, hoo, please Mistress, please don't spank me anymore, it hurts so much, owww, owww."

Cassandra didn't listen to this. Instead, she continued spanking harder.

SMACK "oww" SMACK "OWW" SMACK "owwhoww" SMACK "OWW"

"What did you say? Did you just ask me to stop? You know I decide that not you!"

SMACK "oww" SMACK "ooh" SMACK "owwhoohhh" SMACK "OW"

SMACK "OWW" SMACK "OW" SMACK "owwhoww" SMACK "OWW"

Peyton started to wail.

"Oohhh hooo, hooo, owww, please, I'll be good, I'll never do it again, I promise."

Cassandra pursed her lips.

"Too right you won't be doing it again, or you'll be getting such a spanking you won't sit down for a week."

"But Mistress, it hurts, so much, ooh, ooh, hoo, hoo, hoo," Peyton wailed.

Her bottom was crimson all over, and she was wriggling a little as her bottom was evidently burning red hot.

"Oww, how, how, owww."

Peyton was crying openly now, but Cassandra bore in mind what Peyton had told her. She wasn't finished. The hairbrush felt good in her hand, and she wielded it like an expert having had some excellent practice with the sandal. It was obviously making an impact on Peyton's bottom too.

SMACK "ohh" SMACK "OWWW" SMACK "owwhoww" SMACK "OW"

SMACK "oww" SMACK "OW" SMACK "oooh" SMACK "OWW"

"Remember how you said you deserved this spanking, well now you're getting it, Peyton."

SMACK "owwww" SMACK "OW" SMACK "oooh" SMACK "OW"

SMACK "oww" SMACK "OWW" SMACK "owwhoww" SMACK "OWW"

"But I didn't know it would hurt this much, oooh, hooo, oooh, hooo, oh, oh, oh." Peyton was crying openly now.

Part of it, the crying part, was starting to break Cassandra just a little, and the other part wanted to make sure Peyton was punished properly now she had got going. That part won and she treated Peyton's bottom to another volley of smacks.

SMACK "oww" SMACK "OW" SMACK "oooh" SMACK "OWW"

SMACK "oww" SMACK "OWW" SMACK "owwhoww" SMACK "OWW"

SMACK "oww" SMACK "ooh" SMACK "owwhoohhh" SMACK "OW"

SMACK "OWW" SMACK "OW" SMACK "owwhoww" SMACK "OWW"

"Please, Mistress, please," Peyton begged her.

SMACK "OWW" SMACK "OW" SMACK "oooh" SMACK "OW"

SMACK "oww" SMACK "OWW" SMACK "owwhoww" SMACK "OWW"

Cassandra stopped for a moment.

"Alright, Peyton. I won't ask you if you're sorry for what you did, because I can see that."

"I am, Mistress, I promise, so sorry."

"I know."

Peyton's bottom was a deep shade of red now, and Cassandra was ready to wind up the spanking with a bit of contrition.

"You're going to promise me, Peyton, never to do anything like this again, understand?"

SMACK "oww" SMACK "OWW" SMACK "owwhoww" SMACK "OWW"

"Yes, yes I do, Mistress."

"Go on then," Cassandra pressed her, "Promise me."

SMACK "owwww" SMACK "OW" SMACK "oooh" SMACK "OW"

"I promise, Mistress."

"You SMACK will SMACK never SMACK use Tinder SMACK again."

"Noo, I won't, I promise, I promise."

"You SMACK will SMACK never SMACK fuck another SMACK woman SMACK without my permission."

SMACK "owwww" SMACK "OW" SMACK "oooh" SMACK "OW"

"I won't I never will, Mistress, never again, I promise."

Cassandra smiled. She spoke very quietly to her.

"Good girl. Just remember, I'm here for you, Peyton. I'm here to kiss you, to fuck you, anything you want, and so is Nathan. You should have asked me, I would have said, yes, come over, darling, I will fuck you for sure."

"Yes, Mistress."

SMACK "oww" SMACK "OWW" SMACK "owwhoww" SMACK "OWW"

"I'm also here to spank you, and punish you when you've been naughty just like now. OK?"

"Yes, Mistress."

"Good, so now for your final six, to make sure you truly learn your lesson."

"But I…" Peyton cut herself short, she knew better than to demur. Last time it had cost her a lot more spanks.

"OK. I hope you're ready."

Peyton was silent. She knew the spanks would be hard and Cassandra definitely intended to make them so.

"One" SMACK "Oww hoo"

"Two" SMACK "owwww"

"Three" SMACK "Ohhhh"

"Four" SMACK "Owwwwww"

"Five" SMACK "Ooooh hoooo hooo"

"Six" SMACK "OWWWWWW"

The last two were landed as hard as Cassandra could make them.

Peyton was sobbing. Cassandra put the brush down and eased Peyton off her lap. She held her close and kissed her, talking softly and gently to her. Perhaps she had got a little carried away. Very shortly she felt, Peyton's lips on hers, kissing her and nuzzling her.

"Oh Cassie, Cassie I want you, fuck me, fuck me, please."

Cassandra started to kiss her back, hard and passionately. She pulled Peyton to her feet and laid her on the bed. Then Cassandra reached into her bedside drawer and pulled out her rabbit. She lay down, and slid the rabbit deftly into Peyton's slick wet pussy.

"Oh, God, what's that, oh, my God." Peyton gasped.

"You wanted me to fuck you," said Cassandra softly flicking on the pulsing vibrations.

"Oh, God!" Peyton shrieked. "Cassie, oh, oh, fuck, oh, Cassie, oh, oh, oh oh, oh."

Cassandra flicked up the intensity and Peyton almost screamed.

"Oh, oh fuck, fucking hell, oh my God, oh, Cassie, Cassie, Cassie!"

Cassandra began to move the rabbit in and out, fucking Peyton using her hand. She kept the fronds against Peyton's clit and put the intensity on the rabbit to the maximum setting.

"Oh, God, God, God, Cassie, Cassie, I'm going to, I'm cummmingg, oh, oh, oh, oh, ohhhh!" Peyton shouted at the top of her lungs, her toes curling as she gripped the duvet cover with her hands. "Oh, Cassie, that's so beautiful, so beautiful."

Cassandra removed the rabbit, leaned down and kissed her. Peyton's arms came up around her, and started to pull her down into an embrace. The kiss was explosive, and Cassandra felt heady, lightheaded, as it went on and on. Then Peyton was pushing her onto her back, and she began to lick Cassandra's feet and toes with her tongue.

"Oh fuck, fuck, oh my God." Cassandra gasped in turn. Peyton was licking every inch of her feet, running her tongue down the soles, biting, licking sucking her toes.

"Oh Peyton, Peyton, I love that, I love it."

Peyton took her time, covering every inch of Cassandra's feet with her kisses and licks. It felt heavenly.

"Oh Cassie, I love your feet so much, I love them, oh God, God."

The next moment she felt Peyton's wet pussy against the ball of her foot. She opened her eyes to see Peyton kneeling and moving her pelvis against Cassandra's foot, fucking herself. It was horny as fuck. Cassandra watched in fascination as Peyton closed her eyes and her head went back lost in the motion.

"Oh, Cassie, oh, oh, oh, oh God, I'm sorry, I just couldn't, oh, oh, fuck, fuck, fuck, I love that so much, fuck, fuck, ahhhh!" Peyton climaxed with a scream pulling Cassandra's foot hard into her crotch. Cassandra wiggled her toes as Peyton carried on her orgasm for quite a long time.

"Oh my God, Cassie," said Peyton, "I couldn't help it."

"It's fine, I liked it, it was sexy as fuck, darling." Cassandra smiled, her own pussy was now aching for release and Peyton didn't waste time obliging her.

Peyton's head went down between Cassandra's legs, her tongue began flicking her clit. Cassandra arched her back. She started to push her pussy hard into Peyton's mouth, rubbing herself against the insistent lapping. Everything had taken her right to the edge already. Her orgasm was very close, it had been building all this time, all through the spanking and she felt as if she would burst.

"Oh, fuck, Peyton, oh, oh, oh, ah, ah, oh, fuck, fuck, fuck, fuck, oh, God, fuck, oh, oh, ohhhh!" The dam broke and her climax washed over her in wave after wave. Cassandra cried out her voice rising in pitch as she peaked while Peyton licked her on and on until Cassandra couldn't stand it. Finally, the sensations began to gradually subside. She felt completely sated.

Peyton was lying down beside her. Caressing her cheek and smiling at her.

"Thank you," Peyton whispered.

"For what?" Cassandra whispered back.

"For spanking me, for everything."

"It was my pleasure, darling, really. Was it to your liking?"

"No, it hurt like fuck, but I deserved it, I wanted it, I needed it."

"I'm glad I gave you what you needed then. You did deserve it too." Cassandra smiled.

"And for making love to me, letting me fuck your beautiful foot."

"That's also my pleasure."

Cassandra kissed her.

"It was my pleasure too. I'm sorry about… before."

"Hush, you've paid the price for it. Now let's forget it. Just never think, I don't need you, Peyton, because I do…"

Peyton was looking at her, suddenly very intently. Cassandra felt something overwhelm her. Feelings which she hadn't examined before were surfacing at a rapid rate, perhaps these last events were the catalyst. The sexual chemistry they had felt was sublimating into something much more.

Cassandra spoke without thinking. "I love you, Peyton."

The words hung there between them. Peyton's eyes opened wide.

"Cassie, I…"

"I love you, Peyton, I can't help it. I'm in love with you," Cassandra said opening up her now.

Peyton didn't speak for a moment, and Cassandra's heart was in her mouth. In what was a seminal moment for them both, she wondered if she had spoken out of turn. Perhaps Peyton wasn't carrying a torch for her after all. However, before she could think anything further, Peyton was pulling her closer.

"I love you, Cassie, oh, I love you so fucking much, I love you, I love you."

They were kissing once more and inflamed with passion. Peyton's fingers frantically found Cassandra's pussy and began to finger fuck her.

"Oh, Peyton, oh, fuck, fuck, oh, God, oh, oh, fuck, I love you, I love you, Peyton, I love you, oh, oh, oh, ohhh!" the orgasm was intensified by her deep feelings.

The two of them lay together holding each other tightly. Cassandra felt as if she didn't ever want to let Peyton go. She knew she would have to, as Nathan was going to be home soon. What would happen then? Would Peyton stay and the three of them would fuck? How would she tell Nathan she was now in love with Peyton, as well as Nathan?

They were so different. Peyton was softer. Making love to her was like peaches and cream. Nathan was more visceral and guttural, he was like a tiger or a panther in bed. Their lovemaking was usually much less tender, especially recently. Cassandra liked both. She loved two people. She was polyamorous. There was no doubt in her mind. How else could this be? She could never be satisfied with only one of them. Peyton would be happy to share her, but would Nathan? Time would tell. For now, she was happy to have released something within her which she had evidently been holding back. Her love for Peyton. The future would, she felt, somehow take care of itself.

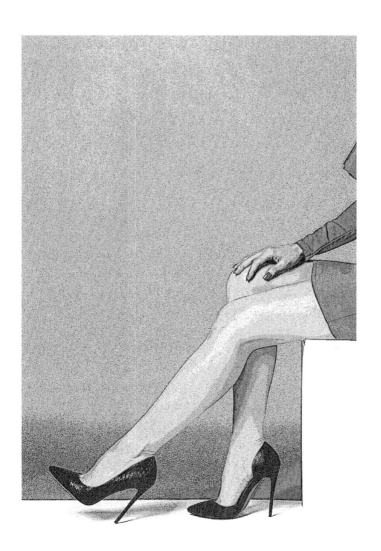

Cassie gives another hairbrush spanking (Book Six)

Emotions had been coursing through Cassandra for several days, since she disclosed her love for Peyton. She found it hard to reconcile the idea of loving, wanting to be with and nurturing two people at once, with her own upbringing. She had been raised on monogamy. A person, particularly a woman, gets married, has kids. Her parents were not particularly strict, nor pious but they were simply ordinary. Her existence was mundane and perhaps that as much as anything had led her to marry Leonard. It was expected of her to do well. He was a man with money, and for all his lack of prowess in bed, a sweet talker. Cassandra had been seduced by him paying attention to her, an admin assistant in his firm. She went from zero to hero when she stepped up to the altar. He put her on a pedestal, gave her a university education, in return for her love. She had loved him too, knowing no other form of love than that. She was a good wife, she did everything a wife should do, and then he died. In her grief, she found herself rich and independent. Then she had met Nathan and suddenly became aware of her profound sexual nature. His ministrations had unleashed the beast, and it could no longer be contained. The spanking was a catharsis from a shy retiring woman to someone who was confident, and felt somehow empowered by her newfound dominance over two very different people. Now she was Cassandra, the spanker, the bedroom bitch, but still inside quite shy and a loner. She had never wanted kids, and probably never would. Fierce passions stirred within her for Peyton and for Nathan. Apparently, this was normal for polyamorous people. She did not really know what she was, the label was perhaps convenient, to help her understand herself.

She and Nathan were having dinner. He had cooked a cottage pie, with peas and broccoli. He was an excellent cook, and this was part of his contribution to the household. They had lived together in harmony, for the most part, for some time. Then Peyton had come on the scene.

"A penny for your thoughts," he said to her as he consumed his own helping of pie. He had a prodigious appetite and at the same time a metabolism which burned it all away.

"Oh, sorry," Cassandra had not realised she had drifted off a little into her own pensive self-examination.

"You've been distracted lately," he continued. "So, what's up?"

Cassandra took a forkful of the pie and ate it, realising she couldn't avoid things anymore. He had to be told.

"Well?" he said cocking an endearing eyebrow.

"I… there's something I need to tell you." She eyed him apprehensively.

"Go on."

"You remember how we talked about Peyton, and you asked me a question, about how I felt?"

"I asked you if you were in love with her," he said bluntly. He fixed her with an unnerving stare.

"Well…" she hesitated, once she said it there was no turning back. What would be would be. "I am… in love with her."

There was silence while he digested this. Just as she had guessed, he might not be quite as cool with it as he might appear.

"But I'm also in love with you, just as much as I ever was, Nathan… and…"

"Stop." He held up his hand. "Just don't talk to me about it, for the moment."

He turned his attention to the pie, and took another helping. They ate in silence while Cassandra wondered what was going through his mind. At length, they both finished, and he cleared the table.

She sat there looking at him when he suddenly said. "Bend over the table."

"What?"

"I said bend over the table, Cassie." Then seeing her expression amended it slightly. "Don't look so worried, I just want to fuck you."

Cassandra who was wearing a short skirt, t-shirt and nothing else, stood up. This was her normal attire for his homecoming, she liked to turn him on. Uncertainly she bent forward over the dining room table. It would not be the first time they had done this, but she felt a little awkward all of a sudden, though her pussy betrayed her, nevertheless. She was wet with anticipation as she heard him undo his belt and drop his jeans. Without preamble, he entered her.

"Oh, fuck, oh God!" she cried out as his thick hard cock filled her up.

"Cassie, you little bitch, I'm going to fuck you, so hard," he grunted beginning to move slowly at first.

His hands came down to grip her thighs.

"Oh, shit, oh, oh, oh, oh, fuck," she cried out unable to resist the feeling he gave her every time they fucked.

"Oh, Cassie, Cassie, oh fuck, fuck, oh. See this, I'm fucking you, Cassie, because you're mine, you are fucking well mine, you bitch." He began to pick up speed, plunging into her and thrusting harder, faster.

"Oh, oh, God, oh, oh, oh, oh, fuck, fuck, oh, oh." Cassandra was now too far gone to think of anything except his thick organ pounding into her. The words he said were at odds with everything she felt but she couldn't process them at all.

"Ah, fuck, ah, ah, oh, oh, oh, oh, ohh! You bitch, I will show you, who you belong to, I own you, you fucking bitcchhhh!" Nathan shouted, beginning to ram his cock home harder and harder.

"Jesus Christ, Nathan, oh God, that's just, oh, God, oh." Cassandra was nearing her climax and it threatened to break at any moment. There would be time enough to recall the words, now the sensations took over.

"Cassie, I'm going to, ahhhhhhhhhh! You fucking bitcchhhhhh!!!"

She felt his cock pulsing and the warm sensation of his spunk inside her. It was a feeling she loved. At the same time, her own climax reached its zenith, and the waves broke within.

"Oh, oh, oh, oh, fuck, fuck, oh, oh, oh, ohhhh!" she cried out as the orgasm washed through her, taking her somewhere else for a few moments, before returning her to earth. Some of the things he had said while fucking her were starting to register.

Quite abruptly, Nathan withdrew and then started to do his belt up. Cassandra stood up and turned around to see him at the kitchen door.

"I'm going out, for a drink with the mates, I'll see you later," he said his voice quite hard.

"What? Just like *that*? You fuck me and go?" Shock registered on her face.

"I'll see you later I'm not in the mood," he growled back.

Anger flared in her suddenly.

"Is that how you assert your fucking male dominance over me, is it?" She shouted at his back. "Bend me over the table and fuck me, then go out for a drink? Is it?"

He said nothing as she followed him to the front door where he pulled on his shoes. Cassandra was almost speechless at his callous behaviour, and in the face of her own emotional turmoil. It was selfish beyond belief. She lost control and let fly.

"Alright then, fuck off and don't talk to me. Fuck off then, Nathan, you fucking arsehole. Go and fuck yourself! Do you hear me? Go and fucking fuck yourself you selfish fucking prick!"

He ran down the steps without a word, got into his car and drove away. Tears were coursing down her cheeks. Tears of rage and shame. He had shamed her just now with what he did. Although she had consented, and enjoyed it, now it seemed almost like a punishment. It was as if he wanted to show her in some primaeval way that he was still the boss, or something like it. Those things he had shouted, too, claiming ownership. What an absolute bastard. She was devastated. She felt used and dirty. She also felt guilty. She slammed the front door and locked it. Then sank down with her back to it and sobbed her heart out.

***

She heard nothing from Nathan overnight, no text and no phone call. Although she wanted to simply leave it, let him get fucked, the guilt began to gnaw away at her. She felt as if she had done something very bad, and that somehow all this was her fault.

The guilt became overwhelming, as if her love for Peyton had somehow driven him away. This was wrong of course, but natural for any human to think so. Cassandra began to desire some form of atonement. As if this could assuage her somehow and put things right.

After breakfast, she got into her four by four, and found herself at the same row of antique shops where she had bought the hairbrush. She felt irresistibly drawn there. She parked up and entered the shop where she had met Faith, the woman who had sold her the hairbrush.

Faith looked up at her smiling, when she saw her. She was, now Cassandra looked properly, devastatingly attractive. With silver hair, full lips and nice eyes. She guessed Faith was in her fifties. Faith was wearing a loose floral shift of dress, but it didn't hide a good figure, and she was wearing thong sandals. Cassandra noticed her bare feet which shown the signs of age, but still were incredibly sexy.

"You came back," Faith observed.

"Yes."

"Did you want to buy something else?"

"I don't know." Cassandra wasn't really sure why she was there at all, and was about to leave. However, Faith somehow picked up her agitation.

"You seem troubled, would you like some tea?" Faith smiled, in a friendly way.

"I… yes… it would be nice."

"Good, well, I'll just lock the door, that way we won't be disturbed."

Faith locked the shop door, and put a closed sign up. Then she returned and led Cassandra through to what seemed to be Faith's kitchen as part of her living accommodation. Faith smiled at her, and set about making some tea. The kitchen was perhaps a little old fashioned with hand-built pine units, and a tiled worktop. It was kind of bohemian, as if Faith was somehow a free spirit.

"You're looking at my hippy kitchen," said Faith laughing. "I'm afraid I'm a bit of a throwback, peace love and all that, it's why I run an antique shop."

She brought two mugs of tea, and slid one over to Cassandra. From a tin, she fished out a lemon drizzle cake, put it on a plate and sliced it.

"Help yourself, it's homemade."

"Thank you," said Cassandra, taking a slice and feeling it would be churlish not to. It tasted delicious.

"So, what's wrong?"

Cassandra though unused to telling her business to strangers, felt peaceful in Faith's company. It almost felt a blessed relief and it seemed easy to pour her heart out, which she did. Faith proved to be a good listener and said nothing judgemental.

"Well, it's quite a story and a tangle you have there," Faith said when Cassandra had finished her tale, and not without a few tears.

"Thank you, for listening. I don't know why I just felt comfortable talking to you," said Cassandra.

"You are welcome."

Faith made them another cup of tea and resumed her seat. She eyed Cassandra with interest.

"Why did you come to me, though, really?" she asked. "I mean don't get me wrong, I'm glad to be of help as a listener, but I don't think it's why you came, is it?"

This was very perceptive, and Cassandra flushed a little.

"Don't be shy, after all, you've told me it all already, there can't be too many more secrets in that pretty head of yours. Especially to a stranger."

"But I trust you…" Cassandra began tentatively.

"And you can, of course, many people do trust me with their secrets."

This was a cryptic utterance and although Cassandra wanted to ask her what she meant by it. She didn't feel she really could.

"I came here because…" Cassandra hesitated and then started afresh. "I thought you might help me to atone."

"Atone? How?" Faith seemed surprised, although there was something about her tone which Cassandra didn't quite believe, almost as if Faith was willing her to spell out what she desired.

She took a deep breath, partly because she wasn't sure herself.

"It's just when I saw you the other day, you know with the cane, and you seemed to know how to use it and…" Cassandra tailed off, unable to finish.

"You thought perhaps it's something I did, on the side, maybe, is that it?" Faith's eyes were twinkling, teasing.

Cassandra nodded and begun to see how Peyton felt, just a little.

"Did you come here to be punished, is that what you mean by atonement?"

This question was blunt and blindsided Cassandra, although it was exactly what she had been thinking.

"I…"

"Do you think it would somehow assuage your guilt? It would, perhaps, make you feel better?"

"I don't know." Cassandra bit her lip.

"Why did you think I would punish you, Cassandra? Do you think I do this for a living? Perhaps I'm a counsellor who dispenses caning and other things…" Faith let the question hang with an amused smile playing on her lips.

"I don't know, I don't know what I was thinking. Perhaps I'd better go." Cassandra wasn't liking Faith's questions and was starting to feel stupid and embarrassed.

As she was getting up, she felt Faith's hand on her wrist.

"Wait, I'm sorry. I was teasing you. I can see you feel distressed, and even awkward. I apologise, I didn't mean to make you feel that way. Stay a little."

Cassandra resumed her seat and looked at Faith, wondering what was to come next.

"You're actually right in what you thought. I erm... I am something of an expert in the field of discipline. I am not a counsellor, although some might see it that way. You sussed me pretty well, although I think, now you've told me about yourself, I read you pretty well too. I was testing you because I'm not sure punishment is going to help you. Your boyfriend, Nathan, is being a dick and if anyone deserves punishing it's him, not you." Faith shrugged.

"I know," Cassandra smiled, "And thank you, you are probably right. But what if I wanted to be punished... anyway..."

"It's your prerogative, of course. And I like you, so if it's what you really want?"

Cassandra swallowed. It wasn't necessarily what she really wanted at all. However, some part of her felt the need and some part of her wanted to experience what it was like.

"I... I would like it, if you would... could... yes..." she said quietly.

"You know I usually charge for this kind of thing..."

"If it's money I can..."

Faith held up her hand, "In your case, I'm happy to do it for nothing, because I like you. You're honest and open, not like so many of my clients and their secrets."

"C... clients?"

"I'm a professional disciplinarian, for my sins. Though I also sell antiques, as a hobby. I hope that doesn't shock you."

"Oh! No, I'm not… shocked… surprised, perhaps. I thought maybe you were an ex-schoolteacher."

"Oh, no, nothing like that. I'm just a woman who likes to give a good spanking and knows how, then I found it paid very handsomely. So, I thought, why not?" Faith studied her a little and then said, "If you want to be punished, then… shall we?"

Cassandra nodded.

"What would you like, do you think?"

"I thought perhaps… you might cane me?"

"That's quite brave, I'm impressed, well, wait here, I won't be long."

Faith disappeared and Cassandra wondered what she was letting herself in for. She looked around and wondered where the caning was going to take place. There was a little flutter in her stomach at the idea of it. What it was actually like would be another story. She was sure it was going to hurt, but somehow the pain was something she felt she needed.

Faith reappeared and she was wearing a pair of black high heeled mules. She had taken off the dress, and replaced it with a tight leather one which hugged her like a second skin. Cassandra could see she had a fantastic body underneath it, and her feet were suddenly incredibly sexy and appealing in the shoes.

"Like what you see? I thought I'd dress the part for you," said Faith noticing the direction of Cassandra's gaze. "I'm also quite the foot fetishist. You've got lovely feet yourself, I noticed them right away."

"Yes, I do like it, and thank you."

Cassandra noticed Faith was holding a thin school cane with a crook handle.

"I thought we could do it in here," said Faith, "It adds a touch of domesticity. I have a proper spanking room of course, but we don't need to go there."

"OK," Cassandra nodded wondering what she should do.

"Just do what I tell you, that's all you need to think about," said Faith in matter of fact tones. She put the cane down and cleared the table of objects.

It seemed quite clinical, cold even, Faith's demeanour. Not the emotion-filled spankings Cassandra gave to Nathan and Peyton.

"Now then," said Faith, when the table was cleared to her satisfaction. She picked up the cane once more. "Stand up, Cassandra, and come to this side of the table." She pointed to the end where she wanted her to stand. Cassandra did so, a little self-consciously. She was wearing a short skirt, t-shirt and thong sandals herself. Perhaps in anticipation of something like this.

Cassandra stood looking at Faith who was smiling and flexing the cane with both hands. The action was quite arousing though in some ways scary too.

"I'm going to punish you now, Cassandra, how many strokes do you think you deserve, six, twelve, or shall I just stop when I think it's enough?"

"You decide," Cassandra whispered.

"I can't hear you, Cassandra."

"You decide," said Cassandra more loudly.

"Very well, once I start punishing you, you are to stay in position until I tell you to move, understood. Normally I expect to be called Mistress or Ma'am, but you can call me Faith this time. OK?"

Cassandra nodded. Faith's voice became suddenly quite assertive, business-like even, but certainly a voice one would obey. This time? Were there going to be other times? Cassandra wasn't sure about that at all.

"Bend over the table, Cassandra."

Cassandra complied at once finding it easier to lie with her arms stretched out in front. She felt completely vulnerable in that position, exposed. The table felt a little cold to her skin. She could tell Faith had walked up behind her by the sound of Faith's heels on the tiled floor. Then her skirt was lifted up, and her knickers pulled down to expose her bare bottom.

"What a very nice backside you have, my dear. So, inviting for the cane. First, though I'm going to warm up your bottom just a tad, so the cane leaves less marks."

Faith bent down and removed one of Cassandra's thong sandals. She could be heard dusting it off.

"I think this will do nicely and quite fitting considering your own track record with sandals and spanking."

Faith moved again, to Cassandra's left-hand side. Faith was obviously right-handed.

"First a little spanking, for you, Cassandra."

Cassandra felt the sole of her own sandal touch her bottom lightly. It was strange to be on the receiving end. The sandal was removed and then came two spanks one on each cheek.

SMACK SMACK

Cassandra gasped at the sting. It wasn't, however, too unpleasant. Before she had time to think it was followed by another half a dozen.

SMACK SMACK SMACK SMACK SMACK SMACK

"Oh God," she said out loud as the sting deepened. Each smack stung as it made an impact and then left a lasting impression.

"Getting through already, are they? Good, that's good," Faith said amused.

SMACK SMACK SMACK SMACK SMACK SMACK

SMACK SMACK SMACK SMACK SMACK SMACK

"Oh God, oh shit, oh fuck…" the second set increased in intensity and they certainly hurt, but still not in a bad way. It was arousing, feeling the heat of them.

"Your bottom is getting nice and pink already, how cute." Faith seemed to find it quite funny rather than emotional.

SMACK SMACK SMACK SMACK SMACK SMACK

SMACK SMACK SMACK SMACK SMACK SMACK

SMACK SMACK SMACK SMACK SMACK SMACK

"Fuck, fuck, fuck, fuck." Cassandra couldn't help swearing as another volley of spanks came one after the other.

"Just a few more I think, before the cane," said Faith.

SMACK SMACK SMACK SMACK SMACK SMACK

SMACK SMACK SMACK SMACK SMACK SMACK

"Jesus…"

"Cassandra really, such a potty mouth you have, my dear."

SMACK SMACK SMACK SMACK SMACK SMACK

SMACK SMACK SMACK SMACK SMACK SMACK

"Sorry, Faith, it's just…"

"I know, well your bottom should be nicely warmed up, as long as you don't want me to stop. Do you? Last chance."

Cassandra paused for a moment. Her bottom was burning lightly from the spanking which she suspected wasn't as hard as it could have been. However now she had started on the course of action, she felt duty bound to experience it to the full.

"No, Faith, I don't want you to stop."

"Now, while I'm caning you, it's a chance for you to think about what you've done wrong. If I ask you a question, you are to answer it. You are to obey me implicitly, understood?"

"Yes, Faith."

"Good, that's very good. Then let us begin your real punishment."

Cassandra felt the touch of the thin bamboo against her buttocks, as Faith lined it up and picked her target. It was removed once, and twice. Then without warning, she heard a swish and the sound of the cane as it impacted her naked buttocks.

SWISH THWACK

Cassandra felt nothing at first and then a searing white heat spread through her buttocks. It was painful and intense.

"Ohhhh!" she cried out involuntarily.

"You've been a naughty girl, isn't that what you want to hear? And now you're getting a well-deserved caning," Faith told her implacably.

SWISH THWACK

The next stroke was just as bad, coming on top of the first. Faith had waited to give the one she just had a chance to subside before delivering another. Cassandra was expecting the rush of pain this time but even so, she cried out.

"Oh, fuckkk!"

"Oh fuck indeed, my girl. That's just two of several, so be prepared. Bad behaviour must be punished. I'm sure you know."

SWISH THWACK

Even after just two, her bottom was beginning to sting and the third just added more heat. She noticed there was a moment, after the almost unbearable intensity of the rush of pain where it felt so good. A moment of clarity before the next stroke came.

"Oh God, God, God," Cassandra whispered.

"I haven't found prayer much help in these instances," Faith laughed. "When you've been a naughty girl then the cane is your teacher and I'm going to make sure you are taught a good lesson."

SWISH THWACK

Faith had plenty of time to speak between strokes and she seemed to enjoy it. She had the kind of voice which was incredibly arousing. In between all of the sensations, Cassandra found herself becoming incredibly wet between her thighs.

"Ohh owww."

"How many do you think you deserve Cassandra, to atone for your sins? Hmmm. One more, two? Let's find out." Faith dropped her voice a little lower.

SWISH THWACK

"Oww fuckk."

If Cassandra had managed to keep count with her mind in a turmoil of agitated feelings, she thought that was five.

SWISH THWACK

"Owww... owww...."

It was beginning to hurt, and her mind started to empty. There was a well inside her which felt like it was about to burst.

"How does it feel now, Cassandra? To have a well-caned bottom?"

SWISH THWACK

"Oh... oh... fuck... oh...."

One more, maybe just one more would do it, came the unbidden thought.

As if she read her mind, Faith obliged but with two in quick succession.

SWISH THWACK

SWISH THWACK

These were harder in intensity one on top of the other. The white heat flashed through Cassandra and suddenly her dam of emotion opened up and she began to sob.

"Oh... oh… ohhh… ohhh…" she cried tears running unbidden down her cheeks.

"Hmm, I think that's enough, come on, get up, darling, get up." Faith's voice changed into one of concern. She laid the cane aside and her arms came around Cassandra pulling her to her feet. Cassandra buried her face into Faith's bosom and cried her heart out.

"It's OK, it's OK, darling." Faith was stroking her hair so gently as if she was a child. "It's OK, precious." She felt Faith kiss the top of her head and looked up teary eyed.

"Here," Faith smiled, "Let me help you a little more."

Without warning Faith's fingers found their way to Cassandra's sopping pussy. Cassandra did not resist while the fingers expertly began to finger her slowly and then faster.

"Oh, oh, fuck, oh Faith, oh God, oh, fuck, fuck, oh, oh, oh." Cassandra stopped crying and laid her head back and allowed the pleasing sensations to go through her.

"That's right, let it take you, darling, surrender to my fingers, sweetheart, that's the way."

Faith's fingers were moving faster, and Cassandra was lost in the moment, with her climax building like a tidal wave. The spanking and the caning had brought her to a height of sexual intensity, and then this. She let herself go. The wave crested and broke as she shuddered deliciously.

"Oh, oh, oh fuck, fuck, fuck, fuck, oh, oh Faithhhhhhhh!"

Faith held her gently, stroking her hair once more, while her orgasm peaked and then subsided. She led Cassandra out of the kitchen, into a living room with soft brown leather sofas, and sat down on one. Cassandra winced as she gingerly settled in beside her.

"Tender?" Faith smiled.

"Oh Faith." Cassandra laid her head on Faith's shoulder. She felt exhausted suddenly, drained. Her bottom was very sore, and she was still feeling the sting of the caning. Cassandra's eyes began to close, and she fell asleep.

She woke later, lying on the sofa covered by a blanket. Faith was sitting in another chair reading.

"Hello, how are you feeling? I let you sleep. I reckon you needed it."

Faith had changed back into her dress and was wearing her thong sandals.

"Oh, God, I should g… owww." Cassandra sat up and her bottom was certainly sore.

"I'm sorry you'll feel it for a while, and it has left some marks, they'll fade though. They would have been worse if I hadn't given you a spanking first."

"You've been so kind to me," said Cassandra, tearing up again.

"Don't cry, my sweet." Faith put down the book and sat down beside her. "I told you I didn't think you needed to be punished, but you wanted it. I can see you needed that, or something, to release your inner demons. I tried to make your experience authentic. I hope I did."

"Thank you, really. Yes, it was authentic alright."

"*Do* you feel better?"

"I don't know," said Cassandra after some thought. "It was cathartic somehow to be on the receiving end. I think I needed it."

"As long as you're happy, then I'm happy."

"You're so nice to me."

"Everyone needs someone nice."

"And I didn't…"

Faith picked up the thought. "As much as I'd love to feel those beautiful lips on my pussy, and I dearly would, I don't think you need the complication. Maybe another time when things are more settled. I was happy to oblige you, and you needed the release. How about some more tea?"

It was early evening when Cassandra drove away from Faith's house. It had been quite an experience, and once she realised she had needed to have. She had stayed for some tea and cake. She and Faith had talked more. Faith had told her a little of her own interesting life, and how she came to be a professional Domme. It was something Faith apparently enjoyed, and it kept her in a decent living. Cassandra didn't enquire further, perhaps there would be another time.

"If Nathan comes back to you, and he will," said Faith as they parted at the door, "Make sure he apologises properly to you and to Peyton, and then give him a damn good spanking, he certainly deserves it."

"I will," Cassandra laughed.

"Promise?"

"I promise."

"Good, because I don't want to have to cane you again." Faith winked and laughed.

Cassandra made a detour to Peyton's. She wanted Peyton, to hold her and to love her. She was going to tell Peyton everything she had done, and hoped Peyton would not be upset. Peyton needed to know how Nathan had behaved. In the back of her mind was also the thought that perhaps one day she should buy a cane from Faith. She wasn't ready for it quite yet.

***

Cassandra lay on the bed face down, while Peyton gently massaged some soothing cream into her bottom. Peyton was only too glad to be picked up and taken to Cassandra's. She had got them a Chinese takeaway, and Peyton had listened wide-eyed to the whole unvarnished story.

"Are you upset with me? I hope you're not upset with me," Cassandra had said anxiously when she had finished.

"Of course, I'm not," said Peyton earnestly. "I love you, how could I be upset?"

"You're not... jealous?"

"No, Cassie, I'm not, not at all."

They had kissed, made love, and now Peyton was caring for her backside. Cassandra had examined the lines curiously in the mirror. They were red and slightly raised but nothing too bad. Faith was obviously very expert as one line was under the other in a nice row down her buttocks. Faith had also tried to keep the bruising down. Getting a spanking first was a good tip. The cream was helping a lot.

"How does *that* feel?" Peyton asked her.

"So much better."

Peyton laid down beside her.

"I wish I could have seen it, your caning," she said wistfully.

Cassandra laughed, "Really? Would you have been turned on by *that*?"

"Yes, I would."

"You're a horny little minx. But you know, I'm thinking of buying a cane…"

"I would love *that*!" said Peyton at once.

"I'm sure you wouldn't, it hurt like hell."

"But I still would love it, if it was you caning me." Peyton blushed a little, all at once quite shy.

"You're a strange one, but I love you. Why do you want to be punished so much?"

Cassandra had wondered about this but never really asked her.

"I don't know, it's just something which has been with me since I was young."

"But you never had a spanking before me?"

"No, never, that part is true, but I wanted one. I've been craving a spanking for years. Then you spanked me so beautifully."

Cassandra remembered Peyton had said she'd never been spanked until she had asked Cassandra to do it.

"You've watched enough spanking porn and stuff, judging by the sound of it," Cassandra laughed.

"I know, I'm sorry."

"Don't be. I'm not going to spank you for that."

She turned to Peyton and pulled her into an embrace.

"What about Nathan? What are you going to do?"

"I don't know," said Cassandra sadly. "I didn't think he would take it like he has. But what he did was almost unforgivable, in the kitchen. I mean not that it wasn't consensual, but it was his way of punishing me or showing somehow, he owned me. I hate that."

"Do you want me to…" Peyton began, her eyes suddenly bright.

"If you are going to talk of leaving me, then you'll be across my knee in no time," Cassandra said severely. "No, you're not doing that. I love you and I'm not letting you go too."

"Are you letting Nathan go?"

"No, I mean I don't want to. I love him very much. I want him in my life and yours."

"I'm sorry."

"For what?"

"For coming between you."

"Now you stop that talk, or else. Nathan had behaved very badly. He's the one at fault. Even if he didn't like it, the way he behaved is beyond the pale," Cassandra pursed her lips.

"What if he apologises?"

"He'll have to do more than apologise. The hairbrush will be waiting for his backside, if he does want to continue with us."

"Will I be able to watch?" Peyton asked hopefully.

"Yes, or I might let you do even more than just watch. We'll see, if it ever happens. I just don't know. He might want to call it quits. I just don't know. If he does, I'm going to be very upset."

"You'll still have me."

"I know." Cassandra kissed her.

"You'll always have me."

"I know, my darling. Stop talking now, and love me."

"OK," Peyton whispered kissing her softly, gently.

***

Several days had gone by since Nathan had left. Cassandra wondered what he was doing and where he was. There had been no word, no text, nothing. She checked his credit card and he had not used it. He had his own money, of course. The pain in her heart increased day by day, as he didn't get in touch.

Peyton had stayed over for a day or two and then gone home. Cassandra could tell she didn't want to. However, Cassandra just felt she could not deal with having Peyton around all the time, as much as she loved her. It was one thing to love someone, another to live with them. It also struck her that if by some miracle Nathan came back then having Peyton living there too would create unnecessary friction. After all, like it or not, Nathan was there first.

Cassandra was not sure what the future held for them. How could they all three live together? How could she sustain it or even afford it? She was wealthy but she didn't have unlimited funds. In her inimitable way, she pushed it to the back of her mind. It would work out, somehow.

As she sat eating a baguette filled with salami, brie, tomato, salad and avocado, her phone buzzed. It was a text. From Nathan. Her heart skipped a beat as she opened it.

"Hi," it said.

"Hi? What the fuck, Nathan?" Cassandra spoke out loud. He doesn't contact me for nearly a week and then says 'Hi'?

Displeased already, she typed, "Hi."

A text came back almost immediately.

"I'm sorry, Cassie."

Cassandra stared at the phone. Was that it? *That* was his apology?

This was followed by another text.

"Can we talk?"

It pulled at her heartstrings at once. When you've been used to having someone around, being with them, and then they're gone, sometimes you bury the hurt. But hearing from him like this brought it all back in an instant. After a pause during which she battled with just telling him to please come home, she wrote.

"You can phone me."

Then she waited, but her mobile rang almost instantaneously. She answered in trepidation at what he was going to say, and what she would say in return.

"Cassie?"

His voice sent chills down her spine, just like it always did.

"Nathan."

"Cassie, I…"

"Nathan why are you phoning?" she got in first, before he smooth-talked her like he always did. Although this time was different, because what he had done was still upsetting her.

"I'm phoning to apologise."

She was silent biting on a retort, on the anger which was surfacing.

"Cassie?"

She tried to keep her emotions in check.

"I have not heard from you for days. You walked out of the house after what you did and what you said. Then you don't text or phone…" she trailed off as her voice began to crack.

"I know, and I'm really sorry."

"Sorry?" she could not keep the hurt out of her voice. "Are you… sorry?"

"I am, Cassie, I really am, I acted like a complete fucking dick to you. I've been a fucking arsehole and I'm ashamed of myself."

"It took you all this fucking time to ring me and say *that*? What the fuck have you been doing for the rest of it, Nathan? After you revenge fucked me in the kitchen?"

He was silent. She had finally put it into words. What he had done. Her voice now throbbed with emotion, as her wrath began to unravel. She waited for him to say something and he finally did. He sighed which only served to wind her up further.

"I was staying with a friend, from uni. I had to think about things."

"What things? What fucking things? You couldn't have the decency to stay and talk to me? Instead, you fucked me like I was your slut and walked away? You left me high and dry wondering where the fuck you were.

You could have been dead for all I know. You could have been fucking well dead."

Angry tears were tracking down her cheeks.

"I know, and I'm sorry, I really am."

"You're sorry but you couldn't even fucking text to say you needed time to think?"

"No, it was a dick move, it really was."

The fact he was taking it on the chin served to calm her down a little. After a few moments, she spoke in more even tones.

"So, what *did* you think about then, Nathan?"

"Do you accept my apology?" he wanted to know that first.

"No, we'll talk about it later, tell me what you thought about."

"OK, I guessed it wouldn't be that easy…" he said in resigned tones.

"Nathan!"

"Sorry, what I thought was that I love you, Cassie, so very much and I've been a fucking arsehole. I was an absolute fuck faced bastard that night. A tosser of the worst kind."

"OK, well I love you too, don't think I don't." She was a little mollified by his self-castigation.

"I thought… if you love Peyton, it's OK with me. I shouldn't be such a jealous piece of shit, which is what I've been."

"OK…" Cassandra waited to see if there was more.

"I know I've got a lot of making up to do, and I don't feel the same way about Peyton that you do. I mean I'm not in love with her or anything but if she is going to be part of our relationship, and our lives then I accept it."

"OK."

"Not many people would let their partner fuck another woman, let alone participate. My friends were astounded and told me what a fucking stupid prick I was being about it."

"Your friends? You told them?"

"Well, only a couple who I really trust, honestly. I mean I had to talk to someone," he said lamely.

"You could have talked to me, and you didn't, you walked out on me. You fucked me and just walked out on me, like I was your whore. I'm not your whore, Nathan, I never will be."

She was determined to punch home the hurtful thing he did, so he would get the depth of her feelings about it.

"I know, Cassie, I know. It was despicable of me. I don't think of you that way, believe me. You've been so good to me, so kind, everything."

"Did you tell them about the spanking?" She wanted to know although for some reason it didn't bother her if they did know.

"I…" he paused. "I did, I'm sorry, and they laughed, and said I most likely deserved it for acting like a fucking arsehole. Actually, they thought it was pretty hot."

"OK." She laughed a little at this, then she was silent waiting for him to make the next move.

After a while he did.

"Can I come back home? Please?"

His voice was contrite, and she desperately wanted him, to feel his cock inside her, fucking her. She wanted his cuddles and his kisses. She had grown used to having him around. She took a deep breath. He needed to pay for what he had done.

"You can but there are conditions."

"Which are?" he sounded as if he had been expecting it.

"I'm sure you can guess. You have to be willing to have a spanking for what you did."

"OK, and?"

"You have to promise never to treat me like that again. Never to walk away from me and not contact me."

"OK, anything else?"

"You have to promise to accept me for what I am. I think I'm polyamorous, Nathan, and so I love Peyton just as much as you. I love you both and I want you both in my life. You have to accept Peyton too."

"Is she going to be living with us?"

"I don't know, not for the moment, no."

"OK, fine, I accept it of course. So, can I come home now?"

She took a deep breath. As much as she wanted him to come, it had to be on her terms. She was resolved to make him wait, and think about it before taking him back into her fold.

"Not today, no. Tomorrow after university you can come home. You will be punished, and Peyton is going to be there. You will have to apologise to her too."

"You told her?"

"Of course, I did."

"Was she... upset?"

"She was upset for me, but you've slighted her, and I want you to apologise to her. She didn't ask me but I'm asking you to."

Cassandra felt it was only fair that he did say sorry to Peyton, after all, he had made nothing of her feelings in his moment of revenge.

"OK, I'll do all of that, anything you say. Any other instructions?"

"Yes, come upstairs, strip and knock, just like before. You will call me Mistress until I tell you the punishment is over. When it's done, we'll put it behind us, all of us, and we won't mention it again."

"OK, well, I'll see you tomorrow then... I guess."

"See you tomorrow."

"I love you, Cassie."

"I love you too."

He disconnected and Cassandra sat for a few moments collecting her thoughts. She felt once more empowered now he had agreed to her terms. As much as she could have accepted his apology outright, she felt it wasn't enough. She'd endured a caning because of him, and he needed to learn never to treat her that way again. He was going to be getting the hairbrush and he wouldn't be expecting it. She dialled Peyton's number, to tell her the news.

***

The following afternoon, Cassandra waited with Peyton in the bedroom for Nathan to come home. It would be the first time she had seen him for a week. She and Peyton had prepared together for the spanking session which was to come.

They had a shower, and inevitably this led to sex under the steaming hot water. Cassandra's tram lines from the caning had thankfully all but faded. Because they had, she opted to wear her red and black lacy satin corset and black high heeled mules, although she would kick them off once Nathan went over her knee. Peyton was wearing a red half corset which sat under her breasts, and red stiletto mules. They both had red painted nails and red lipstick. Peyton had done Cassandra's understated but elegant makeup. The spanking chair was already in position and Cassandra was sitting on it, with Peyton standing beside her.

At the appointed hour she heard Nathan's car pull up in the driveway, and then the front door opened and closed. A very few moments later, he padded up the stairs and knocked at the bedroom door.

"Come in, Nathan," said Cassandra.

Then suddenly, there he was, in all his naked glory. His muscles were toned, and his six-pack looked somehow even leaner than before. His hair was well-groomed along with the beard, and his undercut style. He could not help breaking out into a grin on seeing her and Peyton together.

It took all of Cassandra's resolve not to jump up and rush into his arms. Instead, she smiled back but stayed where she was. Nathan nodded affably at Peyton.

"Thank you for coming on time, Nathan," said Cassandra keeping her tone formal.

"I thought I'd best not be late."

She noticed his cock was standing well to attention, and wondered about milking him. This had been Peyton's idea based upon her ventures into all things spanking on the internet. Last spanking session he had been milked twice. Cassandra decided against it, his cock could strain in anticipation instead.

"You know why you're here, don't you?" she said.

"Yes."

"And that is?" she wasn't letting him off so easily.

"I'm here to be punished because of what I did. I was horrible to you about Peyton, and I went away for a week without contacting you."

"There's more, as you well know, but we'll get to it in due course." Cassandra turned to Peyton. "Fetch me the hairbrush, Peyton."

"Yes, Mistress." Peyton curtsied and went over to the dressing table. She retrieved the bone-handled brush with the smooth back, and knelt in front of Cassandra holding it up as if it was an offering. Cassandra took it and Peyton went back to her place beside her.

"Hairbrush?" said Nathan, eyeing it somewhat askance.

"Yes, Nathan. Your bottom is going to become intimately acquainted with it very shortly." She tapped the back of the brush lightly in her hand. "Peyton knows, don't you. She's already had a spanking with it, and I can assure you it stings. Am I right, Peyton?"

"Yes, Mistress. It stings a whole lot." Peyton flushed pink in recollection.

"I think we shan't waste time discussing it, anyway, come over here and bend over my knee." Cassandra bent down and removed her mules, putting them to one side.

Nathan strode across the bedroom floor, stood beside her, and then knelt down positioning himself across Cassandra's lap. Something which they were both becoming familiar with.

Cassandra took the brush and ran the cool surface of the bone over his naked arse.

"Let's be clear before we start. I am your Mistress in here, and you will address me properly, do everything I say, when I say it, got it?"

She raised the brush and brought it down for the first two spanks.

SMACK SMACK

Two red marks appeared at once on his bottom.

"Owww, fuck!" he said at the unexpected sting.

"I didn't hear your agreement, Nathan."

SMACK SMACK SMACK SMACK

"Oww, yes, yes, Mistress."

"Good!"

SMACK SMACK SMACK SMACK

"Now I want you to be under no illusion as to why you are getting punished. I'm going to spell it out to you. You hurt me Nathan, and it's only fair you get some understanding of that hurt yourself."

SMACK SMACK SMACK SMACK

"Shit, fuck me, that hurts!" he exclaimed.

"Yes, Nathan, it does. So, it hurts me too, when I remember what you did in the kitchen. Do *you* remember?"

SMACK SMACK SMACK SMACK

"Jesus fucking fuck, Cass... I mean, Mistress, yes yes I do."

"Good, and what did you do?"

SMACK SMACK SMACK SMACK

"Owwww, fuck! I bent you over the table, fucked you like a bitch and then I walked out on you and wouldn't talk to you."

SMACK SMACK SMACK SMACK

"Yes, you said it, Nathan. Fucked me like a bitch, like a whore, like a slut who meant nothing to you, and I'm so angry about that, so fucking angry."

Rage rose up inside her as she recalled it, wanting an outlet. She gave it one, with measured spanks on his bottom which began to turn a nice shade of red.

SMACK "Owww fuck" SMACK "Fuck!" SMACK "Ow" SMACK "Shit"

SMACK "fuckkk" SMACK "ahh!" SMACK "oh God" SMACK "Jesus"

SMACK "fucking hell" SMACK "ow ow ow!" SMACK "Owww" SMACK "fuckkkk"

SMACK "fuck fuck fuck" SMACK "Fuck!" SMACK "fuck" SMACK "fuckkk"

The hairbrush was having a satisfying effect on his backside. He seemed to be feeling each spank judging by the swearing. Peyton was watching with wide eyes and her mouth slightly parted. Cassandra could tell it was turning her on.

"How could you do that to me? How could you fuck me like that and leave me? I love you so much, you bastard. But you fucked me like a piece of meat and then just left me, left me, you arsehole, you fucking arsehole!"

SMACK "Owww" SMACK "Shit!" SMACK "GOD!" SMACK "Fuck"

SMACK "fuck" SMACK "Fuck!" SMACK "FUCK!" SMACK "owwww"

SMACK "oh no" SMACK "please!" SMACK "Ow Cassie" SMACK "fuck"

SMACK "Shit" SMACK "Fuck that stings" SMACK "JESUS" SMACK "Fuckkk"

SMACK "Owww" SMACK "Shitttt!" SMACK "Ow" SMACK "God, oh God"

"Good that it hurts you, good! Maybe now you can feel what it's like to have someone fuck you and leave you. You've no idea the pain you caused me, no idea. Well... maybe you do now, just a little."

"I do, I really do, and I'm sorry, Mistress, I'm so sorry," said Nathan.

His bottom was now crimson. Cassandra had measured the spanks to ensure they covered his backside fully.

"I'm glad you are sorry, but it's not over yet. I love Peyton and you have to accept it. Just like you said you would. She is going to be in my life, both our lives one way or another. The way you acted was an insult to her too. So, these are for that insult."

SMACK "Fuck" SMACK "shit!" SMACK "Ow" SMACK "oh fuck"

SMACK "shittt" SMACK "Shitttt!" SMACK "Owwww" SMACK "God"

SMACK "fuck fuck" SMACK "fuck!" SMACK "Ow" SMACK "fuck"

SMACK "Owww" SMACK "Owwww!" SMACK "Owwww" SMACK "Owwww"

SMACK "Ohhh" SMACK "fuck!" SMACK "Ow" SMACK "oh God."

SMACK "Ohh shit" SMACK "fuckk!" SMACK "Owwww" SMACK "owww"

SMACK "OWW" SMACK "OWWWW!" SMACK "OWWWW" SMACK "OWWWWWW"

She paused, his shoulders were heaving, as if he was in the act of sobbing. Perhaps he was silently crying. Either way, he turned his face away from her for a few moments.

"Let it out, darling, you can let it out," she said softly.

He did not reply, perhaps it was humiliating to him if he really was crying from a spanking by a woman. His shoulders were still but Cassandra wasn't finished. There were more grievances to be dealt with.

"You went away, Nathan, you didn't contact me for a whole week. Nothing. That fucking well hurt me. You are never to do that again, do you hear me?"

SMACK "Owww" SMACK "Owwwww!" SMACK "Owwwww" SMACK "OWWWW"

SMACK "Fuck, no I won't" SMACK "Shitttt!" SMACK "oh fuck" SMACK "Oh God"

SMACK "Shit" SMACK "Shitttt!" SMACK "Owwww" SMACK "Fuckkk"

SMACK "OW" SMACK "FUCK!" SMACK "OW" SMACK "SHIT!"

SMACK "Jesus" SMACK "Fuck!" SMACK "Fuckkk" SMACK "GOD!"

"So, you won't ever do that again?" she said quietly.

"No, I won't, Mistress."

SMACK "Owww" SMACK "Shitttt!" SMACK "Ow" SMACK "Jesus"

"Promise?"

"Yes, I promise."

SMACK "Fuckk" SMACK "Wow oww!" SMACK "Ouch" SMACK "SHIT"

SMACK "Ohhh" SMACK "FUCK!" SMACK "Owww" SMACK "God!"

She paused. His buttocks were a deep shade of red. She had also spent most of her ire using the brush on his bottom. She felt perhaps that he had learned his lesson, but she wanted to wrap up the spanking properly.

"Stand up, Nathan," she said.

He sighed a big sigh and did so. His erection was undiminished, but she could see his eyes were indeed wet.

Cassandra put her mules back on and stood up also.

"Now, bend over and put your hands on the chair."

He shot her a slightly anguished look but did as he was asked. When he was settled, she said, "Peyton, put the hairbrush back and bring the riding crop."

"Yes, Mistress," said Peyton obeying with alacrity. She came and knelt before Cassandra holding up the crop with both hands.

"Thank you, Peyton, stand up."

Cassandra swished the crop a few times before speaking to Nathan.

"Nathan, because you insulted Peyton, she is going to give you six strokes with the riding crop. I think that's only fair, don't you?"

Nathan said nothing as Peyton's eyes widened at being told to whip him.

"Peyton, take the crop and give Nathan six of the best with my blessing."

"Yes, Mistress, with pleasure, Mistress." Peyton took the crop from her, and holding it by the handle in her left hand, took a position on Nathan's right.

"In your own time, Peyton. Six of the best."

Peyton lined the crop up on Nathan's red bottom, and tapped it lightly before drawing it back. She let fly with a swish, and lifted it off just as she had seen Cassandra do. She wielded it with evident pleasure.

SWISH CRACK "Owwww"

"That's one," said Cassandra noting a red line on his arse with satisfaction.

Peyton was lining the crop up again. She drew it back.

SWISH CRACK "Fucckkk!"

"That's two."

SWISH CRACK "SHIT!"

"That's three."

SWISH CRACK "Fuck!"

"That's four. Make these last two count, Peyton, as hard as you like."

Peyton smiled shyly and drew the crop back further.

SWISH CRACK "Oh FUCK!"

"That's five."

SWISH CRACK "Fuck!"

"That's six. Good, girl, Peyton. You did that very well. Hopefully, he knows your feelings are not to be trifled with. Now hand the crop to me."

Cassandra took the crop from her and pulled her in for a kiss. She took up her position on the left side of Nathan.

"Are you sorry, Nathan, for insulting Peyton?"

SWISH CRACK "Owwww"

"Yes, yes, Mistress."

SWISH CRACK "Owwww"

"Apologise to her then."

SWISH CRACK "fuckkk"

"I'm sorry, Peyton, really I am," said Nathan.

"Good boy."

SWISH CRACK "OW"

"Now do you promise never to treat me like that again?"

SWISH CRACK "SHIT!"

"Yes, I do, I promise. I never will, I won't honestly."

"And you've learned your lesson?"

SWISH CRACK "ohhhhh"

"Yes, yes I have."

"And you are truly sorry for what you did?"

SWISH CRACK "Owwww"

SWISH CRACK "Ohhh"

"Yes, I am, please, Mistress, I really am sorry."

"Very good. Just remember, if you ever *ever* do anything like that again, the hairbrush will be waiting for your bottom."

SWISH CRACK "FUCK"

SWISH CRACK "OHHH"

SWISH CRACK "SHITTT"

Cassandra flung the crop to one side. His bottom was crisscrossed with red lines. He surely must have a very sore backside.

"You can stand up, Nathan," she said.

He obliged and looked at her. There was contrition in his expression with a little bit of macho defiance, as if he didn't want to be thought of as a pussy.

"Put your hands on your head and don't move," she ordered him

As he did so, she pulled Peyton towards her and began to kiss her. She was wet and her pussy was aching for Peyton's fingers. Peyton didn't need a second bidding and her hand went down between Cassandra's legs, at the same time Cassandra started to finger Peyton.

"Oh, Cassie, oh, oh, oh, I'm so wet, God I'm so wet," Peyton gasped as Cassandra's fingers slid in and out of her slick wet pussy.

"Fuck, fuck, oh God, Peyton, oh Peyton, oh my God, fuck, fuck, fuck." Cassandra was getting close to the edge in a very short space of time.

"Cassie, oh, oh, Cassie, fuck, oh, I'm close, don't stop, don't stop."

"I won't, oh Peyton, darling, fuck, fuck, Peyton, I'm cumming, oh God, fuck fuck fuck, Peyton, I love youuuuu, ahhhhhh!" The wave broke inside Cassandra and she climaxed tensing and untensing as the sensations rushed through her.

"Oh, Cassie, oh, Cassieeee, ooooohhhh, ohhh, ohhhhh!" Peyton screamed as her orgasm hit at almost the same time. Her body jerked and tensed.

As the orgasmic fog in her brain cleared, Cassandra could see Nathan's cock was coated in precum and straining at the leash. His eyes were almost bulging from his head watching their mutual masturbation session.

Cassandra broke apart from Peyton gently.

"Lie on your back, Nathan, in front of the chair. Peyton is going to foot fuck you."

He did so at once, and Peyton squealed with delight. She sat on the chair, and divesting herself of the mules, deftly took his cock between her toes.

"Oh fuck!" Nathan gasped as Peyton began to wank him with her feet moving them up and down on his slick wet cock.

"That's right, darling, very good."

"Oh fuck, fuck, fuck, shit, fuck, fuck," Nathan said through rasping breaths as Peyton's feet relentlessly wanked his cock holding the shaft tightly between her toes. "Fuck, fuck, shit, fuck, fuck, fuck."

"Slow down, darling, don't let him cum just yet," said Cassandra.

Peyton obeyed which received a groan from Nathan.

Cassandra walked over and knelt down to straddle him.

"Let me fuck him, now darling. I want to fuck him. You can sit on his face, and he can lick you."

Peyton stopped wanking him, got up from the chair and positioned her pussy over his mouth. Cassandra lowered herself onto his cock.

"Mmphhh!" muttered Nathan with his mouthful for Peyton's pussy. He began to lick her, and Peyton started to squeal, "Oh Nathan, Nathan, oh, lick me faster, oh God, Oh, Oh."

Cassandra began to fuck his cock, rising and falling, slowly but then faster as if she could not get enough of it.

Nathan was grunting and moaning licking Peyton's pussy, as Cassandra picked up the pace.

"Oh Nathan, oh fuck, I love your cock, God, I love it, I love it," Cassandra cried out feeling the wave rising again and she was ready to cum at any moment.

Peyton was getting closer to her own climax too, "Oh, fuck, oh, Nathan, oh, oh, oh, I'm going to, ohhhhhhh!" She screamed climaxing and pushing her pelvis hard into his mouth.

"Oh Nathan, fuck, oh, oh, ohhhhhhh!" Cassandra started to cum, and felt Nathan's cock pulsing and then his hot spunk inside her.

The three of them had managed to cum at almost exactly the same time, and they held that tableau for a few moments while the sensations subsided.

Shortly afterwards they lay together in the bed. Cassandra lay between them. Alternately kissing each of them.

"I love you both, so much," she said.

"I love you too," said Peyton.

"And I love you," said Nathan.

"You're both special to me, just remember that."

The other two hugged her tight while she smiled to herself. Somehow it seemed as if they had reconciled and perhaps now things would be better. Hopefully, Nathan would no longer be jealous and had learned his lesson. His bottom had certainly had its hardest spanking yet. She had once more exerted her dominance, and somehow it felt good to her. As much as it had been a punishment, the spanking was arousing and horny too, just as it always was. There was so much more to explore with their newfound menage. How things would pan out, she did not know. Then there was her friend Faith. She felt she would visit her again, and perhaps a cane should be her next purchase. Faith would want to know how things turned out with Nathan. She wanted to tell her about the punishment she had given him. On these and other thoughts, her eyes began to close drifting off into a contented sleep held between her two sleeping loves.

Cassie administers a spanking and a caning (Book Seven)

Cassandra was pleased to find the menage between herself, Nathan and Peyton was working out quite well after all. She and Nathan continued to live together in harmony and Peyton would come to stay with them for some of the week. Cassandra wasn't ready to have Peyton move in and she wasn't sure how she could cope financially with the three of them. In spite of an inauspicious start with Nathan throwing a tantrum, they all had a surprisingly loving relationship. Interestingly, no spanking had been needed for some time. Nathan, it appeared, was on his best behaviour as was Peyton.

Peyton was naturally submissive and liked to be punished. However, Cassandra had had no further occasion to do so. She wasn't going to punish her without any reason at all because this didn't seem fair. As things stood, Cassandra was deeply in love with them both. She found she loved them with a passion, and she knew she couldn't choose between them.

Conversely, Nathan had not developed feelings for Peyton, but he tolerated her presence and he liked fucking her. Cassandra didn't know if Peyton had feelings for him. She had not asked Peyton, although it seemed she doted on Cassandra and only had eyes for her. This pleased Cassandra in a perverse kind of way.

There was no doubt, in Cassandra's mind that she enjoyed giving spankings. It made her horny as hell and wet as anything. There was definitely a sexual element to it, and every spanking had been immediately followed by unbridled fucking with Nathan or Peyton, or both. When Nathan was punished, Peyton had been allowed to watch his punishment which had resulted in three extremely turned-on people in the bedroom.

Apart from her somewhat torrid sex life, Cassandra returned to her normal pursuits, reading, painting and drawing, and gardening. She had enough money to live comfortably in a mortgage-free house, all left to her by her late husband. She kept everything in conservative investments, and was careful with her money. She had no real ambition except to live a fulfilled and happy life. Her burgeoning sexual discovery had preoccupied her of late in any case. She also had a degree but no wish to further her education in that respect and she had no need to find a job. Cassandra also didn't really want children. In many ways, she was still finding herself and her own metier. Her life though, had once more settled down into a routine. However, as with all routines, they never seem to last for long without a hitch.

It happened to be Peyton's afternoon to spend with Cassandra, and Cassandra had been looking forward to it. She wore something close-fitting and sexy without underwear, to allow Peyton easy access. She also spent most days with bare feet or wearing thong sandals. She preferred the sandals with thin thongs and thin soles, they made her own lovely feet look very attractive. There were special pairs which she kept for spanking Peyton and Nathan, pink for Nathan and red for Peyton. She wasn't wearing any sandals that day, and felt very sexy without them.

Cassandra was prepared a little light refreshment for them both, salad, cheeses, smoked salmon, and slices of baguette. After they had eaten, she planned to take Peyton upstairs and fuck her. Then she might spend the afternoon drawing Peyton or reading to her. These were two pastimes they had enjoyed together before.

Peyton arrived by taxi which Cassandra paid for. Peyton didn't have a car, and stayed in a small flat in town. She worked at the shoe shop where Cassandra had bought her first pair of spanking sandals for Nathan's bottom. She and Cassandra had got together not long afterwards, and Peyton had had her first ever spanking from Cassandra at her own request. It had proven to be a watershed for them both. There had been more spankings since. Peyton was blonde and beautiful, with blue eyes, a good figure and pretty feet. Peyton had a heart-shaped face, and classic bow lips. Cassandra, by contrast, had brown eyes, long dark hair, and a slim sexy figure. She was beautiful and sensuous. Her strong sexual nature had certainly come to the fore in recent times.

Cassandra saw the taxi from the window and waited eagerly for Peyton to punch in the keycode and come into the house. Peyton was barely inside the door kicking off her shoes when Cassandra took Peyton into her arms, kissing her before the other could speak.

"Oh, my darling, I'm so pleased to see you," said Cassandra with a smile when their lips parted.

"Yes, I'm pleased to see you," said Peyton although her tone was a little restrained.

There was something in her look which gave Cassandra pause for thought. She had seen it once before when Peyton had gone on Tinder and had sex with a stranger. Cassandra had given her a sound spanking for doing so with her newly purchased hairbrush and extracted a promise from her never to do it again. Cassandra had been very jealous at the time. She would probably still be jealous of Peyton sleeping with another woman and sincerely hoped Peyton hadn't repeated the offence.

"What's wrong?" she asked Peyton without preamble.

Peyton burst into tears at once, "Oh Cassie, Cassie, I've… oh… I've…"

She was choking on the words, and could not get them out. Cassandra was nothing if not compassionate, and she took Peyton into her arms and held her.

"Shh, it's OK, darling it's OK," she said soothingly.

"It's not, it's not, I've done a terrible thing." Peyton's voice was full of emotion.

Cassandra's heart sank. What had Peyton done now? And what was she going to have to punish her for this time?

"Come on," she said, "Come into the living room and tell me."

She led the tearful Peyton into the lounge and sat with her on the sofa.

"Now tell me what's happened? Whatever it is can't be *that* bad," said Cassandra hopefully.

"It is, you're going to hate me for the rest of your life," Peyton announced dramatically sniffing back her tears and speaking in a whisper.

"I won't know unless you do tell me, will I?" said Cassandra reasonably.

Peyton shook her head.

"Come on my darling, just tell me what you've done. I am sure there will be a way to sort it out."

Peyton was a little bit wayward, Cassandra knew it, and perhaps needed more looking after than she had expected. She reasoned with herself that Peyton was probably exaggerating.

Peyton sat miserably for a few moments. Then she got off the sofa and knelt down in front of Cassandra.

"What are you doing?" Cassandra asked her.

"This is the only way I can tell you, because you are my Mistress," said Peyton quietly.

"OK, go on then…"

Cassandra waited, if this was how Peyton wanted to confess whatever it was then she wasn't going to object.

"I…" Peyton stopped and then started again. "I took some money."

"What? Who from?"

This certainly wasn't what Cassandra had expected to hear at all. She thought maybe there was something sexual, but this was different.

"You…" Peyton whispered.

"Me? How?" Cassandra could not keep the shock out of her voice. "No, wait. Start at the beginning why did you need to take it, what did you need it for?"

"To pay my rent…" Peyton told her miserably.

There was evidently more to this story and Cassandra need to find out what it was.

"And why couldn't you pay your rent?" she asked patiently.

"Because… because I lost all my salary."

"How?"

Peyton paused, looked at her a little shamefaced and then spoke very quietly.

"Online gambling."

Another shock for Cassandra, she couldn't imagine what Peyton was doing using an online gambling app. The woman was full of surprises.

"Oh Peyton, why?"

"I don't know." Peyton started crying again. "My friend at the shop showed me and said she'd made loads of money and…"

This started to make sense, but it wasn't all of it, yet. Cassandra pushed for more.

"You were tempted and found you lost it."

"Yes…"

"So, you took my money, how?"

"Your… credit card." Peyton's voice was a little stronger now, as with anyone who has confessed a big sin, the confession becomes easier once the initial burden has been unloaded.

They were getting to the nub of it now, and Cassandra was starting to feel sick.

"My credit card? How?"

"I took it from your purse, and I used it."

"But how? You couldn't have known the pin number?"

The world started to spin. It was hard to believe Peyton had done this to her.

"I didn't need it, I just gave the numbers off the card to the agent, and the code on the back. I said you had told me I could use it."

The spinning stopped, it all made perfect sense. Cassandra could feel anger rising within her. She tried to stop it with an effort.

"I see." Cassandra's face was grim.

"I'm sorry…"

"Why couldn't you just come and ask me for the money, instead of taking my card like a *thief*?" Cassandra couldn't help herself saying the words. They stuck in the throat and she was feeling as if a knife had gone through her heart.

"I... I don't know... I was scared... I was ashamed... I was so ashamed...." Peyton started to cry once more, tears streaming down her face.

Cassandra was lost for words, struggling to articulate her feelings. The betrayal was the worst part and it hurt her. Yet her love for Peyton was so strong, she found it hard to know what to say to her, or even to do about it. Anger mixed together with the hurt, it was not a good combination.

"Cassie, Cassie, please say something, please, I'm sorry, I'm so sorry... ooh hoo hoo, ooh hoo hooo." Peyton was crying loudly now sobbing at Cassandra's silence.

Anger won. Cassandra was now furious. She knew there was one way she could get her feelings out into the open.

She stood up.

"Stay there, Peyton, on your knees. I will be back," she said sharply.

Peyton nodded, and continued to cry. Cassandra went upstairs to her wardrobe, retrieved her riding crop and returned to the living room. Her hand was shaking with the effort to control her ire.

"Peyton, get up and bend over the arm of the sofa," she said without preamble.

Peyton looked at her in shock.

"Now," Cassandra spoke firmly but quietly.

Peyton didn't demur. She got to her feet, went to the left-hand end of the sofa and settled herself over the arm.

Cassandra strode up, and lifted up Peyton's dress. Then she pulled down her knickers baring her bottom. Her movements were fast, almost jerky in her haste to give Peyton the spanking she deserved.

"I don't know what to say to you, Peyton, not at the moment, so I'm going to let the riding crop do the talking for me. It will give you a sense of how I feel about this." Cassandra spoke quietly but Peyton must have picked up her tone.

"Oh Cassie," Peyton cried.

Normally Cassandra would correct her and get her to call her 'Mistress' but she wasn't in the mood. She stood to Peyton's left and lined up the crop on Peyton's bottom. This was going to be a punishment spanking and a hard one at that. She lifted off the crop, and brought it down, snapping it off again immediately. It was hard, she knew it and she was channelling her fury into it, but she couldn't hold it back any longer.

SWISH CRACK "owwwwwwwwwwww"

Peyton howled out as a red mark appeared across her bottom. Cassandra whipped her again in rapid succession, fast hard strokes. Tears sprung to her eyes as she did so.

SWISH CRACK "ooh hoooo"

SWISH CRACK "ohhhhhhh owwwwwwww"

SWISH CRACK "owww howwwwwww"

SWISH CRACK "ohhhhhhhhhhh"

SWISH CRACK "ahhhhhhhhhh"

SWISH CRACK "OWWWWWWWWWW"

SWISH CRACK "OHHHHH OWWW OWWW OWWWW"

Peyton's bottom was turning pink, and it now had several lines on it. Cassandra's initial anger was abating slightly. Cassandra had not been light with the crop and was whipping Peyton's bottom with some force.

"You've upset me greatly, Peyton. I feel completely betrayed by what you've done." Finally, she found her voice.

SWISH CRACK "oooohhhh I'm sorry Cassieeeeee"

SWISH CRACK "owwwwwwwwww"

"It's a bit late for sorry, isn't it? After you took my credit card and spent my money without permission."

The anger in what she said was palpable and matched the strokes she was delivering. Peyton was yelling out at each strike almost at the top of her lungs, but Cassandra didn't care.

SWISH CRACK "owwww ohhhhh please I'm sorry, pleaseeee"

SWISH CRACK "OWWWWWWW"

"How can I trust you? HOW? Hmm, after this? Hmm? You tell me?"

SWISH CRACK "eeeeehhh owwww owwww"

SWISH CRACK "Owwwwww ohhhhhhhh"

SWISH CRACK "ooooh hooo ooooo hoooo"

"I'm sorry Cassie, I'm so sorry, please, please forgive me, I beg you, please…" Peyton was pleading with her as Cassandra laid stroke after stroke across her reddening backside.

"Easy to say isn't it? Harder to do."

SWISH CRACK "nooooooooooo"

SWISH CRACK "OW OW OW OW OW OW"

SWISH CRACK "OWWWWWWWWWWWW"

Cassandra stopped, and tossed the crop aside. It wasn't really doing it for her at all. Peyton's bottom was starting to turn very red but even so, she didn't find it satisfying. Her anger had abated somewhat, and she realised there was a massive trust issue which she needed to resolve.

"Stand up," she said to Peyton.

Peyton did so and stood there with silent tears streaming down her face.

"We are going to have some lunch, and then I'm going to decide what to do."

"I'm not hungry," said Peyton sniffing back her tears.

Cassandra was in the mood to be conciliatory.

"You will come and eat with me missy, or I'm going to take my sandal and spank your bare bottom until you can't sit down for a week," said Cassandra direfully. "Is that what you want?"

Peyton shook her head.

"Come on then."

They sat opposite each other in the dining room. Cassandra found she had worked up quite an appetite, but Peyton picked at her food. Cassandra had to admonish her quite a few times to make her eat. Cassandra didn't like waste, and as she had made the lunch, she wanted to eat it. Although, the circumstances were not what she had envisaged. The food did much to restore her senses, and she now looked at Peyton with a considerable amount of love in her heart.

"What am I going to do with you, Peyton?" she said at length with a sigh.

Peyton regarded her dumbly. Cassandra had come to decision, she needed to talk to someone, and she knew exactly who.

"Look, I'm going to take you home now, there's someone I have to see, and then…"

"Noooo!" Peyton almost screamed it out dropping once more to her knees, "Please noooooo, please Cassie, no, please, please, please…."

"It's only for a little while, don't be silly," said Cassandra coming around to try and pull her up. Peyton, however, wouldn't budge.

"No, please, please please don't dump me, please, please Cassie, please, I'll do anything, anything, please, please don't dump me."

Cassandra got down on her knees herself, "I'm not going to dump you, silly, I just want you to stay home for an hour or two."

"Please, Cassie, please, please…"

Peyton looked so terrified that Cassandra relented. She felt unable to leave Peyton alone at the house. She simply had lost her trust for the moment. However, she relented on taking her home.

"OK, well I have to go somewhere, you'll have to come with me and wait in the car then. I might be a while."

"OK." Peyton nodded vigorously.

Cassandra sighed again.

***

Not long after, she pulled her four by four up near the little row of shops where her friend Faith plied antiques in one of the premises. She had bought the hairbrush she used for spanking from Faith, the owner, and also discovered, in the process of developing a friendship with her, that Faith was a professional dominatrix.

The second time she had met with Faith, she had asked Faith to give her a caning, to atone for what she felt was her own part in Nathan's bad behaviour over Peyton. Faith had obliged. Now Faith felt like a friend, a confidante and she needed to talk to her about this latest dilemma. Faith was older, perhaps in her fifties, wiser and more worldly than Cassandra.

Before leaving home, Cassandra made sure Peyton had been to the loo. She knew she might need to spend a little while with Faith and made sure she saw to Peyton's needs. She had taken a bottle of water into the car, and some snacks, and a blanket.

"I'm going into that shop. If you need me urgently just call me, OK? I'll lock the car, but you can get out if you need to. I might be a while. I'm going to see Faith, remember, the one who owns the shop, to talk things through."

Peyton nodded. She knew about the caning and she knew about Faith. She just accepted it, climbed into the back, lay down on the back seat and lay down pulling the blanket over herself. Peyton put her thumb in her mouth and started to suck it like a little girl. Cassandra observed this affectionately. She couldn't hate Peyton for what she had done, but she was still too angry about it inside. Faith would help her, perhaps, to see some common sense.

"See you later," said Cassandra as Peyton closed her eyes. Sleep was probably best for her, Cassandra mused, as she locked the car. Peyton wouldn't be visible as the four by four had tinted windows, so Cassandra felt she would be safe enough. Cassandra walked over the road to Faith's shop and went inside.

The shop was one of those antique shops full of interesting things, furniture and knickknacks. It was a place one could browse for hours, but Cassandra wasn't interested in browsing today. Faith was seated at her desk writing in a ledger. She had silver hair, kind eyes, and was devastatingly attractive. She was wearing a loose dress as usual, and thong sandals. Faith had pretty feet. Something Cassandra had noticed before. In her mind, she had kissed Faith's feet more than once.

"Cassie, how lovely to see you," Faith said looking up.

"Hi, Faith, have you got time… to talk."

Faith frowned and could tell her friend was troubled. She smiled and said in a voice loaded with affection, "Of course, my love, I've always got time for you."

She locked the shop door, put the closed sign on it, and led Cassie into her kitchen. The kitchen was an eclectic mix of hand-built pine units, with colourful tiles and had a comfortable hippy-like feel about it. Just as she always did, Faith made them some tea, put some slices of homemade fruit cake on a plate and then sat down at the table next to Cassandra.

"Now we are comfortable, what's up?"

"It's Peyton," said Cassandra taking a sip of her tea.

"Tell me the whole."

When Cassandra had finished, Faith regarded her shrewdly. She sipped her tea and took a slice of cake.

"Have you never found yourself in dire straits financially?" Faith asked her with a smile.

"No, no I guess not. I was always provided for by my husband and he left me independently wealthy, so I don't need to work." Cassandra shrugged.

"Precisely, so you haven't the experience to understand the desperate straits people find themselves in."

This hit home to Cassandra at once. Faith had the knack of stating the obvious when Cassandra couldn't see it.

"Oh, shit, I've been too hard on her, haven't I?"

"I wouldn't say *that* exactly. Taking your money without permission, using your credit card, those are not acceptable of course. But sometimes people do things because they are driven to it and can find no way out. If you've never been in that position you won't understand."

Cassandra did understand in a way. She had been driven to spank Nathan's bottom and this was how the whole thing had started. But for that, she would probably never have met Peyton at all. There were, after all, consequences to every action. She still couldn't let go of the issue which was upsetting her, that Peyton had not trusted her enough to ask for help. It hurt her deeply because she felt as if Peyton didn't love her enough.

"But she could have asked me. I would have paid it for her, I would have helped her."

Faith cocked a sympathetic eyebrow.

"Perhaps she was too proud. She didn't want you to see how she'd messed up and then she messed up some more."

This also made sense to Cassandra but there was still more to say.

"I don't understand how she thought I would not discover it, I'm very meticulous with everything."

"Panic, fear, desperation. These make unwelcome bedfellows and drive us to acts we couldn't have imagined possible."

Cassandra thought for a long moment sipping her tea. This echoed what she had been thinking earlier.

"That's true, after all, I would never have imagined spanking Nathan. He drove me to it."

"Well, there we are."

"I love Peyton so much. I felt betrayed. I was very hurt. And now I'm afraid she doesn't love me enough to trust me with her problems."

Faith was so easy to talk to. Cassandra could let out her deepest fears without being afraid herself, of being judged. Faith always looked at her with affection, and she felt so easy to be with, so warm and nonjudgmental.

"Of course, you were. I'm sure Peyton loves you very much, or she wouldn't have begged you not to take her home. That being said, Peyton must be punished, for her own good."

Faith was still a dominatrix at heart, and a disciplinarian still thinks like one.

"But I already spanked her with the riding crop."

Faith shook her head, as if the riding crop spanking was a mere bagatelle.

"She needs a salutary lesson. I assume it's why you came?"

Cassandra sighed. "Yes, to buy a cane. It's what I was thinking but maybe I should…"

Faith cut her off, and said, "I know, and I've picked one out for you. I should probably show you how to use it or explain it at least."

"How did you?" Cassandra regarded Faith as if she had magical powers.

"I knew after your own caning that you would be back one day to get one of your own." Faith laughed.

"Thank you, you're like a fairy godmother."

"That's a nice compliment, but don't compare me to your mother, darling, or anyone else related to you. It doesn't gel with what I'd dearly love to do to you, how much I want to kiss your beautiful lips… and other things." Faith spoke softly, suddenly and with a longing in her eyes which she must have concealed so well all of this time.

Cassandra's eyes opened wide at this unexpected revelation.

"I'm not a saint, you know. Nor am I immune to the charms of such a beautiful woman as yourself. Is that too forward of me?"

"No, but… oh, Faith… I…"

"It's OK, I just wanted you to know. I'll always be your friend, but God, Cassie, I want to fuck you so badly. I'm sorry, I couldn't stop myself from telling you anymore. See, that's exactly what I was saying about desperation."

Cassandra was silent for a moment. There was anxiety in Faith's expression where she had previously seemed so calm and composed.

"I do want to fuck you too, Faith. I mean, I've wanted to even the last time when you caned me." It seemed time to admit to her own desires since they were being so honest.

"I know, but it wasn't the right time, and maybe now wasn't the right time to say anything."

"No, it was, it is, I just… it's just I feel this thing with Peyton is my fault as well, for not being attentive enough to her. I feel bad. I feel as if I need…"

"You also want atonement?" Faith cut across her thought. It seemed to have become their code word for punishment.

"Damn, why are you so perspicacious?"

"I find you easy to read, my dear."

"OK, yes, I do, and I feel as if I should, don't you?"

Faith laughed.

"Don't look at me, it's your choice. I'm happy to oblige you if you want it. I think you really do want it, don't you? If it makes you feel better… I enjoyed it last time."

"OK, yes. How much?" Cassandra felt she should ask this because Faith usually charged for her services. She hadn't asked for anything from Cassandra, however.

Faith shook her head. "Oh, nothing for you. I will do it for you any time, for the love of it, my sweet. What would you like, another caning?"

Cassandra thought about this and felt she wanted something more intimate.

"No, perhaps I should go over your knee."

"I have the perfect thing."

Faith got up from her chair and went out of the room. She returned with a large solid looking wooden hairbrush, with an oval head.

"This should do nicely."

Cassandra eyed with misgivings. She had delivered two spankings herself with a hairbrush and she was certain it was going to hurt.

"OK."

"Last chance to change your mind."

Cassandra steeled herself, something within her wanted to feel that brush on her backside.

"No, I want a spanking."

"Very well, we'll go into my other sitting room."

She followed Faith into the 'other' room. Faith took off her sandals and walked in barefoot. Cassandra looked at her pretty feet liking them even more. She removed her own sandals too. They entered a space which was nicely furnished but less cluttered. There was a wooden chair without arms in the middle of the floor.

"That's my spanking chair," said Faith. "It gets a lot of use. Now, you can take off your clothes."

"OK, but…"

Cassandra was reluctant but she had required the same of Peyton and Nathan.

"Come on, my sweet. It's to make you feel vulnerable, you know that." Faith's voice was coaxing, soothing.

"Sure, OK."

Cassandra removed her clothing. Faith looked her over appreciatively and then took off her dress and undergarments. Cassandra was surprised to see Faith was in very good shape underneath, with firm skin and well proportioned. She was incredibly beautiful and desirable. There was something of an undercurrent between them, an unspoken desire. Although in truth both of them had now articulated it in no uncertain terms.

"So much better to spank naked I find," Faith laughed. "Don't be surprised by my looks. I do keep myself well. I do yoga every day."

"You're gorgeous, beautiful. Maybe I should start doing yoga myself," Cassandra observed.

"Thank you for the compliment." Faith sat down in the chair. "You should give yoga a try, but for now, you need to get over my knee, young lady."

Cassandra settled herself across Faith's lap and found it quite comforting. The naked flesh under her thighs sent a thrill through her. She felt the smooth back of the brush on her bottom.

"You've got a beautiful bottom, for sure, it's almost a shame to spank it. I said almost." Faith let out a low laugh. "Now this is going to hurt, my girl. I don't do spankings which don't hurt. But as we both know, you've been naughty, and this is what naughty girls get."

The brush lifted off and snapped down onto Cassandra's buttock cheek. It lifted off again and snapped down on the other.

SMACK SMACK

Cassandra felt the harsh sting of the brush light a little fire in her cheeks. She realised it was going to be painful.

"Oh God," she gasped.

"A bit more than you expected was it? Well, it always is the first time."

The brush was back against her skin. The smoothness of the wood felt nice but not once it started spanking. It lifted off once more, and again smacked down on alternate cheeks. These were just as hard as the first two.

SMACK SMACK

"Jesus wept."

Faith chuckled. "He probably did, my dear, but you are here to be properly punished and I am going to see that you get a sound spanking."

From this point the spanking took on a familiar rhythm, one Cassandra had used herself. Hard smacks timed to allow the sting to bite before giving her another. It was tougher than she thought. The stinging wasn't unbearable, but it wasn't pleasant either. She could not help shouting out each time the brush made contact.

SMACK "Owwww" SMACK "Oh God" SMACK "oooooh" SMACK "Fuckkkk"

"This is what you wanted remember? When your bottom begins to smart as it surely will, you'll perhaps be sorry you asked me to spank you, but it's too late now."

SMACK "ohhhhhh" SMACK "Ahhhhh" SMACK "shittttt" SMACK "Fuck fuck fuck"

It certainly was smarting. Cassandra could feel it. It was on fire in fact, and she knew the spanking had only just begun.

"You know I don't always like spanking bottoms but yours is delightful, so spankable. I love it," said Faith whimsically.

SMACK "OWWW" SMACK "shit" SMACK "fuck oh God" SMACK "Oh God God God"

SMACK "oh oww oww owww" SMACK "nooo ow that hurts" SMACK "OWWWWW" SMACK "Fuckkkkkkk"

"It's starting to get nice and red, just the way it needs to."

Faith liked to give her a commentary as she continued the spanking unabated.

SMACK "ow howwwww" SMACK "shit oh fuck" SMACK "oh fuck" SMACK "ahhh fuckkkkk"

SMACK "oh oh oh oh oh" SMACK "My God" SMACK "bloody hellfire" SMACK "Ahhhhh"

SMACK "oh fuck why did I ask you to" SMACK "oh Jesus shit shit" SMACK "oh no fuck fuck fuck" SMACK "owwwww owwwww owwww"

Cassandra certainly wasn't making up the reactions. Her bottom was genuinely stinging like a bees' nest and then some. She wondered how long the spanking would continue but knowing Faith it probably would not be short.

"You really need to be more empathic, hmm. This spanking will help you to get there."

SMACK "oh howww" SMACK "how will itttt" SMACK "owwwww" SMACK "fuckkkkk"

SMACK "no oh God" SMACK "my God Faith" SMACK "oh pleaseeee" SMACK "Faithhhhh"

"It will teach you not to be such a selfish stuck up little bitch. When you are being a stuck up cow next time, you'll remember this hairbrush spanking and that will encourage you to stop."

SMACK "Owww" SMACK "yes oh yeessss" SMACK "Ahhh" SMACK "Please Faith please owwww"

SMACK "God it hurts" SMACK "ahhhhh" SMACK "fuckkkk" SMACK "oh God, fuck fuck it"

Cassandra's bottom was reaching fever pitch. Faith spanked hard and she didn't let up. It was starting to pulse and throb. She didn't know how much longer she could stand Faith's relentless onslaught.

"Hopefully this spanking will set you on the road to being more mindful of the feelings of others."

SMACK "I willl" SMACK "Oh God please" SMACK "yes I will I willl" SMACK "oww howww"

SMACK "nooo oh my Godddd" SMACK "ohhhhhh" SMACK "ow oh fuck owww" SMACK "OWWWWWW"

Cassandra wanted Faith to stop and perversely she wanted to be pushed over the edge. Faith seemed determined on the latter course.

"Privilege SMACK doesn't SMACK put you SMACK above SMACK a good spanking SMACK and now SMACK you are getting one SMACK."

"Owww oh owwww owwwww."

"Naughty girl."

SMACK "OWWWW" SMACK "Ohhhhhh"

"You naughty naughty girl."

SMACK "OHHHHH" SMACK "OH NOOOO"

The edge was certainly close, but Faith kept spanking.

"You SMACK will SMACK learn SMACK humility SMACK empathy SMACK understanding SMACK"

SMACK "OWWWWWW" SMACK "OOOOH OWWWWW"

SMACK "OHHHHHH" SMACK "OH OH OW OW OW OW"

SMACK "AHHHHHH" SMACK "NOOOOOOO"

SMACK "OH GOD I'M GOING TO" SMACK "CRYYY OOOH HOOOOOOO"

Like a dam overflowing Cassandra burst into tears. Once more she felt the pain and hurt of a spanking flowing through her. She started to cry in earnest.

"Oh owwww owwww, ohhh ooh hoo ooh hoo hoo ooh hoo hoo hoo"

Faith stopped spanking her and began to lightly soothe her back, stroking her while her shoulders shook. Cassandra didn't really know why she was crying except that it hurt and somehow there was a catharsis from it. After a little while, she felt calmer although her bottom was stinging like mad.

"What a red, red bottom, so red," Faith whispered. "I love it so much, your bottom. You beautiful girl. Why don't you kiss me now, now you've learned your lesson?"

A wave of passion came over Cassandra, she sat up tearfully and knelt between Faith's knees. Her lips found Faith's and they were surprisingly soft and gentle. The two of them locked together in a deep kiss, and Cassandra felt transported, just as she did with Nathan and Peyton. The kiss became more intense and then Cassandra pulled away. Her lips travelled to Faith's firm breasts, and she licked and teased each nipple to hardness.

"Oh, oh, fuck, oh, you've no idea how much I've wanted that, God yes, yes, oh yes," Faith breathed.

Cassandra went lower and Faith eased forward to give her easy access to her pussy. Cassandra's tongue found the sweet enclave and she began to lap gently at first.

"Oh fuck, fuck, oh my God, fuck." Faith leant back and closed her eyes, easing her pelvis further forward still.

Cassandra's tongue found her clit and she pushed two fingers up inside her.

"Oh my goddddd, you're so good at thattt, oh, oh, ow, oh, oh, oh, oh, fuck ohhhhhhhhhhhhhhhhh." Faith climaxed quite easily and sighed with pleasure as her body shuddered with the orgasm.

"Oh Cassie, my God, I never thought. I dreamed of you doing *that* but God, that was so good, so fucking good," she whispered smiling down at Cassandra.

Cassandra stood up and straddled Faith's legs, facing outwards. Faith's hand moved around to finger Cassandra's dripping wet pussy.

"Oh, God, fuck, oh my, fuck, oh Faith, Faith, Faith, oh faster, faster, oh, yes, please, that's, ohhhhhh, ahhhhhh, oohhhhhhhhhhh!" The wave rushed through Cassandra under Faith's ministrations. The woman turned her on so much it was uncanny, and she also climaxed rapidly. She turned around still cumming and kissed Faith hard and with so much passion.

"Oh my God, I never expected, oh God, you've… oh…" Faith subsided under the onslaught of kisses.

She slipped off Faith and the two of them went over to the sofa and sat together naked kissing.

"You know, I could keep you here all night, if you'd do that again for me," said Faith softly.

"I would like to stay with you," Cassandra whispered softly. "But I have Peyton in the car."

"I know, and you should go and take your cane."

However, feelings were rising in Cassandra's breast which she felt the need to articulate.

"Faith… I… I'm beginning to care for you, and I don't understand it, how can I care for three people?"

"Hush, darling. This is something for another time. It's possible for special people like yourself. The thing is I'm starting to care for you, and if I'm honest I did from the moment you walked in. It is very much against my better nature to form attachments, especially at my age, but I have."

"What shall we do?" Cassandra wondered.

"Why nothing, see where it leads, I would, and I'd like to. In the meantime, put your clothes on."

Cassandra got dressed, and so did Faith. They returned to the shop and Faith retrieved a wicked-looking crook handle school cane from a place she had put it.

"Here you are, it's a nice whippy one just for you," Faith smiled.

"Is there any trick, you know, to using it?"

"Well, a spanking first helps to stop too much bruising. Make sure you keep the tip in the centre of the far buttock to stop it from wrapping around. Let each stroke leave an impression before the next, that's far the most effective. Otherwise, you'll find out when you try it out on Peyton."

"Yes," Cassandra smiled. "How much do I owe you?"

"Oh, nothing, consider it paid. It's a present. You let me spank your beautiful bottom that is payment enough."

"Thank you."

"You are welcome," said Faith, "How's your bottom now?"

"It's sore and red I expect."

"As it should be, now behave unless you want another spanking."

"I'll try," Cassandra gave her a loving smile. She kissed Faith goodbye and then Faith let her out of the shop.

She returned to the car and found Peyton still asleep in the back covered with the blanket. She woke up when Cassandra opened the back door and looked at Cassandra wide-eyed.

"It's OK, darling, I'm back now," said Cassandra softly.

"You were away a long time."

"Yes, I know, sorry, I did tell you, I had some things to sort out, we're going home now though."

Cassandra felt it wasn't the time to tell Peyton about her spanking. She would one day but not that day.

"OK," Peyton gave her a tremulous smile and scrambled back into the front. Cassandra placed the cane on the backseat, shut the door and got into the driver's seat.

"What's that?" Peyton asked her glancing at the cane, although it was perfectly obvious.

"It's for your bottom," said Cassandra gently, but not unkindly. "You'll be getting a caning tomorrow."

Peyton's eyes filled with tears and she started to cry.

"Oh, come here, my love, come here." Cassandra leaned and awkwardly tried to comfort Peyton. "Darling, darling, I love you, I want you to know that. Whatever you've done." Cassandra kissed her and Peyton continued to cry. "What's wrong? Why are you crying? Is it because of what I just said?"

"No, not really," said Peyton through her tears. "It's just that, I've been so bad, and I do deserve the cane. I'm just glad you've got it."

"Then why are you crying, silly girl?" Cassandra chided her gently.

"I don't know. I think it's because I thought you didn't love me anymore, and now I've seen the cane I know you do."

Cassandra tried not to laugh, but to her, this made a lot of sense. Peyton wanted and needed to be punished. So, in a way, this was part of Cassandra's expression of love for her. To fulfil that need.

"Yes, I do love you, very much, but I really do have to punish you for your behaviour, you do understand, don't you?" Cassandra was worried now. In case it was too harsh. She bore in mind Faith's lesson and she wanted to be sure she was doing the right thing.

"Yes, and I want you to. I deserve it. I need to be punished very severely," said Peyton fiercely.

"Well, you will be." Cassandra smiled at her. "The cane is a severe punishment as you will soon find out."

Peyton sniffed a little and stopped crying. Cassandra kissed her, feeling her beautiful soft lips and was glad she wouldn't have to stop seeing Peyton. She couldn't have borne that at all.

"I love you, Peyton. I'm ready to forgive you and after your caning tomorrow we will put it all behind us."

"Yes, yes we will."

"Good, girl. We'll go home. But you must sleep in the spare bedroom tonight, as part of your punishment."

Peyton's face fell ludicrously and Cassandra nearly relented, but she felt it to be necessary.

"Will you... will you stay with me a little when I go to bed?" Peyton asked her.

"Yes, I will, my pet, and you can stay the next night with me and Nathan, OK?"

Peyton nodded eagerly at this.

"Alright then, let's go home. Have some dinner, hmm?"

As it turned out, Nathan rang Cassandra and asked if she minded him having a boys' night to play computer games. Under the circumstances, which she did not relate to her boyfriend, Cassandra didn't mind, and Peyton spent the night with her after all, snuggled up in her arms which made them both very happy. As Peyton fell asleep, Cassandra felt a fierce rush of love for this tangled young woman. She had perhaps neglected her needs a little too much, and she probably needed to focus on giving her weekly spankings for a while. It might help to keep Peyton on track. The book of Peyton's Infractions had not been used and it was high time she began to do so. As Cassandra closed her eyes, she wondered if what Peyton had done was subconsciously a way of getting punished. It seemed entirely possible though sleep soon claimed her too and the thought slipped away for the moment.

***

The following morning, at breakfast, Cassandra said, "Shouldn't you be going to work, my darling?"

"I phoned in sick," Peyton replied biting into her bacon and eggs.

"What am I going to do with you, my love?" Cassandra smiled.

"Punish me?" Peyton replied sipping her coffee.

"Yes, but more than that, I can see I need to help you to sort out your life. Obviously, without some kind of supervision, you end up going off the rails."

"I'm sorry, I'm such a mess, I know I am, you shouldn't have become involved with me." Peyton's eyes filled with tears.

"Stop it," Cassandra said gently. "Don't put yourself down like that. I love you and because I'm in love with you, I can't help but be responsible for you. I've some ideas about how we can go forward, if you want to hear them?"

Peyton nodded eagerly.

"Firstly, I am going to be keeping a closer eye on your behaviour and you will be getting weekly spankings if it's not up to scratch. I will be writing anything you do which is naughty in the book."

"What would be naughty?" Peyton asked her.

"Being late for work, not *going* to work without a good reason. Doing silly things online. Irresponsible behaviour and more," Cassandra said implacably.

Peyton nodded slowly.

"Secondly, after let's say a month or maybe less, when I decide, if you can prove yourself to become more responsible then I will let you come and have a room here with us. You will have to contribute to the living expenses, and I'll have to talk to Nathan."

"Oh Cassie, Cassie, oh really?" squealed Peyton in delight.

"Yes, really, I've been thinking about it for a while. I can't afford to keep all of us, you will have to work and earn your keep," Cassandra said firmly, but she was smiling.

"Thank you, I will, I promise, I promise I will do better."

"Yes, you will my darling, because if you get yourself into financial problems again you will be over my knee for the hairbrush, is that understood?"

"Yes, yes, oh I'm so happy, so happy," Peyton clapped her hands.

"I'm glad." Cassandra reached out and took her hand. This last incident had made her arrive at a decision and it had been a tough one for her. Love, she realised, comes with responsibility. She was growing up herself, into a more mature and wiser woman.

Peyton looked so pleased, that Cassandra didn't like to bring her back down to earth but she had to.

"Let's finish our breakfast, maybe do some gardening. We'll have lunch, and then it's going to be time for your caning."

Peyton's face fell for a moment, but then she smiled again. It seemed even that could not place a damper on her spirits. Cassandra thought in a way, perhaps Peyton would be looking forward to the punishment she evidently craved.

The morning passed pleasantly enough. The weather was clement and the two of them spent a happy couple of hours in the garden, weeding and planting. Cassandra was extending her vegetable plot at the back of the house, as she liked fresh herbs, salads and vegetables. She and Peyton worked barefoot because Cassandra liked to feel the earth under her feet. If she was doing heavy work, then she would wear shoes or boots to protect herself. They had a shower together but without sex for a change, and then lunch consisting of a Caesar salad with chicken, and hot buttered toast. Once all the dishes were put away, Cassandra said, "It's time to go upstairs, darling."

Peyton nodded and followed Cassandra to the bedroom. Outside the door, Cassandra said softly, "Once inside I'm your Mistress and you will obey me, remember?"

"Yes, Mistress," said Peyton at once becoming submissive, a role into which she seemed to slip so easily.

Cassandra opened the door, and the two of them entered. She closed it behind them.

"Take off your clothes. Then I want you to stand in the corner and face the wall," she said to Peyton.

Peyton removed her clothing and did as she was told without demur.

Once Peyton was in the corner, Cassandra removed her own clothing and went to the wardrobe. She selected a red thong sandal with a thin sole which was one of the sandals she used for spanking Peyton. She also took out the cane which was hanging by its crook handle. Cassandra placed these on the bed, and then took her wooden chair from the dressing table, and placed it in the centre of the room.

Cassandra had decided to spank naked. She wanted to try it after Faith had been naked when spanking her. Although Cassandra liked her corset and red spanking dress this seemed somehow freer and more fitting. She picked up the sandal and resumed her seat.

"Turn around, Peyton," she said.

Peyton's eyes widened a little when she saw Cassandra naked, holding the sandal in her right hand and tapping the sole gently in her left palm. Cassandra remembered what she had done on Peyton's previous spankings.

"On your knees, Peyton and then you can crawl here like the submissive little bitch you are."

Somehow another persona took over Cassandra when she became the Mistress. Things came out of her mouth which she wouldn't normally say. By now she was used to it and went with the flow.

Peyton dropped to her knees, then made her way slowly to Cassandra. She knelt in front of her and waited for instructions.

"Peyton, you've been very badly behaved. You did something which was almost unforgivable by using my credit card without permission. You spent my money without asking. I would have helped you if you had only told me. You also wasted your own money on online gambling. That was irresponsible. I do forgive you Peyton and I'm glad you had the courage to tell me. But you are going to receive a spanking and a caning as a punishment. You need to learn never to do anything like this again," said Cassandra in quite severe tones.

"Yes, Mistress," Peyton said meekly.

"I love you, Peyton and it's because I love you that I'm going to make sure I teach you how to behave from now on."

"Yes, Mistress."

"Good, now get over my knee for your spanking."

Peyton laid herself over Cassandra's knees in a now familiar position and settled herself comfortably. Cassandra placed the sole of the sandal against Peyton's buttock cheek.

"I was very upset with you Peyton."

SMACK SMACK SMACK SMACK

Four spanks alternating cheeks and lifting off the sandal right away. Four red marks sprung up on Peyton's creamy backside.

"Owww, oh owwwww," Peyton cried out at once.

Cassandra was used to Peyton's very vocal responses to spankings and paid it little mind.

"You SMACK will SMACK never SMACK take SMACK my credit card SMACK again SMACK or use it SMACK without asking SMACK."

"Ooh hoo, no, no I'm sorry, I won't, owww owww owwww."

Cassandra smiled wryly.

"Not as sorry as you going to be, my girl, not by a long chalk."

SMACK "Owwww" SMACK "ooo hooo" SMACK "Oh Mistressss" SMACK "OWWW"

SMACK "Noooo" SMACK "ow ow ow ow" SMACK "oooh hoooo" SMACK "OHHHHH"

Cassandra settled the rhythm a bit, letting each spank sink in before delivering the next one. Peyton's bottom began to turn a nice shade of pink. Her skin was quite creamy and light, and blushed easily.

"You SMACK will SMACK tell me SMACK the truth SMACK in future SMACK"

"Owwwww owwww I will I promise."

"And." Cassandra continued, "You will not do any online gambling ever again."

SMACK "OOOOHHH" SMACK "AHHHHH" SMACK "OW OW OW OW" SMACK "Noooooooo"

SMACK "I wontttttttt" SMACK "Please nooooo" SMACK "OWWWWW" SMACK "Mistresss owwwwwwww"

"Do SMACK you SMACK understand SMACK you SMACK little SMACK bitch SMACK"

This last part came from somewhere deep inside Cassandra's psyche.

"Oooooo hoooo, no I won't, I won't I promise, owwwwwwww"

"Good girl, now you're learning."

SMACK "owwwwww" SMACK "wooo hoooo" SMACK "oooohhhh" SMACK "it hurtssss"

SMACK "oooooohhhh" SMACK "oh ow ow ow" SMACK "ahhhhhh" SMACK "owwww so hardddd"

SMACK "ooooooo" SMACK "nooooo" SMACK "ow howwwwwww" SMACK "wowwww owww owww"

SMACK "OWWWWW" SMACK "OW OW OWWWW" SMACK "AHHHHH" SMACK "OH OW OW OH OWWW"

Cassandra had now delivered over fifty stinging spanks to Peyton's bottom which had taken on quite a nice crimson hue. She liked it when it turned so red, and it certainly was making her wet. As she was also going to cane Peyton, she couldn't do too many more spanks. She could also tell Peyton was on the verge of tears. On impulse, she decided it was enough.

"Alright, Peyton, you can stand up and get ready for the second part of your punishment."

Peyton got off her lap and stood in front of her. Cassandra rose to her feet, dropped the sandal to the floor and went over the get the cane. This would be the first time she had used one, but she had learned a few things from Faith already.

She picked it up and swished it experimentally. It made a nice noise. Then she began to flex it while walking closer to Peyton.

"You know why you are getting the cane, don't you? Because what you did was very unacceptable and I need to make sure you understand that, and that you never do it again."

"Yes, Mistress," Peyton whispered eyeing the cane with apprehension.

"This is going to hurt, Peyton, make no mistake, and it's meant to. You might then understand the hurt you gave to me, in my heart, by what you did." Cassandra said quietly.

Peyton paled slightly at this which made Cassandra's heart go out to her. She moved closer dropping her arm with the cane, so she could stand almost touching Peyton with her body.

"Never think I don't love you. I'm caning you because I do love you, and because you need it. But I love you so much, don't forget that."

"I won't, Mistress," Peyton's eyes were moist. "And I want you to cane me, hard, Mistress, don't spare me."

"I don't intend to, darling, your bottom is going to feel the full force of my disappointment."

Peyton bit her lip and nodded.

"Bend over and put your hands on the seat of the chair. Don't you dare move from that position until I say you can," said Cassandra softly standing aside.

Peyton did as she was told, and once she was in place, Cassandra moved over to Peyton's left side. She placed the cane across the middle of Peyton's buttocks, taking care to centre the end on the furthest buttock as she had been instructed by Faith.

Cassandra lifted the cane and tapped it lightly to get her aim. Then she pulled it back a little way, and snapped it forward with her wrist until it made contact, then lifted it off again at once.

SWISH CRACK

There was a moment when Peyton did nothing and Cassandra knew this was just before the stroke would register, then a sudden rush of pain would go through Peyton's bottom.

Peyton screamed.

"Owwwwwwwwwwwwwwww"

"I told you, it would hurt, Peyton," said Cassandra bring back the cane again.

SWISH CRACK

"Oh owwww owwww owwwwww"

Again, the delayed reaction.

Peyton's bottom had two red stripes which were slightly raised where the cane had made contact. Cassandra was concentrating on where to strike and how hard. So far, she hadn't swung it full force.

"Now perhaps you will understand exactly how much you have hurt me."

SWISH CRACK

"oooohhhhh hooooooo owwwwww"

"I will not tolerate this from you from now on."

SWISH CRACK

"Oooh hoooo owwww oh owwwwwww"

Peyton's reactions to the caning were, as Cassandra expected, in line with her own experience. It wasn't a pleasant experience, but it certainly got the message across. Cassandra picked her target each time trying to lay the stripes evenly along her bottom.

"You will never ever go on an online gambling app again."

SWISH CRACK

"Owwww noooo noooo I won't owww oh owwww"

"Do I make myself clear?"

SWISH CRACK

"OWWWWW oh oowwwwwwww owwww yessss owwwww."

Peyton's bottom was turning even redder, with raised red stripes.

"You will tell me, in future, if you have money problems."

SWISH CRACK

"owwww ohhhh owww owww Mistress yessss owwwwwwww"

"You've been naughty."

SWISH CRACK

"owwwwwwwwwwwwwww ohhhhhhhh God owwwwwww"

"Deceitful."

SWISH CRACK

"Ooooowwwww owwww owwww owwwwww"

"Dishonest."

SWISH CRACK

"Oh owwww owwww owwww please owwww owwww owwwww"

"I'm not having it."

SWISH CRACK

"owww wowowowowowow ooh hooo owwww ohhhhh owwwww"

Peyton's cries were getting louder with each stroke. She didn't have a high tolerance for pain, Cassandra knew, but this by no means made her hold back.

"That's why you are receiving a sound caning."

SWISH CRACK

"ohhhhhhhhhhhh owwww owww owww owww oww owww owwwwwww"

"And why."

SWISH CRACK

"owwww oh owwwwwwww owwwwwwwww"

"You will get another one if you ever do it again!"

"Owwww oh owwww noooo I won't please owwww owww owwwwww"

Cassandra paused she could feel Peyton was at the tipping point, and was probably going to burst into floods of tears. This was all to the good in Cassandra's eyes, it meant a lesson learned.

"Do you promise never to do online gambling again?"

SWISH CRACK

"Owwww howwww yesss yesss I promissseee Mistresss I dooo I dooooo"

"And do you promise never ever to use my cards without asking first?"

SWISH CRACK

"Owww howwww yesss I dooo I really dooooo ooo hoo ooo hooooo"

"You will never deceive me or conceal anything from me again, do you promise?"

SWISH CRACK

"Owwww hooooooooo ooooo hoooooo yes I promisssss I promissssss"

Cassandra pursed her lips, she wanted to stop but she felt she had to push the lesson home.

"And I promise you, an even harder longer caning if you break your promises."

SWISH CRACK

"Owwwww hoooo oooh hooo ooohhh hoooo"

Peyton was starting to cry, and Cassandra knew she had to end it. She wanted to give Peyton six of the best to finish but she felt it would be too much and opted instead for a lesser amount.

"Three of the best, Peyton and then it's over."

"Oooh hooo ooooh hooooo," Peyton cried.

Cassandra ignored her. She brought back the cane further and decided to make the last three really count. They would be the hardest yet.

"One" SWISH CRACK

"Oooooooohh hooooooooooooooooo owwwwwwwwwwwww"

"Two" SWISH CRACKKK

"Owwwwwwwwww oooo hoooo ooooo hoooo oooo hoooooo"

"Three" SWISH CRACKKKKKK

"OOWWWWWWWWWWWWWWWWWW WWW OOOOH HOOO OH OH OH MY BOTTOMMMMM"

Peyton burst into a fit of sobbing, but she didn't move from her position.

"Ooo hooo ooo hooo ooo hoooo ooo hooo."

Cassandra let her cry it out for a bit tossing the cane aside. Then she said, "Get up, darling, it's over now, it's finished."

Peyton's bottom had a nice series of parallel lines across it, and it was a deep shade of scarlet which was probably from the combined spanking and a caning. Cassandra was sure it must sting or even throb.

Peyton stood up and Cassandra took her into her arms.

"Hush, my darling, hush, it's all over now. It's all finished. I love you. I love you so much," she said in soothing tones while Peyton sobbed into her shoulder.

"Oh Cassie, it's so sore, my bottom is so sore," Peyton cried in halting tones.

"I know, my darling, I know."

After a few more moments, Peyton sniffed and seemed to recover. Then all of a sudden, her mouth was seeking Cassandra's and kissing her hard and with passion.

"Oh Cassie, I want you, please, I want you so much," she breathed.

"Come on, darling, come on," said Cassandra quickly moving to the bed and pulling Peyton gently by the hand.

As they lay down, Cassandra put her head between Peyton's legs and began to lick her wet and swollen pussy.

"Oh, God, Cassie, oh Cassie, oh, oh, oh, oh, God, Cassieeee," Peyton started to scream out with pleasure as Cassandra's tongue flicked and lapped at her clit.

"Oh, Cassie, oh, God, oh, God, oh, oh, oh, oh, my, God, God, God, oh my, oh."

Cassandra's relentless flicking was bringing Peyton closer to orgasm, and then Cassandra put three fingers inside her. The effect was instant.

"Oh, Cassie, oh, I love you, oh, oh, oh, oh, I'm… oh, oh, oh, Cassieeeeeee, I'm cumminggggg, ohhhhhhhhhh!" Peyton practically screamed as her climax broke, and she bucked against Cassandra's mouth, pushing herself pussy hard into it. She tensed and untensed being extremely vocal with it. "Ohhhhhh, ohhhhhh, ohhhhhh, ohhhhh, Godddddd."

After a little while her orgasm subsided and then Peyton was scrambling to perform the same office for Cassandra. Cassandra didn't demur and begun to moan softly as Peyton's tongue went to work on her own wet pussy. She was dying to cum and was close to it already.

"Oh, oh, oh, oh darling, oh, my darling, oh, oh, oh, oh, oh, oh, oh, ohhhhhhhhhhhhhhhhhhhhhhhhh." The wave crested rapidly inside her and she climaxed curling her toes and crying out. Giving Peyton the spanking and then the caning had made her ultra horny, she had been on a hair-trigger. She was sure they would be making love many more times before Nathan came home.

She slid under the duvet with Peyton and held her close kissing her lightly.

"I'm sorry you had to have such a severe punishment, my darling," she whispered, nuzzling Peyton's lips.

"I deserved it, Cassie. I was bad and irresponsible. I know that now. But with your help, I'm going to change."

"I'm sorry if I neglected to look after you, but that's going to change too." Cassandra smiled.

"Don't say that, never say that. You've been nothing but good to me. It's me who let you down and I got what I deserved," said Peyton fiercely.

"Can I ask you something, I won't punish you if you say yes. But is all this because I had not spanked you for a while?" This point had been niggling in Cassandra's mind since she thought of it.

Peyton didn't answer right away, evidently considering the question.

"I don't know," Peyton whispered, "I mean maybe but not consciously."

"OK, well, anyway, it's all in the past now. We can move on to better things."

"You'll still spank me though, every week, like you said?" Peyton gave her what Cassandra considered her adorable wide-eyed look.

"Yes, of course, I will, darling, you can count on it."

"Good, because… I want it… I… need it."

"Then I will make sure you get it or more correctly that your bottom gets it."

Cassandra laughed and so did Peyton. She pulled Peyton close and kissed her again.

"Let's sleep, my darling, I'm a little tired, aren't you?" Cassandra said starting to close her eyes.

"Yes, yes I am."

"I love you, never forget that. I love you so much."

"I love you too, you mean the world to me."

Peyton kissed her then, and she kissed Peyton back. After a few moments, Peyton closed her eyes and went to sleep. Cassandra lay thinking of all that had occurred. She mused on how much Peyton meant to her and Nathan too. Now there was Faith. She didn't even know what to think about her. What if she had Faith come over and there were four of them. What would sex be like, three women and one man? It didn't bear thinking of.

What was Nathan going to say about Peyton moving in, she wondered. Not that he really had a choice because it was Cassandra's house. Cassandra wanted everything to be harmonious between them. She didn't want any conflicts. The sleeping arrangements would be interesting. Although, Peyton shared their bed when she stayed. Nathan seemed to be getting used to it.

The caning had been quite something for Cassandra. Another watershed crossed into becoming a dominant woman. She had felt somehow fulfilled as she wielded the cane. There was some kind of real power in it. It was also very hot. She had enjoyed it. She had enjoyed spanking and giving a caning while naked. It was horny. Although she was still going to wear her corset sometimes. Cassandra was sure they would be plenty more spankings to come. She had become addicted, and she loved being the dominant one. On which note, she put the thoughts aside for another day, and let sleep claim her too. There would be many more tomorrows.

***

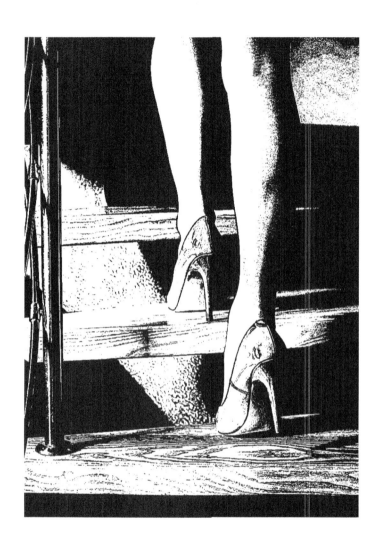

If you have enjoyed this Cassandra anthology, then please do feel free to let us know. If you care to write us a nice review on Amazon and/or Goodreads, we will be very grateful. You can also always write to us at this address:

editor@brookmaxpublications.com

Look out for our other series of hot sexy spanking stories.

The Walter series: A young man's sensual, sexual and spanking journey at the hands of an older woman.

http://mybook.to/walterseries

http://mybook.to/waltermonicaspanks

The Countess Tara series: Countess Tara is a rich independent woman. Anne-Marie, her new secretary discovers that mistakes entail a spanking. Follow Anne-Marie's journey to love and submission in this excellent series.

http://mybook.to/countesstaraseries

http://mybook.to/countesstaraone

The Hotwife Lucy series: Lucy discovers her husband wants her to be a hotwife and she also finds out she has a predilection for spanking. Read all about it in this fantastic sexy hot spanking series.

http://mybook.to/hotwifelucyseries

http://mybook.to/hotwifelucyone

The Sofia series: Sofia is a beautiful polyamorous woman who likes to spank. He has a number of men she loves and in this reverse harem series she tells us a story about each one. This is a hot sex and spanking series you will love.

http://mybook.to/sofiaseries

http://mybook.to/sofiaspankone

Our Brookmax publications website contains links to all of our series

www.brookmaxpublications.com

Printed in Great Britain
by Amazon